The Odd Couple

Q. Kelly

Regal Crest

Nederland, Texas

Copyright © 2008 by Q. Kelly

All rights reserved. No part of this publication may be reproduced, transmitted in any form or by any means, electronic or mechanical, including photocopy, recording, or any information storage and retrieval system, without permission in writing from the publisher. The characters, incidents and dialogue herein are fictional and any resemblance to actual events or persons, living or dead, is purely coincidental.

ISBN 978-1-932300-99-4
1-932300-99-6

First Printing 2008

9 8 7 6 5 4 3 2 1

Cover design by Donna Pawlowski

Published by:

Regal Crest Enterprises, LLC
4700 Hwy 365, Ste A
PMB 210
Port Arthur, Texas 77642

Find us on the World Wide Web at
http://www.regalcrest.biz

Printed in the United States of America

Chapter One

MORRISEY HAWTHORNE COULD not believe it was June already. It did not seem possible that two months had passed since her father's heart attack. She had shivered through his funeral in April, had put up with overcast skies and that miserable, gray drizzle. Now the sky was blue and unblemished. The sun was out in full force for what promised to be a hot summer filled with trips to swimming holes and quality time with Gareth. But Morrisey wanted to go back to April—to April 20th. She could have stopped by her parents' house while her mother was out shopping. She could have called 911 and maybe... Well, maybe her father would not have died alone.

"Damn," Morrisey said. "Two months, Dad." She knelt and studied his tombstone. Elegant and cursive letters chosen by her mother marked his final resting place. The old man would have been embarrassed by all this fancy-schmancy stuff, and Morrisey felt his pain. Adrian Hawthorne. He was just a name now, but he was a giant in Morrisey's memory. He had taught her how to play basketball and how to treat people with respect. He was the only person to hug her when she announced to the family she was pregnant. She had never thanked him, had never said "I love you" to him. "Shit," she muttered. "I'm sorry, Dad."

Morrisey lowered herself onto the ground. A red rose, its petals inviting and plump, was propped against the tombstone. Morrisey reached for the flower, but not to caress it or enjoy its perfume. She needed something to busy her hands and distract her mind. Her mother, the graceful, grieving Margaret Hawthorne, must have left the rose not long ago. Margaret had visited every morning since the funeral, and Morrisey wondered when the vigil would stop. It surprised her, actually—she had not realized how deep her mother's love for her father was.

Morrisey's cell phone rang, and she fished it out of her pocket. She glanced at the screen and saw that her mother was the caller. "Yeah?" Morrisey asked.

"Hey, sweetie."

"Hey. Sorry I'm running late."

"Oh, that's fine. Gareth and I are having a blast. I just wanted to make sure you were all right."

"I'm okay. Long lines. Errands aren't fun."

Margaret clicked her tongue in sympathy. "I wish you'd let me take you clothes shopping. You need more red. That looks so good on you."

Morrisey answered with silence.

"You know, the mall's not far from the cemetery. Five minutes? You should stop by and see your father. He deserves better. He loved you, and you haven't been to see him once."

Morrisey bristled, as she often did when talking with her mother. "Look, I've told you I don't need to visit him to remember him. Why can't you understand that? I'm taking Gareth in a few days, anyway."

"Good. But still—"

"I've got to go. I'm at the cash register." Morrisey snapped her cell phone shut and dropped it onto the grass. "Jesus," she said, ignoring her guilt for concealing the fact she was at the cemetery. She had better things to do than follow her mother's lead and bring roses to a dead man. She had better things to do than weep over a grave and relive the past. She had been mourning her father in her own way, and it was her mother's problem if she thought Morrisey was the devil incarnate for not having visited since the funeral.

"You understand, right?" Morrisey asked the tombstone.

He understood. Of course he did.

Morrisey got up and wiped clinging bits of grass off her shorts. *I'm a fool.* There had been no need to scout the cemetery in advance of Gareth's visit. What had she expected? No cesspools, Venus flytraps or boy-eating trolls had sprung up around her father's grave. The other graves that comprised the Hawthorne family plot seemed inclined to behave themselves, too. Gareth would have a great time. He would be fine, just fine. Her son was no ordinary child.

"Bye, Dad," Morrisey said.

Leaving already? Her conscience squeaked.

"Bye, Dad," Morrisey repeated. "I'll be back soon, with Gareth. He's so happy about coming." She imagined her son, little four-year-old Gareth, at the gravesite. Excitement flushed his cheeks as he babbled with his grandfather's tombstone. "Grandpa!" she pictured Gareth hollering. "I caught a frog yesterday. It was slimy!"

Morrisey grinned, her mood improving. Gareth's fresh innocence was magic, and she found herself missing him desperately even though they had parted only three hours ago. Morrisey picked up her pace as she headed back to her car, but a flash of blue stopped her. It was a toy sailboat in the middle of a row of grave markers. Morrisey's heart stilled. The boat was such an insignificant little thing, but she stared at it for a long moment. Endless possibilities crowded her mind. Had a parent left it for a child? Maybe a child brought it for a parent. Maybe a lover left it for a lover, or...

Morrisey moved toward the boat but caught herself. *Leave it alone.* She would not want strangers poking around her father's grave, violating his privacy.

MORRISEY BROUGHT HER son four days later. She took Gareth's hand and led him up a hill, past the unrelenting march of tombstones and markers. Gareth gripped a bunch of lilies in his other hand, and his eyes were wide as he took in the stillness of the cemetery. He had yet to notice the butterflies, the squirrels — the life surrounding him.

Morrisey's gaze drifted inadvertently to the marker where she had seen the sailboat. The toy was gone, replaced by a scruffy baseball. Morrisey tightened her grasp on Gareth and hurried their steps. If he saw the ball, he would go wild and want to play. *A baseball.* Morrisey's heaviness returned. Her gut said a parent had left it for a child — a boy? Morrisey could not imagine losing her son, bubbly, red-headed, blue-eyed Gareth, her complete opposite in both looks and personality, who had entered her life so unexpectedly.

"Are we there yet?" Gareth asked in a tiny voice.

"Just about." Morrisey guided Gareth to the proper grave and let go of his hand. She noticed that today's rose was even redder and more vibrant than the one four days ago. "Can you read what Grandpa's tombstone says?" she asked.

Gareth stepped forward. "Adrian Hawthorne. My middle name!"

"Yep."

"So Grandpa's down there?"

"That's right."

Gareth edged back toward Morrisey and looked up at her. "Why? Isn't it scary?"

She shrugged. "I don't know. It's just what some people do. Your grandfather wanted to be buried."

"So everyone goes underground?"

"Some do."

"Where do the others go?"

"Some people are cremated. I think maybe that's what I want."

Gareth scrunched his face. "What's that?"

"That's when people's bodies..."

"What?"

"Never mind. But it doesn't hurt. The people don't feel it. They're dead. They're sleeping. They'll never wake up again."

"Like Grandpa. He's sleeping."

"Yes." Morrisey prodded her son forward. "Why don't you put the lilies with the rose Grandma brought?"

Gareth got on his knees and arranged the lilies, using the rose as the centerpiece. "Is that okay?"

"That's great."

"I forgot Grandpa likes roses better."

"Oh, sweetie." Morrisey rushed to reassure her son. Getting flowers had been his idea—charming, little four-year-old Gareth's idea. "Grandpa loves your surprise, I promise. He's tired of roses because Grandma brings them all the time. You got the best-looking flowers in the store. Even the lady said so, remember?"

"Yeah! But she talked funny."

Morrisey wandered off to allow Gareth some privacy. She surveyed the other nearby tombstones and markers. All were family: a couple of cousins, grandparents, great-aunts and great-uncles, great-grandparents. Last but not least was Adrian Jr., the older baby brother Morrisey had never known but whose picture occupied the prime spot above their mother's fireplace. All those decaying corpses.

Morrisey shivered, and for an instant, it was December again. She was freezing cold. Numb, too. She should have beaten her father to his grave, but the car had started, her car had started. The stupid damn car had started—fifteen minutes too late.

Morrisey crossed her arms and stood stock still. She struggled not to think about her own body as blue, pallid, worm food, and six feet under. Her mind latched onto the lonely sailboat and scruffy baseball, but that was just as bad.

Gareth piped up, breaking Morrisey's reverie: "Can we come back tomorrow?"

She blinked. "Tomorrow? Why?"

"Grandpa wants me to draw him pictures and talk to him tomorrow. Can I? Please?"

Morrisey licked her lips. This was not about her. This was about her son, her son who had adored his grandfather. Morrisey looked into Gareth's open, eager face, into his innocent blue eyes. "Sure," she agreed. "We can come tomorrow. But Grandpa's all right. You know? See all those other tombstones and markers? That's my grandparents. That one—that's my brother. This is Great

Aunt Martha, Grandpa's sister. She always pinched my cheeks so hard they turned red."

"Grandpa says they're boring! He wants to talk to me."

"He—but...All right. Never mind. We'll come back tomorrow."

Chapter Two

"I SEE JP everywhere," Charlene admitted as she stared at the drab gray floor. "In my dreams, in the cracks of the bathroom stalls at work, in a child's eager smile."

No one replied. Nobody moved or made a sound. The black silence was so overwhelming that Charlene had to look up. She glanced over the circle of about a dozen people. Their faces, a blur of pity, pain and indifference, only reinforced why she had not wanted to come. "Sorry?" said a pale man with floppy jowls. "I didn't hear you." He cupped a hand to his ear.

"I hike," Charlene said. "Okay. I hike. I volunteer. I go out with people. I went to a therapist, but he wasn't good. I started seeing a new one. She just..." Charlene grimaced. "She told me to *stop* visiting JP. 'Go once a month,' she said. 'No more than that.' So, look, I'm trying. He's the last thing I see before I fall asleep, though. He's the first thing I see when I wake up. I just want to know why he did it."

The group's leader, a smartly dressed woman, spoke, "Tell us about him. Who was he?"

Charlene forced herself to meet the woman's eyes. *Who was he? Good question.*

"Your husband? Boyfriend? Son? Brother? Friend?"

"Son," Charlene muttered.

"When did it happen?"

"Almost three years ago. September 25th, at 5:07 p.m. I know because when I heard the gunshot and ran into his room, the clock was...was...It was the first thing I saw. 5:07."

The group's leader fingered her pearl necklace and attempted a smile. "So an anniversary isn't too far off. That's always a difficult time."

"Anniversary." Charlene stiffened at the feel of the word on her tongue. "How should I celebrate? Throw a party with pointy pink hats and a big old chocolate cake? Happy third year dead? Would y'all like to come?"

The dozen or so faces flinched. "No, of course not," the jowly man said. "She just meant...Hey. We're glad you're here. Is this your first group?"

Charlene hated the gleam in the man's piggish eyes. She knew it all too well. He liked her soft, shoulder-length blond hair, her blue eyes, her small, toned body. He wanted to fuck her. He did not give a damn about her or her son. Charlene stood and slung her purse over her shoulder. "I'm leaving."

The group's leader jumped to her feet. "You just started. Come on, finish telling us about PJ."

"JP," Charlene snapped. "My son's name was John Patrick." She stormed out of the room and down three flights of steps to the parking lot. She stabbed her key into the ignition of her car. *PJ. PJ! The gall of that woman! How hard was it to get a name right?*

A rap sounded at the window, and Charlene jerked her head up. A balding, unnaturally tanned man was peering at her. Charlene had a vague memory of him being in the circle of faces. She rolled her window down, and the man leaned into her. His breath was minty, as if he had just spritzed freshener into his mouth.

"I knew your son," he declared.

Charlene blinked. "What?"

"My kid, Aaron, was on the JV. He practically worshipped your boy. JP Sudsbury, right? All-state, even as a freshman."

Charlene nodded, her spirits brightening. "Yes."

"Yep. I thought so. I knew I'd seen you somewhere. What an arm JP had. His instincts. He never had a problem finding an open man. And his speed...Yeah, he was something."

"He was," Charlene murmured.

"Shame about the accident. I was there that night. Saw it all."

Charlene's throat went dry, and the beginnings of her good mood evaporated. *Shame? Shame? Oh no, you don't.*

The man pulled his lips back into an almost-wolfish smile. "Let me take you for some coffee or ice cream, all right? You can tell me about JP. My name's Alvin Brown."

Charlene rattled her car to life and drove off without a backward glance. Alvin was just someone else who wanted a fuck.

WHEN MORRISEY AND Gareth returned to the cemetery, a model airplane had replaced the baseball. Morrisey could resist no longer. She left Gareth at his grandfather's grave and headed slowly, haltingly, to the grave with the airplane. She held her breath, half-expecting someone to jump from behind a tombstone or tree and holler, "Gotcha! What's wrong with you, sniffing around where you don't belong?"

Nothing happened on the way to the grave, though. Morrisey read the inscription on the marker: John Patrick Sudsbury, Beloved Son. She scanned the birth and death dates. He had been twenty-one and had died almost three years ago. Twenty-one. So young. Still, Morrisey had been imagining a child, perhaps no older than her own son. She glanced over at Gareth, who was holding up a drawing for his grandfather's perusal. Morrisey's heart jumbled with pride, affection and pain. She could not believe that at one time this boy had been the last thing in the world she wanted.

Morrisey redirected her focus to the grave marker below her. She wondered what this young man had been like and what the person leaving the toys was like. Were they mother and son too? Did they look alike or were they, like Morrisey and Gareth, as different as night and day?

John Patrick Sudsbury, Beloved Son.

Only twenty-one. Her father had been sixty years old. Adrian Jr. had been three months old. Morrisey would have been twenty-nine. Now she was thirty-four.

Morrisey shifted her weight to her other foot. She was itching to leave, but something was keeping her — some feeling of obligation, perhaps. The lilies from the day before were still at her father's tombstone. She could get one for this John Patrick Sudsbury, maybe to compensate for her intrusion. *And then what? You'll unnerve whoever's leaving the toys.*

Morrisey rejoined her son. She was done with the cemetery. If Gareth wanted to return, fine. Her mother would only be too happy to take him. "Let's go," Morrisey commanded.

"No!" Gareth howled. "Grandpa wants to see my sticker book."

"Grandma will bring you next week. She wants to see it too."

Gareth's mouth opened with a flurry of protests, but Morrisey was unmoved. "Say goodbye."

Gareth gave in, but not without a scowl. "Can I hug Grandpa?"

"Yeah, fine."

Gareth flung his tiny arms around the tombstone. Morrisey averted her eyes. She waited. And waited. "Gareth!"

"Grandpa misses me."

Morrisey was about to grab her son when she saw a woman. The woman. Morrisey knew who she was right away. Perhaps because the woman seemed as lonely, as lost as the sailboat, the baseball and the plane. Grief in all its proud isolation. Yes, this was the toy-bearer, and she was beautiful. More than beautiful. She might as well have floated to the toy grave in a shimmering white dress and halo instead of the blue jeans and T-shirt she wore. She reminded Morrisey of an ethereal, frail creature.

The woman sat at the grave. She studied the marker.

Morrisey shifted back into guilt mode. *I didn't change anything. Didn't touch a thing. She can't know I was there.*

The woman apparently found nothing amiss. She brought two fingers to her lips, then back to the marker in a kiss.

In that moment, Morrisey felt so ungainly, so clumsy, so awkward, even though she was anything but. *I'm an ogre next to her.* The features that had won Morrisey countless admirers and bedmates—her sharply defined face, her dark hair, her intense, even darker eyes, her long, limber legs, her rich, honeyed laugh, her tan skin, her even, white smile—all vanished.

She was a troll, she really was, compared with that woman.

"What's wrong, Mommy?" Gareth asked.

"Nothing," Morrisey murmured. "Show Grandpa your stickers."

JOHN PATRICK SUDSBURY, Beloved Son, his grave marker read. Even though it had been nearly three years, Charlene faithfully brought toys and trinkets her only child would like. A baseball, a model car, a cool keychain gadget. No flowers, though. JP would have laughed at that. *Mom! What am I gonna do with flowers?*

Charlene talked to her son about anything, about everything: her day, a rude customer, or a generous customer who left a huge tip, the burgundy Plymouth Acclaim they had shared, which was on its last legs. JP had named the car Silver because of its silver driver's door. The prospect of cruising about in such a car would have mortified most teenagers. Not JP. Charlene had scored a deal on Silver and saved five hundred dollars, so JP made the best of the situation. He never grimaced at the mismatched door. He never complained or squawked about it. Within days, even JP's wealthy friends, with their BMWs and convertibles, were affectionately calling the car Silver, too. Her son could have made a friend of anyone, Charlene mused. *Before the accident.*

Sometimes at the cemetery, it was like the old days, before JP's football injury, when they would chat for hours. Of course, JP did not talk back anymore. This Sunday was no different. JP was as silent as ever.

Charlene slipped the airplane from the day before into her purse. She took out a turkey sandwich and a bottle of Diet Pepsi. Sundays were her sole day off most weeks, and she alternately dreaded and relished them for the same reason—more time with her son. She crossed her legs and nibbled at her sandwich. The day was heating up, despite the forecasters' promises that it would stay reasonable. Sweat slithered down Charlene's back, but she did not care. "I should be getting a pay raise soon," she told her son. "Maybe I can set aside some of it for a new car. What do you think?"

She pictured JP — pre-accident, of course — and imagined his response, "Great idea, Mom. Want to go look at cars tomorrow?"

Charlene's heart tightened. She would miss Silver, that ugly, ugly creature. How JP had loved the damned thing. Charlene decided to wait a little longer to replace her car. Silver would be all right for a few months yet.

After Charlene finished her sandwich, she remembered that she was forty-one years old today. Another year had come and gone, another year without her child, another year of unanswered questions. She stuffed the empty sandwich bag into her purse. Miriam, her best friend, and Miriam's lover, Liz, would likely want to take her out that night for dinner. It was their tradition. And to think Liz had been so jealous at first, all those years ago, at how close Miriam was with an ex-lover, an ex-lover twenty years her junior, no less. Charlene fingered her rainbow bracelet, which had been a peace offering of sorts from Liz when Charlene turned thirty-four.

She traced the letters on JP's grave marker. "Remember when you took me downtown that day?" she murmured. "You were so proud you could buy me dinner."

Wind whistled through the treetops and swirled around the graveyard. Charlene closed her eyes, basking in the embrace. JP was telling her he did remember. "I wore my best dress. You were so handsome in your tie and khaki pants. It feels like it was just yesterday."

The wind stopped, and JP, bloody and broken, flashed into Charlene's mind. Her heart caught in her throat, but, as always, she was powerless to resist the abrupt, fractured moment her world changed forever.

The gunshot.

Breaking into his room, flinging herself on him. Shaking him. *Move. Please. Open your eyes. Breathe. Please. Make your heart beat. Anything, anything. Please!* Having the most absurd, ridiculous thoughts — hoping no one else in the apartment building had heard, praying that nobody would come. Postponing calling Miriam and Liz and 911 for as long as she could because this was the last time he would be in her arms, for her to cradle just so. Holding him until he was cool to the touch. Letting go of him as the sun slipped over the horizon. Calling Miriam and Liz then returning to JP. Miriam and Liz — a policewoman — rushing over, the other police and EMTs arriving, trying to coax her into releasing the body.

The body. Charlene bristled at the memory, but her retort had done its job. *This thing you call a body is my child, thank you very much.*

Charlene forced her eyes open. John Patrick Sudsbury, Beloved Son, his grave marker still read.

"Remember what you did for me when you were four? No, you probably don't remember. That was such a long time ago. It was my birthday, and you made the cutest little card for me. You were so excited when you woke me up. 'Mommy, happy birthday!' you said. You'd combed your hair all nice. You brought in breakfast for us. A big bowl of Lucky Charms with extra hearts on top. A glass of orange juice. And..." Charlene chuckled. "That horrible mess in the kitchen." She pictured the child, her JP, with his liberally freckled face, pert nose, carrot-red hair and shining blue eyes. They had eaten the Lucky Charms together and then snuggled in bed. In that world, in Charlene's memories and in her sorrow, JP would always live. She could even hear his laughter now, carefree and unburdened. She squeezed her eyes shut again as her son's giggles continued. What she would give to hear them again, for real.

The laughter continued, and a little voice shouted, "Mommy! The caterpillar tickles!"

Charlene's eyes flew open. That voice was real. Right across from her, just yards away, there he was. Her son, her JP. Four years old again and risen somehow from the grave. There was no mistaking him. He had listened to her, and he was back. Charlene went weak with disbelief. Her heart wobbled. *OhGodOhGodOhGod.* This was it, then. This was how she was going to snap and plunge into the valley of the insane. Because JP was dead. The gunshot. The holes. The lifeless eyes.

He was not back. He never would be. But how to explain this boy? Was he simply a figment of Charlene's grief?

The child laid something—a caterpillar?—on a tombstone and chased after a squirrel, coming ever closer. His laughter was music to Charlene's ears. This boy was no figment. Charlene was not going off the deep end. She was hearing JP.

Without thinking, she leaped to her feet. She opened her mouth to call her son to her. *JP, JP, you're home, you're alive. How? No, no, tell me later. That doesn't matter. Just come here, come here. Let me hug you.*

The boy skidded to a stop. He met Charlene's eyes.

She got a good look at his face, and her heart sank. In the summer, light tan freckles had covered most of JP's features, but this boy was blessed with a mere sprinkling. Charlene thought once more that she must be going crazy. Then the child cocked an eyebrow, just like JP would have, and hope filled Charlene's whole being again.

"Hi," the boy said, and he grinned hugely.

Charlene blinked back tears. Freckles or not, this boy was her son. She was being given a chance to redeem herself, to make things right. But a harsh, logical voice cautioned her to take a deep breath, to calm down, to just think a minute, to not say or do anything she would regret later. How could this boy be JP? She had held him for hours, for hours, those lifeless eyes. Still, she had to ask.

"JP?" she ventured.

The child shook his head and flashed another eager smile. "I'm Gareth. Like in the King Arthur story."

Charlene struggled to reconcile the clash between logic and emotion, between mind and heart. *Gareth. JP. Gareth.* How could it be? How could this child, this so-called Gareth, have JP's blue eyes, his laugh, his hair, his everything, except for the freckles? How? Was it some cruel trick of fate?

Seemingly out of nowhere, a woman, tall and tan, with dark hair and dark eyes, appeared. She tousled Gareth's hair and offered a shy smile. "I apologize if Gareth was bothering you."

A faint thread of hysteria washed through Charlene. She fought to keep it at bay. "Gareth. That's a nice name." *No. No. That's JP. My son! My son! Why do you have my son?*

The dark-haired woman grinned. "I've always loved King Arthur stuff. Anyway. Hi. I'm Morrisey." She stuck a hand out.

Charlene robotically took the hand but let go after a second.

"Are you okay?" Morrisey asked.

Charlene could not bring herself to answer right away. What she wanted to do was fall to her knees and take this other woman's son in her arms. She wanted to inhale his sweet little-boy smell. She wanted to feel him breathe and hear his heart beating. She wanted to tell him everything would be all right, that she was so sorry, so very sorry for having failed him. What she wanted to do was trace his face, look into those familiar, lively blue eyes, and reassure him that everything would be okay now.

She could not do that, though. That would be absurd. JP was dead, and no amount of pleading, no amount of tears and promises and deluding herself about this look-alike boy would change that.

"You okay?" Morrisey repeated.

"It's been a long day."

"I understand. I've had more than my share of long days, too."

"My son," Charlene blurted out. "He reminds me of my son."

Morrisey's eyes narrowed. "Gareth reminds you of your son?"

Charlene's gaze dropped to the grave marker at her feet. "Yes. JP."

"How?"

Charlene looked back at Gareth, into JP's bright blue eyes, and fought to keep herself stiff. "How what?"

"How does he remind you of JP?"

"Oh, just... Nothing, really. I don't know. I'm silly, huh? I'm sorry."

"Don't worry about it," Morrisey said, but her earlier friendliness had vanished.

"Mommy!" Gareth exclaimed. "Can I go back to Grandpa?"

"Sure," Morrisey replied. "I'll be right there, okay?"

Gareth darted toward a group of graves next to a cluster of trees. Charlene memorized every detail of how he moved, of how he played, and an unbearable wave of loneliness hit her. Her son, her JP, was gone, dead. Here was this bubbly boy, though, a haunting reminder of how JP used to be before the accident.

"Come here often?" Morrisey's voice was cool.

Charlene willed herself to look at Morrisey instead of at her son. "Yes, I come here a lot. Do you?"

"No. I don't like cemeteries. I don't belong here."

Charlene replied without thinking, "Do I?"

Morrisey blinked. She softened and took her time answering. "If being here helps you, then..." She shrugged. "Then you should be here."

Charlene liked this quiet, subdued answer. She was so used to Miriam, in her loud, forceful, no-nonsense voice, telling her to stop visiting JP so often, to stop cutting first dates short, to start going on second dates. Miriam loved to promote the virtues of "moving on," but this new woman understood.

Or not. Morrisey went on, "Do you *belong* here? I don't think you belong here, no. This place is for dead people. I see the toys you leave for JP. It just seems... Oh, I don't know."

Charlene took a step back. "What? You just said that... Hey. I go on hikes, okay? I date. I volunteer at the rescue mission. I try. I try, I really do. But I held him in my arms for hours. He's what I see right before I fall asleep. He's the first thing I see when I wake up. I dream about him. Him, the blood, the holes in his head."

Morrisey squirmed. "I'm sorry. I don't know what I'm talking about. I don't know you. Anyway, I should get back to Gareth. Again, I apologize that he bothered you earlier."

Charlene regretted her outburst. Now her tiny, fragile bond with Gareth would be severed. *Don't let Morrisey leave.* "I have a picture of JP if you want to see," Charlene said softly.

Morrisey glanced over at Gareth. He had moved several feet from the cluster of tombstones and was trying to catch a butterfly. "Don't hurt it!" she called.

"I won't!" Gareth scampered back to the tombstones.

JP, Charlene thought. *That's JP exactly.*

"I have a meeting," Morrisey said, all business-like. "Goodbye."

"No picture?"

"No picture."

Charlene knew there was no meeting, so she bent over and got her purse. She quickly found the photo she'd had in mind. It was one of her favorites of JP and had been taken on his third birthday. He was gazing adoringly at a cake with three candles on it. "They look alike," Charlene said as she held out the picture. "That's how Gareth reminds me of JP."

"I said I did not want to see."

"Please. It's amazing. They could be twins."

Morrisey's eyes darkened. "Fine." She snapped the photo from Charlene's hand. She stared at the picture for a long moment. It was as if she was not quite sure of what she was seeing, as if the picture was blurry or faded, which it most definitely was not. Morrisey's lips parted and her breathing became shallow.

Unease stirred throughout Charlene. *Something really is wrong here.* There was something in Morrisey's expression, something more than mere surprise—maybe panic or self-doubt, maybe confusion or recognition. Whatever it was, Morrisey was in a hurry to hand the picture back. "It's amazing. Wow." She mumbled a few polite, trite phrases and returned to Gareth.

Just two minutes later, mother and child got into a red Cavalier that was parked near Charlene's Acclaim. They were gone as quickly as they had appeared.

Chapter Three

CHARLENE WAS IN a daze as she rang the doorbell. She barely remembered the drive to Miriam and Liz's house. All she saw in her mind was the child, Gareth, with JP's red hair, blue eyes and laugh. Not to mention the flash of "something" in his mother's eyes.

The door opened, and there Miriam was, with her usual bright smile. "Charlene! Guess what I'm doing. I'm—what's wrong? You look as if you've seen a ghost."

Charlene studied her best friend for a moment—the graying hair, the lines on the round, matronly face, the concerned tilt of her head. Yes, Charlene thought, she had done the right thing coming here, even if Miriam tended to push too hard. Good old familiar, comforting Miriam would help make sense of it all.

"Charlene? Why are you looking at me like that?"

"I think I have."

Miriam ushered Charlene inside and shut the door. "You think you have what?"

"Seen a ghost."

Miriam stilled immediately. "What? Who?"

"JP."

"JP?"

"JP. Only it couldn't actually have been him, right? He looked like JP, exactly like JP, except for the freckles."

Miriam led Charlene to the couch. "What happened?"

Charlene took a deep breath. She willed herself to remain calm and controlled, to not let excitement get the best of her. "I was at the cemetery, and I saw a little boy. He must've been four years old. He was JP all over again, Miriam. He really was."

"Oh, sweetie."

"He said his name was Gareth. It's a nice name, I suppose. But I kept wanting to tell him, 'You're not Gareth. Don't say your name's Gareth. You're JP, my son.' That isn't possible, is it?"

"No, honey."

"What if it is? You should have been there. You needed to see him! It was just...The timing was so odd. It can't be a coincidence." Charlene began to gesture, trying to get her point across without seeming crazy. No flashes of inspiration came to her, so she simply said, "I shouldn't have let him leave."

Miriam grasped Charlene's hands. "It's all right. It's all right."

"His mother came up. Her name was Morrisey. She didn't look anything like him. And I was so...You have no idea, Miriam. I wanted so badly to just hug him. I showed her a picture of JP."

Miriam raised an eyebrow. "What happened?"

"Her expression changed. She's hiding something."

Miriam got to her feet. "Here's what we'll do. I'm going to fix you a glass of water, and we'll have some of your birthday cake, hmm? That's what I was doing when you rang the doorbell. I was frosting it, putting the finishing touches on it. Or maybe a glass of milk would be better. Sweetie, did you even remember today's your birthday?"

"Miriam." Charlene grabbed her friend's arm, willing her to understand. "Please. Please."

Miriam sat back down and sighed heavily. "Everyone has a twin. People have seen me around town at places I've never been to. It's a coincidence, honey. I can see how it was a huge shock. It's just coincidence, though. Really."

"It was more than that."

Miriam cleared her throat. "Charlene, ah, you know, you ought to give that support group a second chance. I'll go with you."

Charlene tensed at the memory of the faux-concerned faces, the sugary-sweet tones. "I'm not going back to that group or any other group. And I'm done with shrinks. You know that."

"Well, you have to do something. JP's dead. He's gone! Stop grasping at straws. Start living again. Come on! Give Connie a second chance. Or how about Olivia? You liked her laugh, right? She was hot for you. Dinner. A movie. Ice cream. Something. She'll get your mind off JP."

Charlene chuckled, her light tones giving way to a scowl and dark words. "So I'll go on a second date, and everything will be dandy. Fuck that. Stop patronizing me, Miriam."

"Come on, sweetie. Let's talk over some cake."

Charlene wasted no time leaving the house.

MORRISEY SMILED, CHATTED and laughed with her son during the drive home from the cemetery, even though it took all of her self-control not to turn into a panicked, trembling mass. It was after she tucked Gareth in for a nap that she sank onto her living room couch and allowed her disconcerting thoughts to roam free.

"JP," she whispered, testing the name. "JP. John Patrick Sudsbury, beloved son."

Was he the one with the high, squeaky, almost feminine voice, the one who had bit her tongue, the one who kept screaming at the others to force her eyes open?

Or was he the *hoo-hoo-hoo-hoo* one, with the deep, rumbling voice who taunted her after it was all over, towering over her and asking about the gas station?

Or was he the one who had gone last, the one who pleaded with the others to stop even as he helped them hold her down?

Or was he the one who went first, the one who so hungrily tore her winter cap off?

Morrisey felt so stupid, so incredibly foolish. She had wondered about that grave with the toys. She had cared about that young man. She had felt guilty about violating his space.

Did he ever feel guilty about raping her, about leaving her for dead?

She was so stupid, so unbelievably fucking stupid. And there was nothing she could tell herself, no lies, no oh-maybe-it's-just-a-coincidence crap. If it'd just been the picture, sure. Probably. Perhaps. Maybe. It'd given her a start, but she had told herself, "It's just one of those things. Lots of people look alike."

The burgundy Acclaim with the silver driver's-side door clinched it. Proved it. It was no false alarm like the one the previous fall, no sir. That Acclaim she had noticed in the parking lot of the high school where she taught. She had nearly broken down. The driver's-side door was not silver, but so what? It could have been replaced. What if the boys or young men who raped her were students at the school? What if they knew her? What if they had told everyone about it? Morrisey imagined the boys saying, "She was all right. Maybe a 5 on a scale of 1 to 10. She was kinda tight. She needed to loosen up."

Maybe everyone at the school knew she had been raped.

Oh God.

It didn't matter that a white-haired woman, and not four youths, had gotten out of the car.

Morrisey thought she'd never get over seeing that Acclaim at the school. Please. That had been nothing compared with the sight of the car at the cemetery, its silver door glinting like a tooth. How had she done it, how had she kept holding her son's hand, how had she kept walking to her car as if she hadn't a care in the world?

Morrisey shuddered and forced herself from the couch. She surveyed her living room as if seeing it for the first time. Reminders of Gareth were everywhere. There were toys scattered on the floor and a couple of drawings on the walls. Gareth, her opposite. Her love. Now she knew who his father was.

John Patrick Sudsbury, Beloved Son.

"JP," Morrisey said again. "JP." So Gareth's father was dead, at the young age of twenty-one. Morrisey was glad. She would never have to risk running into him and seeing a glimmer of recognition in his eyes as he looked over her and her son, his son. She would never have to worry again about him tracking her down and raping her again or trying to take Gareth from her.

Yes, she was glad he was dead.

But there was his poor mother. Her pain was so raw and open. The woman loved her child just as much as Morrisey loved Gareth. JP had been a person, a son, a real, live breathing person, not just a faceless rapist. It must have been like a knife in the heart for his mother to see a boy who looked like her own son.

"JP," Morrisey muttered, trying to steer her thoughts from his mother. "JP. Which one were you?"

"That lady asked me if I was JP."

Morrisey jumped at Gareth's voice behind her and whirled around. "Don't scare me like that!" she scolded.

He smiled his impish Gareth-smile. "Why did the lady think I was JP?"

"I have no idea. No idea. I don't know."

"Can I have a cookie?"

Morrisey laughed. She got on her knees and drew Gareth to her. She held him close for a few moments. "I love you."

Gareth wriggled out of her embrace. "Why are you sad?"

Morrisey smoothed his bed-rumpled hair so she would not have to meet his eyes. "I'm not sad at all. No, sweetie. Why would I be sad?"

Chapter Four

AFTER CHARLENE FLED Miriam's house, she did what she did best. She cleaned. Cleaning always helped channel her nervous energy, excitement, grief. This was definitely a time to clean. Otherwise, she would go crazy just sitting around her apartment thinking about the little boy she met at the cemetery and the telltale flash of *something* in his mother's eyes and her shallow breathing.

First, Charlene set to work with dust rags and Pledge. After that, she vacuumed, scrubbed and mopped. She did not clean JP's room, though. She avoided that task as much as possible. After she put up her cleaning supplies, she checked the time. One measly hour had passed. *Great.*

She kept replaying Morrisey's reaction to the picture, down to the slight parting of her lips. The woman knew something, and she was not telling. Charlene was more sure of it than ever. She fished her phone book out of a kitchen drawer, her heart hammering. *Please be in there.*

She quickly found Hawthorne, Morrisey. "Yes!" Charlene whispered. "Thank you." After Morrisey and Gareth had left the cemetery earlier that day, Charlene had gone over to the group of tombstones where Gareth had been playing. *Can I go back to Grandpa?* Just about all of the tombstones and markers in that group had the name Hawthorne on them.

Shivering with excitement, Charlene wrote Morrisey's number and address on a Post-it note. *I'm coming. I won't let you get away again, JP.*

Charlene took a deep breath and laid down her pen. What was she doing? Gareth was not JP. She had no intention of crowning this new boy as her JP, as her only child. She could not deny, however, that there was something about him, something. She had felt it instantly with Gareth, that indescribable bond between mother and child. Gareth and JP were connected — and in a big way.

So what was it? Had Mr. Burroughs, JP's father, returned to the city he had fled so many years ago, maybe just for a short visit, and impregnated another woman? That was unlikely.

That left one possibility. Charlene let it enter slowly, carefully and deliciously. It filled her with new life and purpose. She had felt an immediate bond with Gareth, and he looked and acted like JP for a very simple reason. He was JP's son.

JP had left something behind, after all. Not all of him was gone.

CHARLENE THOUGHT ALL that afternoon and evening about her next step. She did not want to scare off her grandson's mother, so proceeding with caution and restraint was imperative — and she was already at a disadvantage. She still lived in the same cramped, tiny apartment where she had raised her son. The place had two bedrooms, and the second one, JP's, was barely more than a closet. Threadbare carpeting had covered the floors when Charlene moved in at age seventeen, and over the years, various new, differently colored carpets had taken their turns. The end effect was always the same — dull, boring, depressing, with all colors pointing to brown.

Charlene had never really noticed it when JP was alive. Now the brown lurked everywhere, and she hated it with a passion. The exterior of her apartment building was exactly the same color as her carpeting and in exactly the same rundown shape. She had some catching up to do. Morrisey Hawthorne was obviously from the right side of the tracks.

Charlene was not. She had always hated the phrase "from the wrong side of the tracks," but in her case, there was no denying its accuracy. She lived in Roanoke, a city in Southwest Virginia that had a notable railroad past. The tracks cut the city into two parts — one part mostly nice and one part mostly shabby.

In the nice part, the Blue Ridge Mountains loomed in the background and were beautiful, breathtaking. Perched atop Mill Mountain was an old friend, the neon, man-made star, second-largest in the world, which had given Roanoke its nickname as the Star City of the South. In the nice part of town, the Roanoke River was not as muddy. In the shabby part, the mountains in the background clashed with the faded buildings and worn people. The river was brown. The star was just... well, it was a star. It was an old, reassuring sight, yes, but it was definitely out of reach.

Morrisey Hawthorne lived just a stone's throw from the city. She was in Roanoke County where big houses, nice cars and lush grass were plentiful. She lived on West Haverwood Drive. Charlene used to clean house for someone on East Haverwood. The houses there were huge, dripping with insane wealth. Why would West

Haverwood be any different? Clearly, Morrisey had money. The mystery deepened. Just who was she? What had she been doing with JP? He was so much younger than Morrisey.

Yes, JP had looked a few years older than he actually was, with his muscular chest and the rock-solid arms that came from years of playing football. Most of all, there was the guarded, knowing look in his eyes signaling he had grown up all too quickly.

JP had a son. Had JP known?

Did Gareth already have a daddy? Charlene strained to remember if Morrisey had worn a wedding ring. Her fingers as she took the picture and then held it were long, slim and lovely. Morrisey really was a beautiful woman. Her eyes were so dark, so expressive, flitting through so many emotions. No. No wedding ring, so she probably was not married.

Charlene brimmed with vigor and purpose as she riffled through the clothes in her closet. After her shift at The Log Cabin the next afternoon, she would knock on Morrisey's door and hope for the best. She would wear her nicest clothes and bring a present for Gareth—maybe one for Morrisey, too. Charlene hoped she would get the answers she needed. She knew almost nothing of JP's post-accident life. She had no idea about any girlfriends or any women he might have been seeing. The only friend she had met, once and for five minutes at that, was a string bean of a youth named Ralph. She had never caught his last name. He had a squeaky, almost girly, voice, and his shoulder-length hair was a mishmash of dyed colors. His eyes were hidden behind a pair of cheap sunglasses.

She had not liked him, but Ralph was one of the precious few people who attended JP's funeral. She would always be grateful to him for that. He had lingered from afar, and Charlene had noticed him only when she turned to leave. He scurried off without a backward glance, just like a cockroach, and she had not seen him since. All those answers had hovered just out of reach for almost three years. Maybe now closure would come. Not from Ralph, of course, but from Morrisey, from the mother of JP's child.

The telephone shrilled, shattering Charlene's happy contemplations. She scowled and let the answering machine pick up. Miriam's worried, anxious voice floated across the bedroom. "Charlene, let's go out for your birthday. You shouldn't be alone. Call me, please. I know you just need to vent, that you just need someone to listen. I'm up for it, promise. Me and Liz. Hey, we'll stop by tonight, okay? How's 8:00? We'll go for dinner."

Charlene snorted and fingered a pale blue polo shirt. *Nah. Too casual.* Miriam did not understand. She was not a mother. She had not lost a child, had not held her son's lifeless body in her arms. She had not cried and clutched him to her, and then one day, seen a way out. No, Miriam was the last person Charlene wanted to be with right now.

THE NEXT AFTERNOON, Morrisey studied herself in the bathroom mirror. She hated what she saw. Haggard circles defined her eyes and her mouth was pinched. *Great. You'll make a lovely date.* Janet Raines was a construction worker and had the muscular, tanned body to show for it. Her hair was close-cropped and sun-bleached. She was very nice, but perhaps too bland. This would be their fourth date, and Janet had been asking when she could meet Gareth. Morrisey did not know when that might be. She was not even sure why she had agreed to go out with Janet in the first place. Maybe it was to prove to herself she was moving on just fine from the rape. Janet was nice. She was cute and had a great smile. She seemed safe enough. She had never set Morrisey's heart aflutter, though. There had been no moments of giddiness, no racing pulses.

Morrisey had forgotten those electric sensations until the day before, at the cemetery, when she had first set eyes on the wraithlike woman who turned out to be JP's mother. Morrisey grinned and shook her head. She smoothed her shirt and checked her teeth. The woman from the cemetery certainly had sent her nervous system into overdrive for a few minutes, but Morrisey would be very content to never see her again.

The doorbell rang, rousing Morrisey from her reverie. She frowned. She knew that ring, a brisk jab, very well. It was her mother, who would be baby sitting Gareth. She was early, as usual. Gareth was not even home yet from playing with a friend down the street. That was typical Margaret Hawthorne, always dropping by early or unexpectedly, which annoyed Morrisey no end.

Morrisey headed to the front door. She opened it without thinking, breaking her own rule of checking to see who was on the other side.

The visitor was not Margaret Hawthorne. It was the woman from the cemetery, Gareth's other grandmother. She clutched two small, wrapped packages to her chest. "Hi," she said in little more than a whisper. "First of all, I wanted to say that, uh..."

Shock paralyzed Morrisey. She could not find her voice, especially with the Acclaim looming in the driveway, mocking her with its silver door.

JP's mother displayed a shaky smile. "I just wanted to, well, I just wanted to...I wondered if you could help me. I didn't introduce myself yesterday, did I? My name's Charlene Sudsbury."

Morrisey was unable to answer. All she saw was that stupid

car and feeling *them* exploding inside her, and the —

Charlene reached for Morrisey's hand, but Morrisey jerked back. "What do you want? How did you find me?"

"Can I come in? Just for a minute."

"No. How did you find me?"

"Please," Charlene pleaded. She drew her brows together, and for a fleeting second, it was as if Morrisey was looking at Gareth. *Good God.* They had the exact same expression.

"No," Morrisey repeated, struggling to conceal her dread. "I said no. How did you find me?"

Charlene shifted guiltily. "After you left, I went to the tombstones where Gareth was playing. They all had the same last name. Then the phone book. Look, please, I just want to talk. Did you know JP, my son?"

The Acclaim must have been washed and waxed right before Charlene came over. It shone, just like it had that night, with the pristine snow and the full moon. *Did I know your son? Why, yes, I believe we met once. Didn't he rape me and leave me to die? Yes? That's the one? Jolly good fellow, he was.*

"He killed himself a few years ago," Charlene went on. "Maybe you already knew that. He shot himself in the head. Out of the blue. I don't know why. And I...I've just..."

Morrisey kept her expression indifferent. *Suicide. Wonderful.* "Sorry, I don't know who he is."

"Are you sure?" Charlene leaned in, and Morrisey caught a hint of lavender. "Maybe he gave you another name. Please. I just want to know why he killed himself, why he couldn't come to me. And if your Gareth is his son."

Morrisey replied automatically. "Again, I'm sorry about your loss. But I didn't know your son. I had Gareth through artificial insemination." It was the same story she had told everybody, even her own family.

Charlene brightened. "Well, that explains it!"

Morrisey flinched. "No. He wasn't the donor."

"How do you know?"

"I just do. Look..." Morrisey sighed and crossed her arms. "Okay, Gareth's father is a man I met in Europe. An older man, a doctor."

Charlene was not buying it. "Why did you say you were inseminated?"

"You have no business acting as if I owe you an answer. But, fine. I'm telling you Gareth's father is a wealthy, very married European man, if you get my drift. Again, I'm sorry for your loss. Goodbye." Morrisey started to close the door, but Charlene wedged herself in the doorway.

"Wait," she begged. "Wait. Just one second, please."

Morrisey looked into Charlene's blue eyes and remembered the sailboat, the baseball and the airplane. Charlene took advantage of the mental lapse and slipped inside. She set the gifts on the hallway table. "Look," she said. "I'm not going to judge you. That's the last thing on my mind. I'm not in the business of judging people. I don't care how you met JP and what you two did. I don't care if he was nineteen and if you were, what, in your late twenties? I don't care if you met when he was seventeen. Or sixteen! Whatever! I don't care if it was a drunken, one-night stand. Maybe he gave you a fake name. Maybe you never knew his name. I don't care about any of that. I just want to try to get into my son's mind, to know why he killed himself, and I'm hoping you can help with that. You knew him! I can see it in your eyes, in the way you bite your lip. You recognized my car, the car JP and I shared. I make you uncomfortable. That's the last thing I want. I don't care how you and JP met. I just want to know all you can tell me about my son. And please, please, I want to know my grandson."

Morrisey rubbed her forehead and tried to will the dull throb of a headache away. This woman was not going to give up.

"I will do anything you want," Charlene continued. "Anything. Just please give me a chance."

Morrisey cleared her throat. She ignored the desperate passion radiating from Charlene's eyes. "Again, I really am sorry—"

Charlene picked up the gifts. "This one's for Gareth." She indicated the present covered in baseball wrapping paper. "This one's for you." She proffered the second, which was wrapped in solid white paper. "Please, just talk to me."

Morrisey was at a loss for words. What was she supposed to do or say? This was all so surreal. "I really am sorry," she began haltingly. "I can see how much you loved your son. But, I'm very sorry, he's not Gareth's father."

"I won't do anything to you. I promise."

Morrisey bit her lip and looked away. "Please," she said in a little, weak voice she did not even know she possessed, "I mean it when I say I didn't know your son. Now please go."

Charlene took a step back and studied Morrisey for a moment that stretched into another, and then into another.

Go away. Go away. Go away. Leave me alone. Morrisey knew all she had to do was walk to the door and open it, but her limbs refused to cooperate.

A glimmer of understanding appeared on Charlene's expression. "What are you saying?"

"I'm not saying anything except that I didn't know your son and, therefore, he is not Gareth's father."

"JP hurt you."

Morrisey winced. *Hurt.* She hated that word. Why not say rape? Hurt was too nice, too ambiguous. She had bled. She had barely been able to walk. Hurt was not shattering her insides like glass and leaving her to freeze to death. But now was not the time for semantics.

"I didn't know. I'm sorry. Oh, God, I'm so sorry."

Morrisey blinked back tears. So a stranger, the mother of one of her rapists, knew what Morrisey had been unable to tell her own mother. Morrisey turned and strode into the kitchen. She grabbed a paper towel and dabbed at her eyes. *Go. Please, just go.*

Charlene remained rooted to the floor.

Morrisey took a deep breath. *Stop it. No more crying. You're fine. You're a big girl. Suck it up. You're in control.* She returned to Charlene. "I told you that Gareth's father is a man I met in Europe. What part don't you understand?"

"Okay," Charlene replied. There was no fight in her anymore, no more passion. "I'm sorry about the misunderstanding. I won't bother you again."

Anger washed through Morrisey. "I don't need that," she snapped.

Charlene stopped in mid-step. "Need what?"

"You know what! That pity, feeling sorry for me. That's total bullshit. I'm doing fine. I'm doing just fine."

Charlene's eyes widened. "No, no, I wasn't. I was just—"

"I know what you're thinking."

Charlene slumped, clearly miserable to her very core. "Okay. Tell me."

"Poor woman. I better leave her alone. It's so sad, that poor woman. It's like she has a disease."

"I'm not thinking that. Not at all," Charlene said, but her tone was not persuasive.

Morrisey snorted. "Enlighten me. What are you thinking?"

"Nothing."

"Nothing?"

They stared at each other for a long, horrid moment. Emotions flickered across Charlene's face—the same shock and revulsion as before, but this time, shame dominated. Charlene wrapped her arms around herself. "I'm just thinking I should leave."

"A few minutes ago, you were all gung-ho, and now you can't escape fast enough."

Charlene tightened the grip on herself. "I don't want to hurt you more than I already have. I'm sorry. I'm so sorry."

The doorbell rang.

"I'll get that on my way out," Charlene offered.

"It's my mother. She's baby sitting. I have a date."

"A date? God. Look, I'm just going to get out of your way. I'm sorry I've been such a—"

"No. I do not want people feeling sorry for me."

"I didn't mean—"

The doorbell rang again, more insistently this time. A nanosecond later, Gareth burst through the doorway, pink paint speckling his clothes. "Mommy!" he cried, but he stopped when he saw Charlene.

One of Morrisey's neighbors, Bruce Smith, was behind Gareth. Bruce was a broad-chested man with an easy grin. "Hey, Morrisey. Hope those clothes weren't expensive." He chuckled. "Gareth and Bryan got it into their heads to paint our doghouse, in pink."

Morrisey noticed that Charlene was trying to avoid Gareth's curious gaze. Bruce held out his hand to Charlene. "So you're Morrisey's date? Poor you. Ha. No, I'm just kidding. I think she means it when she says she doesn't bite. I'm Bruce. We live a few houses down."

Charlene blinked but took Bruce's hand. "Date?" She turned to Morrisey. "You're going out with a woman?"

Morrisey gave Charlene a black look. "I'm gay. You have a problem with that?"

"No!" Charlene dropped her gaze. "I just...I just...sorry."

"Okay, uh..." Bruce smiled uneasily. "See ya around, Morrisey. Good luck with the paint." He made his escape.

"You're the lady from the cemetery!" Gareth cried.

Morrisey reached for her son. "Let's get you cleaned up. Grandma will be here soon."

Gareth dodged her touch. "Grandma's boring!"

"Too bad. You're stuck with her."

"I don't wanna," he protested. "I wanna finish the doghouse."

"Grandma's taking you to a nice restaurant."

"She's boring!" Gareth wailed.

"Gareth. Go get ready. Now."

Gareth changed tacks and directed his protests toward Charlene. "My grandma's boring!"

Charlene did not answer, and Morrisey tightened her hold on Gareth. "Go change your clothes. I'll be with you in a minute."

He wriggled out of her grasp, his scowl deepening. He pressed his case with Charlene again. "Grandma chews with her mouth open! She tells me not to do it, but she does it!"

Charlene replied with a stiff: "You should listen to your mother."

Gareth narrowed his eyes. "Go on, sweetie," Morrisey urged. "Get cleaned up. I'll be right with you."

"Fine." Gareth trudged off.

Charlene straightened her shirt and said, "I don't know why I..." She faltered. "I shouldn't have..."

The doorbell interrupted, and Morrisey threw her hands up. "That'll be my mother, finally."

Charlene nodded. "Have a good evening. I'm sorry I bothered you."

"Wait." Morrisey reached for Charlene's arm.

"Should I leave the back way or hide?"

"We need to talk."

"I won't bother you again."

The door swung open, and Margaret Hawthorne stepped through. "Hello! Grandma's here!" She glowed, as usual. Her graying hair was swept up, and a sparkly black dress and high heels showed off her trim, svelte body.

Morrisey let go of Charlene and whispered, "My mother doesn't know about the...what happened."

Charlene's eyes clouded over. "Okay."

Margaret went right over to Charlene. "Hello! You must be Janet. My, you're a tiny thing! So gorgeous! I never would've thought you were in construction."

"I'm not Janet."

"This is Charlene, an old friend of mine," Morrisey intervened. "She dropped by to say hello. Charlene, this is my mother."

"Margaret," the older woman affirmed. "It's so nice to meet you!" She threw Morrisey an irritated smile. "Morrisey's always so secretive. I can't remember the last time I met a friend of hers." She addressed Charlene again. "How long have you known my daughter? How'd you two meet?"

Morrisey answered in Charlene's stead. "We met a long time ago. Hey, I need to check on Gareth. He was playing with Bryan, and they got into some paint. Both of you stay here. All right?" Morrisey studied Charlene pointedly. "Let's finish catching up, okay?"

"If you want."

"Yes. I'll be right back." With that, Morrisey went off to find Gareth.

Chapter Five

CHARLENE FELT AS though she were floating outside her own body. She felt unworthy to be in the presence of this woman with the distinguished bearing and the diamonds. Charlene bet that it would cost her a week's wages and tips just to afford Margaret Hawthorne's dress. *I am the mother of your daughter's rapist*, Charlene thought. How could she have been so blind? How could she not have seen it?

"Morrisey didn't mention how you two met," Margaret said.

Charlene mumbled the first thing that came to mind. "High school."

"I don't remember you. You do look quite familiar, although not from that far back. Where have I seen you?"

"No, uh, Morrisey and I weren't friends at the time. We were a few years apart, anyway. But we ran into each other at the store last week."

"You're an ex-girlfriend. From college?"

Charlene's stomach knotted. "What?"

Margaret chuckled, apparently interpreting Charlene's reaction as an affirmation of sorts. "How long were you together?"

Charlene fumbled for an answer. "No, really, we weren't together."

Margaret flapped a hand. "Fine. Whatever you say."

"It's true."

"Oh, bull. I saw it the instant I came in here. You could cut the tension with a knife."

"I better go," Charlene said. "It was nice to meet— "

"Which high school?"

The question stopped Charlene cold. "Cave Spring," she said, hoping she sounded convincing.

"Ah."

Charlene allowed herself to breathe. "Well." She stuck out a hand. "It was nice meeting you."

Margaret did not take the hand, so Charlene dropped it.

"Don't hurt my daughter," Margaret warned.

"What?"

"You heard me. Don't hurt my daughter. Morrisey's been through enough already."

Charlene swallowed. "I don't want to hurt her. I'm going to leave. Okay?"

"Morrisey wanted you to stay. So stay. Come on. Want me to get you a drink?"

"No, thank you."

Morrisey rounded the corner, Gareth at her side. "Here he is," Morrisey said. Gareth's face was shiny from a fresh scrub, and he was dressed in khaki pants and a white polo shirt.

"Hi, Grandma," he said, none too eagerly.

"Hello, darling." Margaret kissed the top of his head. "Aren't you cute enough to eat?"

Morrisey escorted her mother and son to the door. She saw them off with a wave. Charlene hovered back in the hallway, willing herself not to break down. Not here, not now, not in front of this woman.

Everything was so wrong. She had never hated herself more. JP had raped Morrisey, and Charlene had come barging into her life as if she were entitled to her grandson. Instead, she had ripped open the wound that JP had inflicted, and Morrisey's pain was so raw and so naked, it hurt just to look at her. Gareth, too. Every time Charlene had looked at him in the past few minutes, she had not experienced any of the joy or new life that had filled her before she came to Morrisey's house. All she had seen in her mind's eye was JP after the accident, a shadow of his former self, cursing at her and shoving her around. She felt again his ugly, hateful gaze, heard the mean words and smelled the alcohol on his breath.

Morrisey returned from the door. "Come with me," she said.

Charlene obeyed, following her into the kitchen.

"Want a drink?" Morrisey asked.

"I'll leave. Your date, remember?"

"I'm going to cancel."

"Don't let me ruin your evening. Go out. Have a good time. Please."

"You and I need to talk. I wasn't looking forward to the date anyway." Morrisey reached into a cupboard for two glasses. "What do you want? Water? Diet Pepsi? Coke? Tea? No alcohol, though. I've been meaning to get more wine."

"I don't want anything." Charlene studied Morrisey, so tall and beautiful, and obviously hurting but trying to put on a brave face.

"Coke it is." Morrisey filled two glasses.

"Why can't I go?"

Morrisey handed Charlene a glass. "Because I said so. Because you came here wanting answers. You can't leave just because they weren't the answers you wanted. If I can't get out of this, neither can you."

"Oh." Charlene tried to sip from her drink but set her glass down because her hands were trembling. "Don't you hate me?" she asked. "Me and JP?"

Morrisey pulled her lips back into a feral smile that chilled Charlene's heart. "There. See. That's why you're staying."

"What's why I'm staying?"

"That pity," Morrisey said. "I don't need your pity. I am doing just fine, and so is my son. Let me tell you about him. He is the most wonderful, most perfect child in the world. He is a child of love."

"Child of love?"

Morrisey's eyes narrowed in challenge. "Child of love. You have a problem with that?"

"No."

"When I look at him, I see Gareth. That's all. I see my son, a little red-headed boy who's too smart and too curious for his own good. I will not, I repeat, I will not have you looking down your nose at him and me. Don't you ever dare pity me and my son. Ever. Understand?"

Charlene met Morrisey's defiant gaze. Morrisey lifted her Coke and drank easily. No shaky hands.

"What do you want me to say?" Charlene asked. "What's the proper thing to say here?"

The question apparently gave Morrisey pause, for she looked away.

"I'm sorry." Charlene pleaded. "What do you want me to say? That I'm happy about having a grandchild? Well, I'm not. I'm angry. So fucking angry! I'd kill JP myself if he wasn't already dead. I raised him to be better than this. I did. You think I like knowing my son was a monster? Now I'm wondering if there were others. How many other women did he rape? He...what he did to you—"

Morrisey cut in. "I don't want you thinking of me as some poor rape victim and of Gareth as a rapist's child. That's exactly what you're doing. Why, the minute you found out, you were about to slink out of here!"

"I didn't want to hurt you any more! Why would you want me around?"

"Why would I want you around if, say, JP had been a sperm donor or a one-night stand? Huh? That didn't bother you. But the rape—oh yeah, you couldn't wait to escape. Well, guess what? I'm doing just fine, and so is Gareth."

"I know you are. Okay, what can I do? Please tell me what I can do."

Morrisey's nostrils flared. "Do? You mean like to make up for the rape?"

"Anything to help. Money? Name it."

Morrisey growled. "Haven't you been paying attention? I don't need help. I'm fine. Just fine. You get your wish. You can go now." She flung a hand toward the hallway. "Bye. Toodles. Sayonara. Ciao."

Charlene met Morrisey's angry eyes. "No." It did not feel right any longer to go, to flee, to leave Morrisey fighting her demons alone. "I'll stay. We'll drink our Cokes and talk."

Morrisey's shoulders sagged. "No. Just get out of here."

AFTER CHARLENE LEFT Morrisey's, she drove around aimlessly. Where was she supposed to go? Home? To the place she'd shared with her son, who had done such a ghastly thing? No, she did not dare go home just yet. She was afraid of herself, of what she might do to all of JP's things, which she had carefully stockpiled and maintained over the years: the pictures of him, his artwork from elementary school, his trophies and awards.

So where to? JP's grave? The thought made Charlene sick to her stomach. Miriam's? Absolutely not.

After about an hour of wandering, Charlene took the long, winding road to the Mill Mountain Star. She was glad there were only a few cars in the parking lot, but she did not bother to get out of Silver. She shut off its engine and slumped against her seat. Her breaths came in quick heaves, so she forced herself to inhale slowly. When she was under control, she squeezed her eyes shut.

"How could you?" she asked her son. JP was not the person she pictured, though. It was the person whose image had been seared into Charlene's mind for the past hour. Morrisey.

Charlene would do anything, anything, just to make the pain in Morrisey's eyes go away. She would give anything to go back two days and to never have seen Gareth and Morrisey, to never have ripped Morrisey's wound open.

"Fuck," Charlene muttered. "I'm so stupid."

Her son had raped the woman.

"How could you?" Charlene asked again. He came to her, the adorable, eager-to-please little boy, followed by the wild, drugged-out twenty-one-year-old with the ratty hair and shifty eyes. The boy who promised he would always take care of her. The young man who rarely had a kind word to say.

Charlene was too angry, too weary to cry, so she just clenched her jaw shut and stared out the window. After a few minutes, she got out of her car and stepped onto the overlook. It was still light out. Below her stretched the city, and all around her were miles and miles of mountains. Charlene immediately picked out the spot where Victory Stadium had stood. The stadium was gone now, demolished. Just like JP. It was where he knew glory in high school, where thousands of people cheered for him.

This overlook had been one of Charlene's favorite places, before JP's football accident. She and JP had hiked the Star Trail sometimes, and they would usually chat for a while at the overlook before heading back down. Charlene had loved to gaze into the distance, as far as she could see, and wonder if a better life awaited her and her son beyond the mountains. Now she felt more lost than ever. So many mountains. So many unrealized dreams. A raped woman and her little red-headed boy.

"SO." MORRISEY STUDIED the grave marker. "Which one were you?"

The words stared back at her: John Patrick Sudsbury, Beloved Son. There was no toy on the grave. No baseball, airplane, sailboat or anything else. Morrisey was not sure if it meant anything. Charlene had probably just forgotten to leave something the day before. Morrisey lowered herself to the ground. She crossed her legs and took care not to sit directly on the grave. She tucked a strand of hair behind her ear and reread the letters. It was funny, wasn't it? She hated cemeteries and had sworn not to return. Yet she was back already, and not to visit her father, but one of her rapists. Unlike at her father's grave, though, she sensed something here, some kind of presence at JP's resting place. Nothing good, nothing bad. Just a presence.

Beloved Son.

The four youths who raped her had been people. Sons, friends, cousins, brothers. This one was Gareth's father. Morrisey took a deep breath. How many other people were there who might look at Gareth and say, "Hey, wait a minute. He looks just like this guy I used to know," just as Charlene had? What if Charlene and JP had a big family and lots of friends? Yes, Morrisey mused, she was lucky she and Gareth had lasted this long. She had been so tempted to move far away after her son's birth, to get away from it all, to start anew and go to a place where she would not run the risk of her rapists seeing her and Gareth. But her family was here, probably the only family Gareth would have. He deserved a family.

Now Gareth had another grandmother. Morrisey allowed a small smile as she compared her own mother and Charlene Sudsbury. They could not have been more different. Margaret Hawthorne was a traditionalist, a strong family-values type woman. She frowned upon anything unconventional. She sat on several prestigious committees and spearheaded drives for the poor and homeless. She did not actually interact with them herself, though. That would not do. Margaret kept her distance while doing her share. It had taken her years to just accept Morrisey for who she was, but Margaret was getting there. She had been very fond of Rebecca, Morrisey's most recent ex, and blamed Morrisey for the breakup. Of course.

Margaret never said out loud that she wished Morrisey were more like her sister, Betsey, or her brother, Bobby, but the disapproval was there, and sometimes it was none too subtle. Morrisey tried to not let it bother her. Above all, she was sorry for her mother, for all the woman was missing out on by being so closed-minded. Morrisey did not get that feeling with Charlene Sudsbury. She knew next to nothing about Charlene, really, other than that she and Gareth shared some DNA. There was just something about her. The way Charlene carried herself with no artificial airs, the eyes that conveyed so much emotion. Once again, Morrisey flashed to the first time she saw Charlene, here at this very cemetery.

Charlene had been the epitome of quiet dignity. She certainly did not dress or talk like Margaret Hawthorne. And she looked young enough, probably was young enough, to be Gareth's mother. Morrisey wondered who JP's father was. Was Gareth going to have another grandfather as well? How about aunts, uncles? Was this going to turn into one huge mess? Morrisey cringed at the thought. Why hadn't she asked? *Stupid, stupid.* Was a new family member going to show up on her doorstep every day?

She plucked several blades of grass and let them fall through her fingers. She and Charlene had left things so up in the air. If only there had not been that look of pity in Charlene's eyes. "God," Morrisey muttered. "Fine." She might as well admit it. Pity or not, she wanted to see Charlene again, and she hated herself for it. Charlene lit something in her that Janet Raines did not, that no else had, not even Rebecca.

How wrong was that? How weird and creepy was that? Charlene was the mother of one of her rapists. She was Gareth's grandmother.

The chirps of crickets brought Morrisey out of her disquieting thoughts, and she returned her attention to the grave marker. Dusk was beginning to fall, and she did not want to be at the cemetery even if the darkness was slight. "So, John Patrick Sudsbury, beloved son, which one were you?" she asked.

The trees whistled, and Morrisey shivered, goose bumps covering her skin. The trees fell silent just as she arrived to her car.

CHARLENE LAY IN bed and gazed blankly at the ceiling. Blinds and curtains muffled the morning sun, lending the usual dimness to her room. She had to be at work in an hour but could not force herself to clamber out of bed and go about her day as if all was right with the world. She should not have let JP get away with hitting her. It did not matter that it happened only once. "He cried. He hugged me," Charlene whispered. "He apologized. He meant it."

I know he did.

She saw it happening all over again, as if were yesterday.

She had arrived home from work to the usual—plates of congealed food, a dozen empty beer cans, an apartment that smelled and looked like an ashtray, and a zombie son in front of the TV. She was fed up at last and asked him, bluntly and forcefully, "What's happened to you? Yeah, you lost your football scholarship. So what? You have brains and a good heart. Use them."

He had ignored her and scratched his crotch.

She refused to back down.

He came inches from her face, his breath stale and liquor-laced. Veins pulsed from his neck, and he slammed her against a wall. Not once, not twice, but three times, until her tears came. He stopped, his mouth going wide. He repeated over and over, "Sorry, Mom, I won't do it again."

She said with a calm firmness that belied her shock: "Get out, JP. Get out of this apartment. Now."

JP swallowed. He took a step back, his face crumpling. Then he lunged forward and threw his arms around her, clinging to her for dear life. His chest heaved as he sobbed. "SorryMomI'msosorryGod I'msorryIloveyouMommyMommyIloveyou."

She let him stay, her poor lost soul of a son. He got part-time work the next day, scooping ice cream. The job lasted a week, but he never hit her again. Still, he had not learned his lesson, had he? He had simply taken his rage elsewhere.

Yes, he had hit her and she let him get away with it, because of the tears, the apologies, the little boy "Mommy."

"Shit." Charlene got out of bed and forced herself to the present, to a world in which her son was dead and buried. She made her way to the bathroom. "I'm sorry," she muttered. "God, Morrisey, I'm so sorry."

A FEW DAYS passed. Each of Charlene's mornings started the same way. She lingered in bed, her heart heavy. She thought about JP, Gareth and Morrisey: JP, ugly and brutal, Gareth, who no longer filled her with joy, and Morrisey, beautiful and wounded. Charlene struggled to come up with something she could do to help Morrisey. What was there, though? She did not have a magic wand.

More and more, thoughts of Morrisey haunted Charlene. Morrisey had so casually prepared the two glasses of Coke, as if Charlene had just stopped by for a chat. Morrisey had tried so hard to be brave, her voice fierce, her eyes unwavering, as she defended her beautiful little son as a child of love. Her desperation, gone almost as quickly as it appeared, when she said her mother did not know about the rape. Who had Morrisey told? Was Charlene the first? The possibility dismayed her.

After sorting through her thousand thoughts, Charlene would get out of bed, wander into JP's room and pack a few things. Then she would unpack them. Pack and unpack. Pack and unpack. She would also dust and clean the room. Afterward, she would walk through the apartment. JP surrounded her in pictures. He morphed from a cherubic bubbly baby into a grinning, freckle-faced boy. Almost overnight, he became a gap-toothed skinny ten-year-old. Then he was a strong, handsome sixteen-year-old.

Charlene yearned to take the pictures down. JP did not deserve to be up there, but every time she went to remove a photo, she stared at it, paralyzed. The pictures stayed.

Heartache, anger and love pulled Charlene every which way, rendering her hopelessly indecisive. She could not do a damned thing except flounder. She had not even visited JP's grave. Five days had passed since that Sunday, and never before had Charlene let more than three days in a row go by before visiting.

Several more days dragged past. No answers, no brilliant insights, were forthcoming. One morning, when she did not have to be at work until noon, Charlene decided to stomach her revulsion and visit JP's grave. Maybe this time she would find what she needed. She got into Silver and drove the route so familiar she could have done it blindfolded.

The day was turning out to be refreshingly cool, a welcome break from the smothering humidity of the past several days. Charlene made her way to her son's plot and stood over his marker.

John Patrick Sudsbury, Beloved Son.

Beloved son.

Charlene sank to her knees. "Why, JP? Why did you do it? Why did I let you get away with all you did?"

The wind started blowing, as it did so often when Charlene was talking to JP. As always, her ears perked, listening for answers that would probably never come.

The wind stopped trilling. Charlene sat and buried her face in her hands. She should have stayed home. *Did you really expect to learn anything?* She was about to get up and leave, but the voice stopped her.

"Excuse me. Charlene?"

Charlene jerked up in surprise, and her heart sank. *Morrisey's mother.*

Margaret Hawthorne held two long-stemmed roses. Her expression was concerned and curious. "Are you all right?"

"Yes. I'm fine."

"We met the other day. I'm Margaret Hawthorne."

Charlene scrambled to her feet. "I remember."

"I knew I'd seen you somewhere before. Now it's coming back to me. You were sitting here many times when I visited Adrian, my husband."

Charlene proffered a weak smile. "Really? I haven't noticed you."

"You've always been wrapped up in your own world," Margaret said kindly. "Who have you been visiting?"

Charlene refused to let her gaze drop to the grave marker. "My son. JP."

Margaret drew in a breath. "Your son? I'm so sorry."

"Thank you."

"What happened?"

"He killed himself." *He blew his brains out—with me in the next room. Wasn't that considerate?*

"Killed himself? Oh my. I'm so sorry."

"Me, too."

Margaret studied the grave marker. "Almost three years."

"Yes. Sometimes it feels like yesterday. Other times, it's another life."

Margaret extended one of her roses to Charlene. "For your son."

"No, I couldn't. Those are for your husband, aren't they?"

"He'd want John Patrick to have it. Take it," Margaret urged.

Charlene had no intention of accepting the rose. If Margaret Hawthorne knew what JP had done to her daughter, she would raise bloody hell. She certainly would not be offering a rose. "I really can't," Charlene said. "You don't know us."

"I can see you loved your son very much. I'm a mother too. I've lost a child."

"You have?"

"Yes. Our firstborn, Adrian Jr. He was just a baby. Born with all sorts of troubles. The doctors said he wouldn't last the week. He lived three months, three wonderful, precious months." Margaret let out a heavy sigh. "Not a day goes by that I don't think about him. If he'd been born today, in this day and age, he'd be fine. All those 'what ifs'." She held out the rose again. "Please, take this. This isn't for my husband, anyway. It's for my son. I always put a rose on his grave too. John Patrick should have his today."

Charlene took the rose. "Thank you." She inhaled its strong and sweet scent. "It's lovely."

Margaret beamed. "It's from my garden. Adrian's, really. I never was into gardening, but he loved his flowers. So I'm learning."

Charlene carefully arranged the rose on JP's grave. "Thank you."

"Have you talked to Morrisey lately?"

Charlene's heart stilled at the mention of her grandson's mother. "No. How is she?"

Margaret shrugged, but her gaze was keen. "She's fine. Should she not be?"

"I was just asking."

"Tell me, please," Margaret implored. "What really happened between you and my daughter?"

"Nothing."

Margaret shook her head. "Morrisey and I never were close. Mostly my fault, I suppose. We never understood each other. She always did her own thing, pushed against me. Now with my husband gone, I've come to realize I made mistakes. I want to be close to my daughter. I can't do that because she won't tell me anything. Can you help?"

"Tell her what you just told me."

"I should. It's easier said than done, though."

"Does she love Gareth?" Charlene asked.

Margaret's eyes widened. "Of course she loves him. He's her son. He's the best thing that happened to her."

The pit in Charlene's stomach deepened. She still could not believe Morrisey had not told her family, or at least, her mother, about the rape. She had held it inside for years, which must have been torturous.

"Morrisey used to be so standoffish," Margaret went on. "She was always in her world, doing her own thing. She had to have things her own way, all the time. She had no sense of humor. That's probably the Morrisey you knew back then, right? Then after Gareth, my daughter loosened up. She was happier, so much happier."

"Really? Happier?"

"Yes. Happier. Why are you so surprised?"

Margaret saved Charlene from having to answer by continuing. "I was as surprised as I've ever been in my life when Morrisey told us she was pregnant. And through artificial insemination! She'd been so against having kids, and out of the blue, there she was, six months along. It all worked out, I suppose."

"I suppose," Charlene concurred.

Margaret studied JP's grave marker again. "How old were you when you had him?"

"Seventeen."

"Then you didn't know my daughter in high school. Why, you two must've been at least six years apart."

Charlene scrambled for an explanation. "Ah, is that what I said? I was in high school. Morrisey was in junior high."

"Charlene, what's going on? Why can't you admit you're an ex-girlfriend?"

"Nothing's going on. I promise."

"Well, whatever it is, Morrisey still likes you. It just took one look at her for me to know. I don't want to sound like a broken record, but be careful. Whatever you do, don't hurt my daughter again, please."

Charlene was tempted to laugh at the absurdity of the statement, even though a tiny, guilty part of her clamored to be heard. What would it say? That while Morrisey might not like her, Charlene certainly was attracted to Morrisey, whom she foolishly, ignorantly, had wounded. Morrisey had been on her mind for days and days. Morrisey was beautiful. Lovely. Lonely. No. Charlene refused to even think about it.

"Trust me," she said in a voice that left no room for doubt. "Your daughter most definitely does not like me."

"Well, you like her."

"No, not like that."

Margaret only sighed.

Chapter Six

MORRISEY WAS BLOWING bubbles with Gareth in their front yard when her mother's familiar gray Buick Park Avenue pulled into the driveway. "Grandma's here!" Gareth cried.

"Yes, I see," Morrisey replied. *What's Mom up to now?*

Gareth set down his bubble blower and ran to the Buick. Morrisey was much slower getting to her feet, and she greeted her mother with a tight, thin smile.

Margaret hugged Gareth. "What have you been doing today?"

"We were blowing bubbles!" Gareth exclaimed. "And later we're going to the zoo!"

"The zoo? Wow!"

"Yeah! We can see dinosaurs and tigers and monkeys!"

"Not dinosaurs," Morrisey corrected. "They're at the museum."

Gareth was not deterred. "Grandma! Wanna see my new dinosaur book?"

"Sure. Run in and get it."

"Okay!" Gareth dashed into the house.

Morrisey crossed her arms and cocked an eyebrow at her mother. "What brings you here?"

"Can't I drop by and say hello?"

"I'm not in the mood for games. What do you want?"

Margaret looked offended. After a couple of seconds, though, she nodded. "I saw your ex-girlfriend today."

"Rebecca? What's she doing here?"

"No, not Rebecca. Charlene."

Morrisey snorted. *That's what you're up to.* "Charlene is not an ex of mine."

"Oh, pshaw." Margaret shrugged the denial off. "Then what's with all the tension? I know that tension, sweetie. Only from an ex!"

"Yeah, well, she's not an ex," Morrisey snapped.

"You know, I didn't much like Charlene when I met her here.

Something rubbed me the wrong way about her. I thought she was going to be bad for you. After today, I like her."

"Good for you," Morrisey drawled.

"She cares genuinely about you, sweetie. But she thinks you don't like her."

"Mother," Morrisey said tersely, "I don't like being the subject of gossip hour. Stay out of my business."

Gareth flew out of the house with his book. "Here it is, Grandma!"

"Will you get me some water? A bottle?" Margaret asked.

"Okay!" Gareth ran back inside.

"I saw her at the cemetery and just wanted to say hello. Did you know about her son?"

"Yes," Morrisey replied quietly.

"I gave her your brother's rose, to put on John Patrick's grave."

Morrisey's mouth went dry. "Oh." An image of JP in his casket floated into her mind. He was pale, and his eyes, Gareth's eyes, were open. His lips parted in a sinister smile. His teeth were straight and white.

"Does that bother you about the rose?" Margaret asked.

"Doesn't bother me. That was sweet."

"Charlene wouldn't accept it. I had to persuade her."

Gareth barreled out again, book in one hand, a water bottle in the other. He gave the water to Margaret and dragged her to the porch. He flipped the book open to the first page. Morrisey paid him and her mother little mind. *Charlene.* No matter what, Morrisey could not erase the woman from her mind. It was not just because Charlene made Morrisey's pulse race. It was also because Morrisey had a feeling Charlene could give her some, if not all, of the answers she had been seeking. Answers about the rape, about Gareth's father—which of the four he was. Who the other rapists were and what they were doing now. Perhaps Charlene could bring closure. Finally, closure.

The night before, Morrisey had picked up the phone book and located Charlene's name, address and number. She wrote the information on a Post-it note. Then she ripped the note into shreds. She was not ready to call. She was still too afraid.

AFTER MORRISEY TUCKED Gareth into bed that night, she went to the kitchen. She picked up the phone receiver but replaced it right away. She pricked her ears, hoping Gareth would cry out for another story or a second round of tickles. No sound was forthcoming, and Morrisey forced herself to get the phone again. She felt as if she were floating outside herself as she watched her long, slim fingers punch in Charlene's number. What was she doing? *Crazy. Stop.*

The phone rang. *Hang up, hang up.* Two more rings. "Shit," Morrisey muttered. She was about to abandon her task when there was a click. A soft, breathless voice followed. "Hello?"

Morrisey's stomach fluttered, and she stared at the phone as if it would tell her what to do.

"Hello? Hello?" It was definitely Charlene.

"Hello," Morrisey said.

A sharp intake of breath sounded. "Morrisey?"

"Yes. Hello." Morrisey kept her voice steady.

"I'm sorry about today."

"What?"

"Your mother and I ran into each other at the cemetery."

"Right. Yes." Morrisey pulled the telephone closer to her. "Yes, she told me."

"I know I'm the last person you want to hear about. I haven't been going to the cemetery."

Morrisey cleared her throat. "Look, we need to talk."

"No, we don't. I'll leave you and Gareth alone. I promise."

"We need to talk."

"About what?"

Morrisey gestured, even though she knew Charlene could not see it. "Please. We need to talk."

"Okay," Charlene whispered.

"Can you meet me for lunch tomorrow? Or dinner? No, wait, I can't do dinner."

"I work tomorrow. I'm off Sunday."

Sunday was only two days away, but to Morrisey the time would hover like a shimmering mirage. *That's too far off.* She did not want to go through the next couple of days in constant anxiety and tension, worrying over her meeting with Charlene. No, she had to see Charlene as soon as possible and get it over with. "Can you come now?"

"Now?"

"Yes. Can you?"

Charlene replied in a scratchy voice. "I, uh...yes. I can. Are you sure?"

"Do you remember where I live?"

"Yes."

"See you soon." Morrisey sank into a chair, trying to steel herself. She told herself that she had done the right thing. She and Charlene would have to meet again at some point, and better sooner than later.

Morrisey began preparations for Charlene's arrival. She

changed from her pajamas into newly washed jeans and a T-shirt. She brushed her hair until it shone. For good measure, she brushed her teeth and washed her face. Afterward, she studied herself in the bathroom mirror. She smiled, hoping she appeared nonchalant, carefree, unburdened.

Her next stop was Gareth's bedroom. His door was open, and a Bugs Bunny night light shone from an electrical outlet. Gareth, clad only in shorts, was tangled under his bedcovers. His chest rose and fell steadily. Morrisey held her breath and tiptoed toward her son. She loved watching him sleep, but she would not linger this time. She bent down and grazed his forehead with a kiss. "I love you, sweetie," she whispered. She then retreated into the living room to await her guest.

CHARLENE ARRIVED TEN minutes later, her presence signaled by two beams of light turning into the driveway. Morrisey headed to the door. She did not want a knock or the doorbell to wake Gareth.

Charlene took her time getting to the porch. The moon was out in full glory, and its light framed Charlene just so, highlighting her fragility and vulnerability. Her hair was tousled, and there were lines on her face where none had been before. She had been suffering for her son's crime, but that did not detract from her beauty. Far from it. Yet again, Morrisey felt like an ogre—stupid, awkward, clumsy. Charlene was a woman she could easily, very easily, fall head over heels in love with.

Be careful.

Charlene's expression was fearful, and Morrisey tried to reassure her visitor: "I won't bite. I know you're not responsible for what JP did."

"Oh. Okay." Charlene's voice was tiny and full of doubt.

Morrisey stepped aside and gestured for Charlene to enter. Morrisey closed the door behind them. "Want something to drink?"

Charlene gripped her purse. "A drink?"

"Yes. Or something to eat. Both?"

Charlene blinked and fidgeted.

"Please don't be afraid of me," Morrisey said.

Charlene took a step back, bumping into the door. "I'm not. Well, I don't think I am. I just don't know what to say."

Morrisey inclined her head. "That makes two of us."

"So why'd you call?"

Morrisey shrugged. "Like I said, we need to talk. Coke again?"

Charlene gaped. "How do you do it?"

"Do what?"

Words poured out of Charlene's mouth. "I'm a mess, a horrible, frightful mess. My hands were shaking so hard when I tried to put the key in the ignition. I could hardly drive over here. I keep feeling like I'm going to throw up. And look!" Charlene tugged at her mussed blonde hair. "It's a mess! I'm a mess! I dropped the brush twice, and I couldn't do anything. I've been awful ever since I found out, so angry at JP, sick to my stomach. You're so cool, calm, collected. How do you do it?"

Morrisey stifled a smile. She felt so much better. She even had the urge to laugh but did not want to embarrass Charlene. "Hey," Morrisey said. "Your hair's fine. Okay? Really. It looks great. How's mine? Just remember hair's the only thing that matters."

Charlene's response was a tiny smile, one that wanted to be bigger but was not brave enough. Color rose in her cheeks, and the Charlene-smile unconsciously expanded.

"Is that a 'wow, your hair's amazing?'" Morrisey asked.

"Yes," Charlene said, laughing.

"Good. I'm glad we have our priorities straight now."

A FEW MINUTES later, Morrisey, bearing two Cokes, joined Charlene on the couch.

Charlene took a sip. "Thank you."

Morrisey spied a GI Joe peeking from under the ottoman. She scooped up the toy and fiddled with it.

"What's that?" Charlene asked.

"This?" Morrisey indicated the little plastic man. "One of Gareth's GI Joes."

"He likes them?"

Morrisey studied the action figure's unnatural smile. "Yes."

"What does Gareth do with them?"

Morrisey forced herself to look at Charlene. "The usual war games and stuff. Sometimes he dips them in paint. Don't ask."

Charlene's expression grew wistful. "What is he like?"

Morrisey shrugged. "He loves to play outside. I'll throw a baseball with him a lot, and he always manages to sneak frogs and other nasty critters inside. Ugh." She wrinkled her nose. "He's smart. He really is. He's friendly and outgoing. He's very sweet. He hates to see people and animals hurt. He's a curious boy. He goes up to people all the time. He asks them all sorts of questions. I was never like that. No one in my family is. Or was." Morrisey left the question unasked. When Charlene did not respond, Morrisey prompted, "Is anyone in your family like that? Was JP like that?"

Charlene shifted in her seat and avoided Morrisey's eyes. "Yes, he was, before the accident. I'm sorry."

Morrisey ignored the apology. "What accident?"

"Football accident." Charlene took a moment to collect her thoughts. "JP was a golden child. He was a star, a quarterback. He had a scholarship to Virginia, and he had an extensive laundry list of goals. He kept saying that after he turned pro, he'd buy me a big house with a pool, a fancy car, everything I never had, to thank me for all I'd done for him."

"So he was injured in a game?"

"Yes. In his senior year of high school, our team made it to the district championship. With four minutes left in the game, JP was sacked really hard by three guys. He lost consciousness. He had broken ribs and a permanently damaged knee. He'd never be able to play again. Football had been his life. Football was his way out. That injury killed him. He lost his scholarship. I kept telling him, 'You will be fine. Go to college, I'll help you. Don't worry about me.' He didn't listen, and he was never the same person again. He started hanging out with the wrong people and got into drugs. Charlene shuddered. "Then one day, he ended it all."

Charlene's despair was so naked and intense. Morrisey wanted to help, but she felt like an idiot when all she could muster was a weak, "I'm sorry."

"He wasn't JP anymore. He was some person I didn't know. I kept making excuses. Oh, that football injury, blah, blah, blah. But maybe the injury just brought out something in him that was already there, though. Maybe that was the real JP. I never thought he'd hit me. My own son."

Morrisey stiffened. "He hit you?"

Charlene's eyes widened. "What? Of course not. Oh God, did I say that?"

"Yes."

Charlene flapped her hand dismissively. "Once. No big deal. Didn't hurt."

"Ah." *Change the subject.* "What about JP's father? What is he like?"

Charlene flinched, and Morrisey knew she had hit a nerve. She pressed on, asking, "Who is he?"

"He was—you really want to know?"

"Yes."

"He was my junior-year English teacher in high school."

"Wow."

"I was stupid back then." Charlene slumped. "He made me feel so special. Do you know what I mean?"

"Maybe."

"I was lonely. I don't know. Never mind. It's a long story, and I won't bore you with the details."

Morrisey met Charlene's eyes. "You won't bore me. I promise."

Charlene looked away. She sighed. She scratched her nose. "I was in love," she murmured.

"With your teacher." *With a man.*

"No, not with him," Charlene clarified. "Not with Mr. Burroughs."

"Then who?"

Charlene turned distant, as if she were detaching from herself. Her words became slow and measured. "My best friend Jamie. I was head over heels in love with Jamie — or so I thought anyway. Now I realize it was just a stupid crush. Anyway, Jamie didn't like me back and wouldn't talk to me anymore. My mom was into a lot of bad stuff like crack cocaine. I was juggling school and working full time. My life was shitty. Then there was Mr. Burroughs, this beautiful, passionate, intelligent person who paid attention to me and told me I was the best thing since sliced bread. When he gave me that secret, special smile one afternoon, I knew what he wanted. And I let him have it. Once a week for about three months. Why not?"

Morrisey looked into Charlene's serious eyes and digested her words, discerning the hint of defeat. Morrisey set down the GI Joe and said, "So your teacher used you."

Charlene bristled. "I was using him too."

Morrisey was incredulous. "How? Was the sex that amazing?"

That made Charlene laugh, just a little. "No," she admitted. "The sex was horrible. But when I was with him, I wasn't my old boring plain self anymore. I was having an affair with my dashing, gallant teacher. That's exciting, isn't it?"

"Could be."

"I told you I was stupid."

"No. It happens. It's human."

Charlene grinned. Shyly? Gratefully? "When I told him I was pregnant, he gave me money for an abortion. Then he moved away with his wife. She was pregnant too, and he said he really did love her."

"Asshole."

"Eh. I didn't mind that he left. I was afraid he'd ask me to marry him."

"Why would that scare you? You wouldn't be your old boring self anymore, right?"

"I didn't love him, never did. Like I said, I was young. I was stupid. It was just the excitement of a fling, of not having to be myself anymore, even if it was just once a week."

"Did JP ever want to track down his father?" Morrisey asked.

"Nah. JP said we didn't need him, and I was glad. I didn't want that man in my life. He had his wife and other child, and that was fine by me."

"Ever wonder about them? JP's half-sibling, about the same age as him. Was it a boy or girl?"

"Don't know, don't care. I had my own life, and Mr. Burroughs wasn't in it."

"What did he look like?"

Charlene's lips pulled back into a knowing smile. "Like Gareth. Like JP. Every time JP smiled, a perfectly symmetrical, even smile, it was like I was looking at Mr. Burroughs all over again. Now there's Gareth, too."

"But Gareth has your smile," Morrisey pointed out. "Just a little off-kilter."

"Really?" Eagerness crept into Charlene's voice. "I hadn't noticed that."

Morrisey picked the GI Joe up again. "Yes. I love that smile." She traced the lines of the GI Joe's camouflage fatigues, her heart hammering. *Come on, do it. Just don't look at her.* "Charlene," Morrisey began, "one reason I asked you over tonight was so you could tell me about your son. You've already shared a lot, and I appreciate that. Thank you. I'd like to know a few more things, though."

"Medical histories, you mean? Well, my family's been pretty healthy. Gareth has nothing to worry about there."

Morrisey squeezed the GI Joe. "Not that."

"No?"

Morrisey shivered as if the air conditioning was on full blast. "Forget it."

"What is it?"

Morrisey blurted out the words before fear could get the best of her. "I just want to know which one he was."

"I don't understand."

Morrisey swallowed, and a shudder, half anticipation and half dread, ran through her at the realization that she was going to talk about the rape. Not with a friend, not with a psychiatrist, not with a relative, not with a lover, but with the mother of one of her rapists, a woman she barely knew. But it was time.

Morrisey clenched her jaw and looked into Charlene's eyes. "There were four of them. It wasn't just JP."

Charlene blinked, not quite absorbing Morrisey's words right away. "What? You mean..." She paled with understanding. "Oh, God."

"There were four of them. I never got good looks at their faces. I could have. I didn't want to. Maybe I should have. Maybe I'd know which one was Gareth's father."

A strangled sound gurgled up from Charlene's throat. She glanced desperately in the direction of the front door, but Morrisey willed herself to continue. All she had to do was keep talking. No stopping to think or feel. "It was December, a couple of days before Christmas. I was driving back from visiting Betsey, my sister. She had just moved to the lake. It was snowing pretty hard, and my car suddenly started making a weird, hiccupping noise. I pulled over, and the car died on the shoulder. I got my flashlight and looked at the engine and all around the car, but I couldn't figure out the problem. I tried to call for help with my cell, but there was no signal. I'd passed a gas station about a mile back, so I started walking to it. A car—sorry, a SUV—passed. I waved for help. The driver ignored me or didn't see me. Then another car came. The wind was blowing hard, but I heard the voices before I saw the car."

"Silver," Charlene murmured.

Morrisey ignored the interruption. "Its windows were rolled down. The guys were sticking their heads out, their tongues lapping up the snowflakes, and they were whooping. I didn't wave for their help. They stopped anyway. They pulled over and spilled out. All I had was the flashlight. I was stupid. I didn't keep mace or anything like that in my car, but come on! A flashlight? I should've brought something else too. I just wasn't thinking because I was so pissed at my car."

Charlene protested, "No, no, no, it wasn't your fault. You don't need to tell me any more. I understand. It's okay. You don't need to tell me."

Morrisey's heart sank. *In other words, you don't want me to tell you.* "Okay," she whispered. "Okay. Fine." *Never mind that I've come this far only to be cut off.* Why was she subjecting Charlene to this? What mother would want to hear about her son raping a woman? "Sorry," Morrisey mumbled.

Charlene reached for Morrisey's hands and slowly entwined their fingers. Morrisey's mouth went dry and her pulse skittered. *Don't touch me. Don't you dare touch me, Charlene Sudsbury.*

Charlene tightened her grip. "Please tell me."

Morrisey felt as if her hands were on fire. She hated Charlene's touch. Hated it and loved it. She needed her hands out of Charlene's, right then and there. She was paralyzed, though, just as afraid to let go of Charlene as she was to keep the touch. Their hands fit together so perfectly, it was absurd. Morrisey wondered if Charlene noticed. Probably not, because at the moment, she was busy peering into Morrisey's face. "Morrisey," Charlene said, her gaze serious. "You want answers, and I want answers. Tell me what happened, and we can help each other."

Morrisey tried her best not to feel that night all over again. It happened anyway. The snow, which had been merely a pretty nuisance just a few moments ago, had become her enemy. It cloaked everything in its white, freezing blanket. Including her. "I was so cold," Morrisey said. "It was so cold. The snow, it just kept coming. And coming. So did they. The boys. That's what I remember most, the cold, inside and out. I remember how they smelled and how I watched the car go away. Your car. I could see it just fine through the snow and the darkness. The silver door, like it was in a spotlight. I was freezing. So cold, so numb. And then I saw my blood, all that blood. I didn't know what—"

"Morrisey, you're shaking. Let me get you a blanket."

Morrisey took a deep breath to compose herself. *Fuck. You're here, not there. It's a warm summer night.* The air conditioning was not on high, but here she was, transported back into that 20-degree nightmare. She shook her head. *Get a grip. You're fine.* "Thanks, Charlene, but I don't need a blanket."

"Are you—"

"I tripped backwards over a root. Can you believe it? A root, under the snow. They swarmed all over me, holding me, pushing me down, making sure I couldn't break free. I never had a chance. One had a really high, squeaky, almost feminine voice. I can still hear it as if it were yesterday. And God, he bit my tongue so fucking hard. I bled, and he sucked me dry. I couldn't see any of them very well. I didn't want to. I ignored them. Well, I ignored them as best as I could, considering. I tried not to feel anything. I just kept my eyes shut until they were done. I tried to turn my ears off.

"They smelled awful. Cigarettes, alcohol, just rancid. I can't even go into a bar without smelling them. So I don't go to bars. I couldn't feel my tongue because of the one who bit it. They had left me to die. I knew it, and they knew it. There was no way I could make it to the gas station. Somehow I stood and pulled my pants up. My sweater wasn't even my sweater anymore. It looked like a bear had...Anyway, I went back to my car. I tried it, just to see. And fuck, the car started perfectly. First try, it purred. I had to go home and act like nothing happened, like life was the same as always."

"Ralph," Charlene said in a muted whisper.

"Ralph?"

"Yes. He was the only friend of JP's I met after the accident. He had the most squeaky, girly voice. He showed up for the funeral too. Oh my God." Charlene was suddenly animated. "Morrisey, you have to call the police. We'll track Ralph down and make him pay."

"No!"

"Yes!" Charlene replied with just as much force. "You can't let them get away with what they did. There's no statue of limitations for rape in Virginia, right?"

"Don't tell me what to do. You think I want a trial, that I want to talk to reporters? You think I want to go to the police and tell those strangers all about it? I couldn't even tell my own family."

"I'm a stranger."

Morrisey jerked her hands out of Charlene's. "Go home."

Charlene betrayed no reaction. She asked, "Who were the others?"

"I said, go home. We're done here."

"You wanted to know which one Gareth's father was. So tell me more about the others."

Morrisey paced to the other side of the living room. She felt as though her body was a heated, angry current, but Charlene sat, unblinking, unmoving, hands folded in her lap.

"Must be nice," Morrisey said. "Just sitting there, acting as if—"

"Please. I didn't mean what I—please. Just tell me."

Morrisey gave up and finished her story from the fireplace. "Fine. One had a really low, rumbling voice. Like sandpaper. After it was all over, he kneeled down beside me. He said, 'Hey. Get up. You wanted a ride to the station, didn't you?' He laughed. I'll never forget that laugh. He enjoyed it. He enjoyed taunting me. And then they all left. The guy with the squeaky voice—Ralph? He went second. The one with the rumbling voice went after. One guy kept yelling at the others to stop. They didn't listen. Finally, he did it, too. He was the one who went last. And, the guy who tore my winter cap off, he dove in first. He was the quickest one. He also hurt the most. Down there, I mean. Anyway, those two who went first and last didn't have distinctive voices. Just, you know, typical." Morrisey paused for a second, startled at a new memory. "The first one had a moustache. I can't believe I just remembered that. It was a tiny moustache, just stubble really, but still..." She readied herself to meet Charlene's face. "Which one was JP? Do you have any idea?"

Charlene's eyelids fluttered.

"Take your time."

A muscle trembled along Charlene's jaw. "JP was the one who kneeled down and reminded you about the gas station. The third one. That's his voice, exactly."

"Oh." Disappointment ran through Morrisey. She had hoped, for Charlene's sake, and perhaps for her own and Gareth's, that JP had been the reluctant one.

Morrisey and Charlene were still for a long time, thinking.

After years of wondering which of the four Gareth's father was, Morrisey finally knew. *Gas station guy is Gareth's daddy.* Now what?

Charlene stood and approached Morrisey. "Sure you don't want a blanket?"

"I'm not shaking anymore."

They fell silent again. Morrisey hated the tension, hated being vulnerable, especially in front of Charlene. Morrisey wanted to crack a joke, to make herself and Charlene laugh, to show that she was okay, that she wasn't normally a weakling. What came out of Morrisey's mouth was not a joke, though. "What did you get Gareth?"

"Huh?"

"The present from the other day."

"Oh! It's about a boy named Tommy and his dog. It's kind of a combination coloring book and drawing book."

"And what did you get me? I'm not so easily bought."

Color stained Charlene's cheeks, and Morrisey found herself enjoying the reaction. *Good girl.* She was back in control, and now it was Charlene's turn to squirm.

"Well?"

"I have it in my car. Want to open it?"

CHARLENE COULD BARELY look at Silver as she approached the car. She felt sick, remembering the way JP had patted the door and proclaimed with a grin, "Handsome car. Let's call him Silver." How charming he used to be. "Silver," Charlene whispered. "God damn you." Silver, who had always filled Charlene with warm fuzzies but never would again. Charlene grabbed Morrisey's and Gareth's presents and darted back into the house.

Morrisey was in the kitchen and greeted Charlene by wriggling ten long, eager fingers. "Gimme."

Charlene handed the present over. She looked into Morrisey's sparkling dark eyes, at her well-defined face, her mischievous lips. The haunting thoughts about Silver drifted away, and butterflies Charlene had thought were long extinct fluttered to life. She was rendered breathless just as she was the first time Jamie's crystal-clear green eyes met hers for a second too long, giving her hope that maybe, just maybe, there was potential for more than friendship. *Yeah, right.* A week later, after more lingering eye contact, after long, delicious touches, Charlene dared kiss Jamie. Jamie had yelped and screeched, "What the hell?"

Charlene's face burned, then and now, with the sting of rejection. *Stupid damned butterflies.* "Don't open the present."

Morrisey frowned. "Why?"

"Let me get you something better for later." *Something practical, like a blender. Something proper for the mother of my grandchild.*

"Hmm." Morrisey turned the box over in her hand. "Can I shake it or will it break?"

"Really, please. Let me have that back. I'll get you something better."

Morrisey cocked an eyebrow. "I'm not expecting the Hope Diamond." She flashed an impish grin. "Although if that's what this is, I won't complain."

Charlene's dread increased despite Morrisey's attempts at playfulness. Morrisey was going to laugh at her and then reject her, just as Jamie did.

"Well, I'm going in," Morrisey declared. Seconds later, crumpled wrapping paper lay on the kitchen counter.

Charlene held her breath. She watched and waited. Morrisey really was beautiful. Lovely. Sexy. More and more features became apparent to Charlene, like the crinkles in Morrisey's smile, her tiny dimples, the way her eyes shifted color depending on the light. Her graceful movements were nothing like Charlene's clumsy self. Charlene loved Morrisey's slim, elegant fingers, fingers that were now caressing a King Arthur figurine.

"Do you like it?" Charlene asked, hoping that she wasn't telegraphing her attraction. "You don't already have one like that, do you? Because I'll take it back. I had no idea what to get. I was at the mall for such a long time, but I just couldn't find what I wanted, so I went to a place downtown. See, I remembered what you said about loving the King Arthur stories."

"Oh, this is beautiful." Morrisey turned the figurine every which way, taking in every detail. Charlene's stomach performed a back flip. Not even Jamie had earned a back flip.

"It's exquisite. Oh, Charlene. You shouldn't have."

Charlene shrugged modestly, trying to hide her immense relief. *She likes it. She loves it!*

"I can't believe you remember what I said about King Arthur."

"Gareth's an unusual name," Charlene explained. "And the truth is, the King Arthur story has always been one of my favorites, too. It's actually what brought me and Mr. Burroughs together, though I'm sure he was just using it as an excuse."

"Yeah?"

"Yep." Charlene forced a laugh. "We had to do papers on a book by Samuel Clemens, and of course, I picked *A Connecticut Yankee in King Arthur's Court*. I turned my paper in, and a few days later, Mr. Burroughs asked me to stay after class. He said my work was great, but that I needed to expand in several areas."

"Expand? As in your legs?"

Charlene stammered, "No. No. That came later. He gave me that look, the look that said, 'You're beautiful, smart, wonderful. I want you, need you, crave you.'"

"The look you wanted to see on Jamie's face."

"Yes. Oh, well. It wasn't a big deal."

Morrisey nodded. "Well, thanks for the present. It's lovely."

"You're welcome."

"Lunch Sunday?" Morrisey asked.

"What?"

"Do you want to have lunch with me and Gareth on Sunday?"

"I don't understand."

"Lunch. I can't promise the food will be anything fancy, though. How's Sunday? Here."

"I — wow. You said you weren't easily bought."

Morrisey laughed. "I'm not, but you can give Gareth his present Sunday. I wouldn't mind another one, either."

Charlene licked her lips. *Is she flirting? No, she can't be. But — shut up. It doesn't matter.* A wave of gratitude seized Charlene, and she wrapped her arms around Morrisey. "Thank you. Thank you so much."

The hug turned out to be quite possibly one of the longest of Charlene's life, but she hardly noticed. How could she, when Morrisey smelled so good, like cotton candy and Play-Doh and roses all in one? How could she notice when Morrisey was so soft, yet so firm? How could Charlene notice something so insignificant as time, because Morrisey was hugging her back, and Morrisey was a wonderful, wonderful hugger, so much better than Miriam and JP and Mr. Burroughs and Jamie combined? *God how can she smell so good and — oh, fuck.* Charlene drew back with a jerk.

Morrisey was silent for a long moment. Then she said, "See you at noon."

"Bye," Charlene muttered. She stumbled out of the house.

Chapter Seven

THOSE DARK EYES haunted Charlene long after she left Morrisey's. She tossed and turned all night thinking about them and the little dimples, the smile, the soft playful voice, the hug—the lingering, agonizing best hug ever. The more Charlene tried to banish thoughts of Morrisey, the more overpowering they became. For twenty-five years, JP, alive and dead, had been Charlene's life, her world. She had been too busy supporting herself and her son and then coping with his death to pay much attention to anybody. Her longest relationship, if it could be called that, was with Miriam, when JP was four years old.

She and Miriam had gone on three wonderful dates. At the end of the third one, they had sex, awkward, awful sex. Miriam knew Charlene had been anxious, and because they got along so well, she suggested another date. She arranged for her mother to watch JP and took Charlene on a romantic weekend at her cousin's cabin in the woods. A roaring fire, candles and wine completed the picture-perfect setting.

The sex was even worse. It was time to call it quits. "We're meant to be friends, best friends," Miriam said, and she was right. From then on, Charlene had not gone out more than a few times with any woman, though she had sex with some—blessedly, much better experiences than with Miriam. But Charlene had not thought about dating in a long time, despite Miriam's efforts to set her up with Connie or Melissa or Hope or Ursula or whomever. The suicide of a child had that effect.

But now?

Charlene's tossing and turning wore her out, and she drifted off to sleep. It did not last long. The alarm jerked her awake at 6 a.m. and Morrisey flashed into her mind immediately. *God, no. Not again.* Charlene felt so dirty, so sleazy. She shuddered as if cockroaches were crawling all over her. *My son raped the woman.* Charlene kept replaying the undeniable pain in Morrisey's eyes and her barely controlled voice.

Despite having bathed the night before, Charlene stripped her pajamas off. She showered. Scrub, scrub, scrub. *Don't think about her.* Wash hair, rinse hair. Scrub, scrub, scrub. *Why her? Why now?*

Charlene left the shower and got ready for work. It was only when she walked inside The Log Cabin that she realized she had not once thought of JP that morning, at least not in the "I miss him so much; how could I have saved him?" context. No, it was Morrisey who occupied Charlene's mind. Morrisey with her laugh and long dark hair and gentle touch. Morrisey who let Charlene hold her hands. Morrisey whom Charlene could not wait to see again.

Charlene came to an abrupt stop in the middle of The Log Cabin. She turned around slowly, surveying the place. She wanted out, to quit and tell her co-workers she was moving on to something better. The restaurant was such a boring place. It really was. It was generic and cheap, blah and frequented by families looking to save a few bucks while getting a decent meal. None of that had bothered Charlene much before. Now she wanted to rip out the worn and faded gray linoleum from the dining room floor and replace it with vibrant red tiles or carpeting.

Why was the place so damned dark, even at breakfast time? More light needed to get in. The place needed to be brighter and more cheerful. It needed to sparkle, like Morrisey sparkled. *Fifteen years*, Charlene thought. *I've been here fifteen years.*

"Hey," called the manager, Jay Wilson, from the other end of the restaurant. "Let's get going. Don't forget your Log Cabin smile!"

Charlene ground her lips together. "Right."

Hi! Welcome to The Log Cabin. What can I get you folks?

AFTER THE LUNCH rush ended, Jay called Charlene into his office. She went slowly, dreading a scolding. Ever since she had run into Morrisey and Gareth at the cemetery, she had not been herself. She was easily distracted, her patience with customers wore thin quickly, and she was prone to messing up orders. She calculated bills wrong and dropped dishes with alarming frequency. Even after JP's football accident and then his death, Charlene had been nowhere near this distracted. *JP had raped a woman.* Charlene would never forget Morrisey's raw, naked pain.

She let herself into Jay's small, sparse office. Jay indicated the metal folding chair across from his desk. Charlene sat, and he fixed her with a concerned gaze. "Are you all right?" he asked. Jay was a tall, wiry man in his late twenties, and he was going prematurely bald.

Charlene gave him a vague look, not wanting to appear too

cheerful or too contrite. "I'm fine. I know that—"

"You've been spacey for days. What's going on?"

Charlene intertwined her fingers in her lap, where Jay couldn't see them. He was a nice enough guy, probably the best boss she had worked for. He would understand if she phrased her explanation just right.

"Charlene?" he asked. "What is it? I hope you don't mind, but I spoke with Miriam earlier. Something to do with JP?"

Charlene bit her lip. *Great.* Ever since her birthday, she had avoided Miriam's frequent questions and entreaties to get together. How could she look Miriam in the eye and tell her the awful truth about JP, that he had raped a woman? That the little boy called Gareth was Charlene's grandson? And that the child's mother was so impossibly beautiful and hurting.

"Well?" Jay prodded.

Charlene offered him a weak smile. "It's nothing to do with JP. Well, maybe that's not exactly true. I did see a boy who looked a lot like him. I've actually kind of befriended his mother. It's just brought a lot of memories back. I'll be okay. Thanks for putting up with me."

"Well, all right." Jay reached for a pen and used it to keep his hands busy. "That's good. Because I've been thinking about something else too. It's about your position here."

Panic gripped Charlene. Jay could not be thinking about firing her after all the years she'd put in!

"It's not that." Jay chuckled as if he was reading her mind. "I'm leaving in a few months. I'm taking a job at a computer company."

Charlene let out a relieved sigh. "Wow. Congratulations."

"Thank you." Jay pulled at his tie. "I'd like you to take my place. You practically do everything anyway. You and Miriam. She's agreed to be co-manager. You two would mostly work opposite shifts, all that." Jay let go of the pen and held his hands out. "So what do you say?"

Charlene was sure she must have misheard. "Are you serious? Manager?"

"You deserve it. You've busted your ass at this place for years. You'll do a much better job than anyone else could. I'm going to get the powers-that-be to waive the requirement that you have a college degree. I'll arrange for training classes instead. What do you say?"

"Wow. Oh my God." Charlene covered her mouth, but a laugh escaped her. "Yes. Yes, of course. This is wonderful!" She thought about the darkness, the drab surroundings. Maybe she'd be able to spruce up The Log Cabin after all, to make it sparkle.

"It should've been done a long time ago," Jay observed. He and Charlene talked a few more minutes, sorting out the details. Then Jay showed Charlene to the door. "Go celebrate. Take the rest of the day off."

Charlene stumbled into the dining room. *Manager? Manager!*

Miriam darted over. "Well? What did he say?" She did not wait for an answer and crushed Charlene to her abundant bosom. "I know! I'm so happy for you. This calls for ice cream. My treat!"

A FEW MINUTES later, Charlene and Miriam slid into a booth. They dug into two generous bowls of chocolate ice cream. "So, are you finally going to tell me what's been on your mind?" Miriam asked.

Charlene avoided the question by spooning ice cream into her mouth. "Come on, you can tell me," Miriam prodded. "You went to see her."

"Who?"

Miriam rolled her eyes. "You know who, the woman from the cemetery. Morrisey?"

"Yes," Charlene whispered.

"What happened?"

"She's pretty nice, I suppose. She invited me for lunch Sunday."

"Why?"

"I don't know. Maybe she could be a good friend. Oh, that reminds me. Could I borrow your car for lunch with her?"

"Why?"

Knots twisted and untwisted in Charlene's stomach. She was not going to tell Miriam about Silver and the rape. "I want to impress Morrisey, and your car's better than mine."

Miriam's response was a knowing half-smile. "So you're interested in her."

Charlene fiddled with her spoon and watched the melting blobs of ice cream smearing her bowl. She struggled not to picture Morrisey.

"Sweetie?" Miriam prompted.

Charlene scooped more ice cream into her mouth but barely tasted it. "Yes, I like her," she admitted.

"She doesn't like you back?"

Charlene remembered the intense look Morrisey had given her, how Morrisey had hugged her back just so, with absolutely no move to break away. But Charlene had thought, could have sworn on it, that Jamie liked her too. "I don't know if she likes me," Charlene answered. "She's gay, though. She told me so herself."

"She knows you're gay?"

"I haven't told her."

Miriam opened her mouth but closed it without saying anything. After a moment, she just nodded and polished off her ice cream. "Yes, you can borrow my car. But I'm worried about you. Isn't it odd that you're drawn to the mother of a boy who looks like JP? After saying you don't want to date and acting as if wild horses couldn't drag you to any of the dates I've tried to set up for you?"

"It's not like that," Charlene protested.

"Maybe not consciously."

Charlene slid her half-empty ice cream bowl across to Miriam. "You can have this."

Miriam brushed the bowl aside. "Okay, I'm just going to come out and say it." She reached for both of Charlene's hands. Something indefinable in Miriam's eyes scared Charlene, and she could only nod a mute yes. "You don't need to lie to me," Miriam said. "You're connected to Gareth, aren't you? Is JP his father?"

Charlene gaped at her best friend. Miriam's expression was weary, knowing and sympathetic. "No," Charlene croaked, her tongue awkward. "Of course JP isn't Gareth's father. That's ridiculous."

"You can tell me."

"There's nothing to tell."

"Charlene, you've been a zombie for two weeks. You've been avoiding me like the plague."

Charlene bit her lip, clenched her teeth, and held her tongue down, but the secret was too ugly and overpowering. It came tumbling out. "JP raped Morrisey."

Miriam's shoulders sagged. "I was afraid of that."

"I can't believe it. I wonder if I ever knew my own son."

"You did," Miriam said firmly. "JP was a good kid before the accident. It broke his spirit."

Charlene lowered her eyes. "I don't want to like Morrisey. You understand now?"

"Yes."

"I most definitely do not want to like her. I can't help being attracted to her though. Last night, I wanted to kiss her. I wanted her to kiss me. Isn't that weird? Sick?"

Miriam sighed and shook her head. "I'll have your ice cream after all."

FLICKERING CANDLES ILLUMINATED Janet Raines's lean, tanned face. "More wine?" She held up a half-empty bottle.

"Hmm?" Morrisey stifled a yawn.

"More wine?" Janet repeated.

Morrisey glanced at her watch and feigned surprise. "Wow, it's late. I should be going. I want to tuck Gareth in. Thanks so much for having me over, though. Dinner was great."

"When can I meet him?"

Shame clenched Morrisey's chest. "Actually, I've been thinking. We should just be friends."

Janet's face fell. "What's wrong? Is there someone else?"

"No," Morrisey replied cautiously. "I'm sorry. You're wonderful, you really are. I just don't feel 'it' with you."

"I don't believe you. There's someone else."

Morrisey stood and reached for her things. She had never felt right with Janet, never felt that deep, aching burn for her, but, yes, there was someone else. Morrisey's mind had been on Charlene nonstop. What to wear for their lunch, what to serve, how to make sure Charlene was at ease. Janet Raines had not merited even one lousy thought.

Morrisey knew when a woman was attracted to her, and Charlene Sudsbury most definitely was. The attraction had been there from the beginning, at the cemetery. She had seen it in the way Charlene searched her face. Morrisey realized last night that Charlene had seen her as a woman, not simply as a rape victim, not simply as the mother of JP's child. There was no denying the faint eagerness in Charlene's eyes, her quickened breathing, the flash of desire on her face, the hug. Morrisey could not wait for their lunch "date" to arrive, to see if whatever had happened was just an aberration.

First, though, she had to say goodbye to Janet. She did so with a hug and another apology. On her way home, Morrisey was stopped by just about every traffic light, giving her plenty of time to think. She knew she ought to feel bad about her attraction to Charlene. And she did. After all, this was the mother of one of her rapists and her son's grandmother. However, when Morrisey looked at Charlene or remembered the lonely sailboat, baseball and airplane, these pesky facts didn't matter anymore. What mattered was that Charlene was in pain, and so was Morrisey. Together, helping each other, they could move on. Or so Morrisey hoped. Gareth had been born of the rape, and maybe something else wonderful would be, too. Still, as Morrisey pulled into her driveway, she shuddered as she thought, *my rapist's mother.*

CHARLENE STOOD IN Miriam and Liz's bedroom. She studied herself in the full-length mirror one more time, determined to hunt down and eliminate all of her flaws.

"Enough!" Miriam chided. "Get going already. You'll be late."

Liz, tall and blond with some white in her hair, ambled over to Charlene. "Stay," Liz drawled. "Stay with us two boring old coots. It's your life's dream to watch me mow the lawn, right?"

Charlene ran a hand through her hair, which fell into feathery layers on her shoulders. She and Liz had spent thirty minutes styling it with a curling iron. "You sure it looks better down? And explain to me again why this shirt is better than the other one."

"Out. Now." Miriam encircled Charlene's waist with her hands. "Don't make me drag you."

"Okay, okay!" Charlene escaped Miriam's grasp. "I'm out of here. Thank you." She kissed Liz on the cheek, and when she drew back, Liz was beaming. "What's that grin for?" Charlene asked.

"You have purpose now. It's good."

"Purpose? That's good? When Morrisey's been hurt so much and—"

"It'll be fine. Really," Liz urged.

Miriam took Charlene's hand. "Come on." She escorted Charlene to the door. "You look great. You're hot. You're the woman all the other women hate because no matter what you do, you're gorgeous. Got that? I hate you! We all hate you."

Charlene rolled her eyes. "Your nose is looking rather brown."

"Hush. Get in that car. Have fun!"

ABOUT FIFTEEN MINUTES later, Charlene arrived at Morrisey's house. She took a deep breath, but her uneasiness escalated even more. What if she could not look at Gareth without thinking about what JP had done? What if she simply could not bring herself to love the child? What if she could not look at Gareth's mother without wondering what it would be like to kiss her? What if, what if, what if?

Charlene got out of the car, slung her purse over her shoulder, and clutched Gareth's present and a new one for Morrisey to her chest. Little step by little step, she drew closer to the porch. The front door flew open before Charlene was even halfway to it, and Gareth bounced out. "Helloooo!" he cried. "Mommy said you had a present for me." He barreled to Charlene, and his eyes went wide. "Oh! Two!"

Charlene's pulse raced as she took in the dancing boy with the carrot-red hair and shining blue eyes. She stopped herself from thinking he was JP all over again, because he was not. This was a whole new boy, not her dead son.

Gareth squealed, "What is it? What is it?"

"Gareth!" A voice called from the front doorway, and Morrisey stepped out. "Gareth, no." Smiling apologetically, she joined Charlene and Gareth. "I should've known better than to tell him. He goes ballistic whenever he hears the word 'present'."

Morrisey was wearing jeans that accentuated her long, limber legs. A tight V-neck T-shirt helped bring her shapely assets to the forefront. Charlene had to restrain herself from looking there, but with such a shirt, the task was next to impossible. Morrisey smiled slowly, almost as if she was enjoying Charlene's discomfort. "You did bring something for me."

Charlene ignored her light-headedness. "I didn't want you to feel left out."

"Thanks." Morrisey clasped her wriggling son's shoulders and turned him around. "Gareth." She leaned down and looked him in the eyes. "Can you think of a better way to greet our guest?"

Gareth greeted Charlene a second time. "Hello, how are you? Can I open my presents now?"

Morrisey snorted. "One's for me."

"Okay!" Gareth wasn't daunted. "Which one's mine? Can I open yours?"

"Gareth." Morrisey's voice held a warning note.

Charlene brushed hair out of her eyes. She should have just gone with a ponytail. She would be fiddling with her mop all afternoon. *How attractive.* "Can I just give it to him now?"

"Good idea."

Gareth grabbed the present Charlene held out. He ripped the wrapping paper apart and crowed, "A book! Cool! A dog, Mommy! See! A dog! That's Lassie!" He jabbed a finger at the cover, which displayed a toothy boy and a huge golden Labrador retriever.

"No, sweetie. That's a lab, like Bryan has. Lassies are collies."

"Can we get one? Please? Like him?"

"Maybe," Morrisey equivocated. "Now what do you tell Charlene?"

Gareth flashed Charlene a huge grin that made her heart go wobbly. She could not resist comparing Gareth to four-year-old JP. This boy certainly was his father's son. JP had been the sweetest, most adorable child, too. "Thank you!" Gareth exclaimed. "Can I open Mommy's present now?"

Charlene knelt down so that she was at Gareth's eye level. "Your mom said you like to draw."

"I do," he replied seriously.

"You can draw in there," Charlene explained. She opened the book to the last few pages, which were blank.

"Cool!"

Charlene flipped to a random page in the middle of the book.

A round pink pig winked at her.

Gareth was indignant. "That's not a dog! That's a pig."

"There are lots of other animals in here too."

"Dinosaurs?"

"Yep."

"Snakes! I want to draw snakes!"

"I saw one or two."

"Hey, what's that?" Gareth reached for Charlene's keychain, which was poking out from her purse. "That's cool!"

"This?" Charlene drew the chain out.

"Cool!" Gareth's cheeks flushed with excitement at the mini Etch-a-Sketch and mini Mr. Potato Head that were the main attractions on the chain.

"Want to play with them?" Charlene asked, guilt welling within her. The mini-toys had been JP's. The entire keychain had been JP's.

"Yeah!"

Charlene nudged the toys off the chain. "Do you have big ones?"

"I had a big Mr. Potato Head. He ran away. I miss him." Gareth fiddled with the knobs on the Etch-a-Sketch, and Charlene could not take her eyes off his shining face. No, this boy was not JP. He had come into the world as the result of a violent act, but he was wonderful. He was lovely, her grandson.

Charlene swallowed and looked up at Morrisey. "May I hug him?"

"Fine." Morrisey's voice was strained.

"You sure?"

"Yes."

Charlene returned her attention to Gareth. "Can I have a hug?"

Gareth nodded. "Thank you for the presents, Charlie!"

"You're welcome." Charlene took Gareth into her arms for a long moment, memorizing the beat of his heart, his steady breathing, the fresh little-boy smell, his still body as he let her hold him. At last, he gave a little wriggle, and she broke away, acutely aware that tears were burning her eyes.

GARETH DASHED TO the kitchen table and flung open his new book. Meanwhile, Morrisey led Charlene to the refrigerator. "Want to help me cook?" Morrisey asked.

"Sure. What're we having?"

"How do peanut butter and jelly sandwiches sound? I'll need help. I burn them all the time." Morrisey reached into a cupboard. She drew out a jar of peanut butter. "Crunchy or not?"

"Not."

Morrisey set the jar down. "You can play with Gareth. You don't need to help me. I was just kidding about that."

"Okay." Charlene went off to join Gareth. He handed her an orange crayon, some glitter, and a piece of paper. Excited words shot from his mouth.

Morrisey could not make out what he was saying, but a pang of loneliness stabbed her. She felt like an intruder, like she did not belong in the kitchen. She was the odd man out. Charlene was a natural with Gareth. With their fair skin, identical smiles, pert noses and shining blue eyes, they absolutely looked the part of mother and son. Morrisey's discomfort intensified as Gareth leaned against Charlene and pointed something out in the book.

"Lab!" he cried.

"Boston terrier," Charlene corrected. "That's a Lab. Do you know what this big fellow is?"

Gareth frowned then broke into a smile. "Beethoven! St. Bernard. They're messy!"

"Yes." Charlene giggled and looked up.

Morrisey hastily turned back to preparing the sandwiches, but she felt Charlene at her side a few seconds later. "You okay?" Charlene asked.

Morrisey occupied her hands with the jar of jelly. "I'm fine."

"You know you can kick me out anytime, right?"

"I know." Morrisey set the jelly down and gave Charlene a smooth smile. *I'm jealous, aren't I? Yes, just a little.* She was jealous because this woman looked much more the part of Gareth's mother than Morrisey ever would. It took just one second with them to tell that Charlene and Gareth fit together perfectly, maybe even better than Morrisey and Gareth did. *My rapist's mother. It isn't fair. Well, shit happens.*

"Mommy!" Gareth ran up, waving a piece of paper. "I drew a picture of Lassie and Beethoven."

Morrisey struggled to decipher the shapes. "Wow. Very good." She injected some cheerfulness in her voice. "What's Lassie doing to Beethoven?"

"No!" Gareth howled. "That's Beethoven! He's trying to get Lassie to go swimming. See? That's the pond."

"Oh, I see. Well, they're both big dogs."

"Charlie!" Gareth grabbed Charlene's hand. "You draw Lassie and Beethoven swimming."

"I'm going to finish fixing lunch. Your mother will help you."

"No, Charlene will go with you." Morrisey smiled at the other woman. "Go. It's fine. Really."

Blue eyes full of doubt looked back at Morrisey, but Charlene did not press the issue. "All right," she said, and she let Gareth drag her back to the table. Morrisey finished making the sandwiches and refused to sneak peeks at her son and Charlene.

Chapter Eight

LUNCH CENTERED AROUND Gareth's animated babbling. Charlene caught Morrisey's gaze on her twice. They both looked away and acted as if it meant nothing. Charlene knew she had a problem, a big problem. She was falling even more for Morrisey, no matter how hard she tried to steel herself. And Morrisey's playfulness with Gareth was endearing as hell.

"Can we have pizza for dessert?" Gareth asked once he was done with his sandwich.

Morrisey raised an eyebrow. "Why pizza?"

"'Cause it's yummy! Can we? Please?"

"That's a good enough reason. What do you think?" Morrisey directed her query to Charlene.

Charlene got the feeling Morrisey was testing her and smiled noncommittally.

"Can we?" Gareth was about to fall out of his chair because he was so excited.

Charlene returned his grin. "Do you have pizza a lot for dessert?"

"Never!" he exclaimed. "But once we had French fries and one time we had brownies and another time we had cake first then hamburgers!"

"Really." Charlene nodded slowly, wondering how in the world Morrisey wanted her to reply.

Gareth wrinkled his nose. "I told Grandma we had French fries for dessert, and she got mad. She said it wasn't proper. Remember that, Mommy?"

Morrisey rolled her eyes. "I remember."

Gareth giggled. "Grandma's funny when she gets mad." He ballooned his cheeks out and rounded his eyes. "Well, I never!" he said in a high, squealing voice. "That isn't proper!"

Charlene covered her mouth to keep from laughing out loud, and Morrisey chuckled. "I bet he does that when he's with my mother. Makes fun of me. Don't you, huh, Gareth? You and

Grandma laugh at me."

"No."

"Yeah, yeah." Morrisey reached over and mussed her son's hair. "So, pizza? Okay."

Gareth's eyes lit up. "Ice cream too! Can we have that? And M&M's."

"Sure." Morrisey went to a cabinet and got a small yellow bowl out for Gareth. "Whatever you can fit in there, you can have."

Gareth frowned. "Pizza won't fit in there."

"Sure it will. Roll it up."

"Okay!" Gareth headed to the refrigerator and drew out leftover pizza.

Morrisey leaned against the counter. "Want a bowl too?" she asked Charlene. "I have chocolate ice cream."

"You're so good with him," Charlene said, wishing she didn't feel a twinge of envy.

THEY WERE ALMOST finished with dessert when Gareth fiddled with the mini Etch-A-Sketch again. "I'm making my name," he explained. "I messed up. Charlie! Was this JP's?"

Charlene's heart jumped at the sudden, unexpected question, but Morrisey betrayed no emotion. "Yes," Charlene whispered.

"What happened to him?" Gareth asked.

"He died," Charlene said.

"Like my grandpa?"

"Yes."

"And he's under the grass near my grandpa?"

"Yes."

Gareth nodded, satisfied. "Good. Grandpa can talk with JP. JP isn't boring. Grandpa says my great-aunt Martha is boring." Gareth resumed playing with the Etch-A-Sketch, and Charlene stared in horror at her grandson, at his cute, innocent little face.

Talk with JP? Oh, God. I don't think so. She was too afraid to look at Morrisey, afraid that if she did, Morrisey would come to her senses and banish her from her life, from Gareth's life. After a few moments passed, Charlene looked up. Morrisey's chair was empty. *Great.* Charlene reached for Gareth's shoulder. "Be right back." She headed down the hallway, toward the front door. "Morrisey?"

Morrisey was gazing out of a front window, and Charlene could only see her side profile. Her heartstrings tugged again with the pain of knowing she had hurt Morrisey.

Morrisey crossed her arms and turned to face Charlene. Her expression was cool, and Charlene withered under the intense aloofness, so different from Morrisey's earlier friendliness. "I'm sorry. I shouldn't have let Gareth play with the toys," Charlene said.

"I thought I could do this. Maybe I'm just deluding myself."

Charlene's heart crashed to her stomach, but she maintained eye contact with Morrisey. "I understand. I do, really. I'm just going to go. If there's anything I can do, anytime, don't hesitate to call."

"No," Morrisey replied quietly. "You're staying."

Charlene took a tentative step forward. "You don't need to invite me into your home, into your life and into your son's life. No reasonable person would expect that. I don't. You've done so much already. More than enough."

"You're the only person I've told," Morrisey said. "Isn't that funny?"

"I don't know."

"Don't you think it's pathetic how I told people, even my own family, I was artificially inseminated? I mean, I waited until I was six months pregnant and beginning to show a decent bit before I told my family."

"What did you say to them?"

"We were having dinner. My mother was in the middle of a huge, thick slab of roast beef. Really getting into it. Her mouth would be occupied for a while. So I said it then. Said I was six months pregnant and that the father was some guy who got paid $50 to jerk off in a cup. My mom choked."

Charlene was not sure how to answer. She said, with the vivid image of a red-faced, spluttering Margaret Hawthorne in her mind, "Wow."

Morrisey laughed. "It was pretty funny. Not to her, though."

"I imagine not."

Morrisey turned back to the window. "I didn't tell people because I didn't want them feeling sorry for me."

"That makes sense. I might have done the same thing. I hate the way people withdraw or treat me with kid gloves after they find out my son killed himself. They tiptoe around me as though I'm a porcelain doll."

"Yeah. It sucks."

"I want to help you," Charlene said. "Not because I feel sorry for you, but because you're a cool person. I like you. Tell me what I can do."

Morrisey rubbed her forehead, and her mouth tightened. "You're doing fine."

"Whenever Gareth asks about JP, I'll steer the conversation away. Definitely nothing more of JP's for Gareth."

Disapproval pinched Morrisey's face, but she said nothing.

Her silence concealed so many emotions, so many simmering issues.

Charlene wondered what exactly Morrisey had gone through after she found out she was pregnant. Charlene imagined the whole scenario: Morrisey going for an abortion and seeing the place so sterile and fake; the doctors and nurses being overly nice and syrupy sweet. Morrisey must have hated the men who raped her even more for forcing her into this decision. Had Morrisey felt as if she was not even in her own body? Had she decided she would rather live with a baby than with guilt?

Charlene pictured Morrisey going home from the abortion clinic. She worried and fretted. She passed her additional AIDS and STD tests but agonized that she would not be able to love her baby. Her family must have asked about the sperm donor. Charlene imagined Morrisey retorting, "What does it matter? This is my child, no matter his or her skin color."

Charlene saw it all in that one moment.

GARETH HELD UP a picture when Morrisey and Charlene returned. "I drew a frog!"

"Wow. I've never seen a pink frog before," Morrisey said.

Charlene added, "He's pretty."

"I want to put lipstick on him. What color?"

Morrisey shrugged, so Charlene suggested purple.

"Okay! And purple eye stuff, too?"

"Sure."

Charlene and Morrisey stood in comfortable silence for a few moments. They watched Gareth as he stuck his tongue out and put the finishing touches on his frog. A sense of contentment came over Charlene. She had never felt more at peace in her life, in the company of this beautiful, kind woman and her adorable, mischievous son. It felt right, yet her brain was telling her it was wrong. It was weird and sick.

Morrisey ran a hand up Charlene's back, startling her. "What are you thinking?"

"Nothing," Charlene whispered. "What are you thinking?"

"That I'm glad I invited you over for lunch."

"Me, too. Thank you."

Morrisey squeezed Charlene's shoulder. "It's Gareth's naptime. I'll put him down when he finishes with Mr. Frog there."

Charlene looked up into Morrisey's eyes, craving more touches. She did not want to go, but of course she would have to.

"I thought we could talk some more while Gareth was sleeping unless you need to be somewhere," Morrisey said.

Charlene stifled the smile that sprang to her lips. She pushed away the nagging voice that told her to leave Morrisey alone. *I'm doing it to help her because of what JP did. That's all.*

"YOU LIKE CHARLENE, right?" Morrisey asked Gareth as she tucked him in for his nap.

He stifled a yawn. "She's not boring."

"No," Morrisey said softly. "She's not."

"I feel bad for her."

Morrisey was surprised. "Why?"

"Dunno."

Morrisey studied her son. "Okay."

"Will she bring me another present?"

"Oh, sweetie. I don't know. Now go to sleep." Morrisey pulled the covers to Gareth's chin and watched as he drifted off to dreamland. Although her eyes were on Gareth, her mind was on Charlene. Fear bubbled inside Morrisey, along with indescribable giddiness. Suddenly, she was afraid that she would have regrets, plenty of them, later. Was she in over her head already? Would she get her heart broken? When she made up her mind to do something, she gave a hundred percent. Apparently without quite realizing it, she had decided to allow free rein to her feelings for Charlene.

Morrisey shook her head and focused on her son, who was mumbling in his sleep. Gareth was so beautiful. He really was. And then it hit her, like a heavy weight, but in slow motion. *Oh, God.*

She had let Charlene hug Gareth. She had let Charlene play with him. And why? Because she was so relieved, so unburdened now that she had told someone? Because Charlene had given her that look in the kitchen and set every nerve in her body on fire? Because of that wonderful, incredible hug, which Morrisey had hoped would never end?

Stupid. Foolish. Charlene was the mother of one of her rapists. Of course nothing would come of Morrisey's feelings for Charlene. Those sorts of things just did not happen. And this was not just about Morrisey. This was about her son, too, about what was best for him. Maybe Charlene was okay for now being "Grandma" from a distance. What if her tune changed, weeks from now or years from now? What if she started trying to meddle in Gareth's life?

"Slow down," Morrisey muttered. "Slow down." Enough was enough. Charlene needed to go. Morrisey contemplated playing nice for a few minutes and then showing Charlene the door. This was not the time to develop into a lovesick puppy. What Morrisey needed to do, she decided, was take time to think, to recover. She needed to pace herself, maybe even get over Charlene. The regrets were already overwhelming.

WHEN MORRISEY RETURNED to the living room, Charlene was studying a picture of Gareth and his grandfather on the mantel above the fireplace. The photo had been taken the previous Christmas and showed Adrian and Gareth on the floor, playing with a new train set.

Charlene looked up, met Morrisey's eyes and smiled. Morrisey's heart fluttered, and she clenched her teeth. *No.*

"Is that your father?" Charlene asked.

Morrisey nodded. It was time to start saying goodbye — nicely, of course. She could say something like, "Well, it's been fun. Thanks for coming, but I ought to take a nap, too." She had to say or do something, anything.

Charlene returned her attention to the picture. "He seems like he was great with Gareth. You must miss him."

Morrisey swallowed. "Yes, I do. He seemed to be in perfect health. He ate all the right things and exercised. He was in great shape. Then one day, poof, a heart attack. My mom went out shopping, and she came home to find him in the—" Morrisey stopped. *Goodbye time, remember?*

Charlene nodded, probably misinterpreting Morrisey's hesitation as painful reluctance to get into the details of her father's recent death. "I really am glad you asked me over," Charlene said. She continued talking; Morrisey only half-listened.

Morrisey struggled to muster the courage to ask Charlene to leave, to ignore the light in her eyes, the crinkles her smile made, the rushed eagerness in her voice, which Morrisey would usually interpret as one that went past friendly. But was Charlene really...? No. Charlene was just thrilled about her grandson, thrilled that his mother was being so nice to her.

Goodbye time. Now. Morrisey interrupted Charlene's background monologue, saying, "You should..."

Charlene's eyes clouded over. "You want me to go? Okay. I'll go."

Morrisey's heart refused to coordinate with her brain. Such a task was impossible when Charlene looked so disappointed and deflated, yet smiling and trying to cover it up.

"No," Morrisey amended. "Want to sit on the swing out back? It's not too hot outside."

Charlene's answering grin, huge, brilliant and beautiful, made Morrisey's day.

Fuck.

"SO, NO TROUBLE getting Gareth to sleep?" Charlene asked once she and Morrisey were settled on the swing.

"No." Morrisey shook her head. "He had a busy morning, wore himself out playing with a neighbor's puppy. He'll wake up good as new in thirty minutes."

"He's a great kid. What an imagination."

Morrisey laughed. "Yeah. It's nice seeing the world through his eyes."

"I miss that."

"How old are you? Forty, forty-one?"

"About that." Charlene's smile was tight-lipped.

"Didn't want any more kids? What about after JP died?"

Charlene made an incredulous noise. "No. Oh, no. I could hardly function for months, much less think about having another child. How about you? How old are you? Do you want more kids?"

"I'm thirty-four. And, maybe. It'd be nice for Gareth to have a brother or sister. Someday. I'm not ready for that just yet. I don't want to get pregnant again, so I'd probably adopt. It's hard enough taking care of one child on my own, though." Morrisey grinned. "Listen to me. I was so anti-kids before Gareth came along, and here I'm talking about having another one. Rebecca would hardly recognize me now."

"Rebecca?"

"Oh, yeah. My most recent ex. We were together about two years. She wanted kids badly and as soon as possible. I didn't. That's why she left me."

Charlene settled back into the swing. "Do you keep in touch with her?"

"No. Last I heard, she was living on a farm somewhere in Montana. I'm sure she's happy. I'm happy for her, too. She deserves it."

"Hmm." Charlene's expression took on a meditative quality.

"What?" Morrisey wondered.

"Nothing."

"No, what?"

"Do you miss her?"

Morrisey grimaced. "Not in that way. We weren't right for each other. The kids thing was just one of many problems."

"When did you realize you were gay? If you want to talk about that. I'm sorry. That was a stupid question. Never mind." Charlene studied Morrisey almost fearfully.

"It wasn't a stupid question," Morrisey reassured Charlene. "Well." She took a moment to collect her thoughts. "I always knew. In high school, I admitted it to myself and told my family. They weren't thrilled. They came around eventually—as best as they could, anyway. I can't imagine myself any other way. How sad it would be to go through life without knowing another woman's caress, the feel of her lips on my skin, her hands on my body." Morrisey's gaze traveled over Charlene's face and searched her eyes. What she found there, uncertainty mixed with desire and longing, caused her stomach to turn over and her heart to flutter. "What about you?"

Charlene only stared, her lips slightly parted.

"Charlene? What about you?" Morrisey repeated.

"Sorry. What do you mean?"

"I don't know. What's it like being straight?"

Charlene flinched. She clasped her hands together and puckered her lips. She started to reply but stopped. When her answer came, it was uncertain. "I suppose it's how you feel about women, but just with men."

Morrisey looked straight ahead, at the wood fence separating her yard from a neighbor's. She felt wounded and wondered why Charlene was lying.

Charlene sighed heavily. "Morrisey."

"Yes?"

"You probably won't believe this."

"Try me."

Charlene's expression was pained. "I'm a lesbian, too."

Morrisey allowed herself a smile, but Charlene's discomfort bothered her. "You don't like being a lesbian?"

"What?"

"You don't look very happy."

Charlene's gaze moved to the fence. She spoke slowly and carefully. "I've been afraid to tell you."

"Why?"

Charlene fiddled with a few loose hairs on the side of her neck. "I don't know. Maybe you'd think I was making it up to score points with you. Or something. It is unusual, don't you think, that we're both gay?"

"Oh, Charlene." Morrisey was touched by Charlene's stricken worry. "Don't lie to me about yourself because of...Hey. I believe you. All right?"

"All right. Thank you."

Morrisey decided to interject some humor into the conversation. "All women are gay, anyway. Bisexual at the very least."

"I bet you've converted lots of straight women."

Morrisey was not expecting such a reply. "Yes. In college and for a bit afterward."

"You have that look."

"What look?"

"Lady killer."

"Lady killer, huh?" *I'd better not be blushing.* Morrisey liked the sound and feel of the words. "That'd be accurate enough. How about you?"

"Me?" Charlene was incredulous. "Please. No. I was the girl who fell in love with her straight friends and let them stomp all over her heart. You were the girl who got them to fall in love with you, and then you broke their hearts."

Morrisey squirmed. Charlene's assessment hit closer to home than she cared to admit. "Maybe once or twice," Morrisey said. *I was an asshole.*

Charlene grinned. "I used to be jealous of your type."

"Used to be?"

"Maybe still am. A little. You people had bucketfuls of charm and could conquer anyone you liked. It was all so effortless. People like me would just stammer and blush."

"I don't miss those days, though. Not really. Oh, they were fun and heady while they lasted, but they were empty. Know what I mean?"

"Sure."

Morrisey and Charlene sat in silence for a few moments, then Charlene asked, "So, have you — you know, since the rape?"

The intimacy of Charlene's question did not surprise or bother Morrisey. "Sex? No."

"Are you afraid to?"

Morrisey shrugged. Her nonchalance belied the fact that she felt as if she were floating outside of herself, talking about this with *his* mother. "I'm not afraid to," Morrisey said carefully. "I just haven't found somebody. I have new priorities. I have a child to take care of."

"Ever been truly in love?"

"Maybe with Rebecca. But, I don't know. No, not really. Well, unless you count my son."

"Do you think you'll find somebody?"

"Maybe, but if I don't, that's fine. I'll be happy either way. I'm not going to just settle. How about you?"

Charlene shook her head vaguely. "I've been bad. Canceling a lot of dates my friends set up for me. I should start going on them."

Morrisey studied the wood fence yet again. Jealousy was rearing its ugly green head. *Great.* Morrisey remembered how she used to be — the lady killer, decisive, sexy, oozing charm and smiles. Knowing the exact things to say to make a woman swoon and spread her legs. Now, though, Morrisey wanted to run, yearned to run. Lady killer, indeed.

It should have been easy, a piece of cake, to ask Charlene to lunch again the following Sunday. Maybe Morrisey could have, if Charlene had not reminded her of how she used to be. But Morrisey choked. Her charm from all those years ago, from before the rape, did not return. Her smoothness, her suaveness, remained buried. Her tongue tied itself. She was helpless. She was a lady killer reduced to a pile of rubble. Worthless. The stupid fucking rape had changed her. She was no longer in charge of her own emotions, her own body, her own life.

Morrisey felt herself choking up and was afraid she would need to excuse herself to retrieve some tissues. Somehow, she steeled herself against crying but found no pride and solace in that. She and Charlene stared at the wood fence. After a while, Charlene left.

Chapter Nine

CHARLENE SAT ON her couch. A bland 1960s comedy flickered on her TV screen, but the actors could have been speaking Martian for all she knew. How had she gotten through work earlier that day? She had no idea.

Morrisey. Morrisey. Morrisey.

Being with her the day before had been heaven. Charlene kept replaying flashes from their time together, the big moments, the seemingly insignificant ones. Her favorite was that long instant on the swing when Morrisey's gaze had traveled Charlene's own face. The meaning in Morrisey's eyes was unmistakable. Morrisey was attracted to her. And neither of them was sure how to proceed, or even if they should.

Charlene clicked the television off. *Morrisey.* A woman JP raped, her grandson's mother. She wandered into the kitchen in search of food for her rumbling stomach. She shut the refrigerator door without selecting anything. The prospect of spending another night at home with that horrid brown carpeting, alone in front of the television in a living room haunted by pictures of her dead son, did not appeal to Charlene. She could call Miriam and Liz, see if they were up to anything. *No.* The person Charlene wanted to see was Morrisey Hawthorne. Her heartbeat quickened just at the thought.

Morrisey Hawthorne: a most lovely woman with a most lovely name. They had made no plans to meet again. Charlene was sure Morrisey wanted to, though. Morrisey may have been a lady killer when she was younger, and she certainly still knew how to turn on the charm. The rape and Gareth had changed many things, however. Now Morrisey was more like Charlene—fumbling, awkward, unsteady. She was trying to find her way in life as the single mother of a little red-headed boy. In many ways, Charlene held the reins in this situation.

No regrets.

She grabbed her car keys and jumped into the Acclaim before doubts could stop her. About thirty minutes later she was a couple of streets from Morrisey's house. She realized she had no clue what she was going to do. Was she really just going to drop in, uninvited, with Silver, of all cars? Was she going to needlessly bother the mother of her grandchild, a woman her son had raped?

She had spent most of the afternoon with Morrisey and Gareth just the day before. What she needed to do was exercise some patience and wait for Morrisey to call. *Don't press your luck and wear out your welcome.*

Charlene pulled over to a curb and cut Silver's engine. Children biking nearby shot her curious glances, but she ignored them. She needed an excuse, a reason to be stopping by. She could go back home and bake a couple of cakes, some brownies or cookies and say she'd had plenty left over and wanted to drop some off. Was that too lame? Charlene frowned. Lame or not, it was the only thing she could think of. She started the engine again. She would go to the grocery store and get the ingredients for her baking spree. Or maybe she would just drop by Morrisey's and say hi. Get it over with. She would stay a few minutes. That should be all right. She just needed a little fix—or maybe she should do the baking thing after all.

Charlene let out an agonized cry and put her car into drive. *I'll decide when I get to Morrisey's house.* She made a right, and then a left. She crept past her destination, but Morrisey's car was not in the driveway. Charlene's heart sank. *Baking spree it is.* She drove to the nearest grocery store, and in the baking goods section, in the middle of the aisle, was the woman Charlene yearned to see.

Morrisey and Gareth were laughing and examining a box. Morrisey's hair was in a ponytail, and her red tank top and cut-off jean shorts showed off an incredible tan. Gareth had never been so starkly his mother's complete opposite—he so pale, his bright hair a mess and Morrisey so dark and lean.

Charlene's heart grew heavy as she took in mother and son. *That's true love.* They were so obviously crazy about each other and had such an easy, gentle, teasing rapport. It was something Charlene had never quite experienced with JP. He had been more of her protector, and she had worked so hard to provide for him. Their relationship had been more serious and goal-oriented, especially as JP got older.

Charlene pictured herself bouncing down the aisle and opening her arms to Morrisey and Gareth. She pictured herself laughing with the same carefree abandon her grandson and his mother did. The image she conjured was all wrong. Her laughter was stilted and forced. *Get out of here. You don't belong with them. You never will. Stop deluding yourself.* But Charlene could not tear her gaze from Morrisey. The longer she watched, the more her stomach clenched and the faster her heart beat.

Morrisey had such long, slim fingers, supple legs, that gentle laugh, the dark, sparkling eyes. She was laughing like mad with her son. Morrisey would undoubtedly move on from her demons and return to being a lady killer while Charlene flailed about in her own muck.

Go already, before you drag them down. Charlene turned to leave. She would not intrude on Morrisey and Gareth like this.

WHEN SHE GOT home, Charlene demolished the John Patrick Sudsbury Museum — nonprofit and established for uncertain purposes. Maybe she had established it as torture or self-punishment; perhaps it was testament to her denial, despair, confusion, love or hatred.

First, Charlene surveyed her living room. Her son stared at her from everywhere. It had not always been this way. About a week after his suicide, Charlene went crazy and yanked countless JP things out of boxes. For almost three years, the living room had been a photographic museum of sorts. There was JP, at four, on the entertainment center, in the middle of a popsicles frame he'd made in elementary school.

JP at seventeen, again on the entertainment center, his expression neutral as he posed in his cap and gown. That picture had been taken a few months after the accident, and the contrast between that picture and the one next to it, of a broadly smiling JP as a junior in his football uniform, was stark.

Hanging on the wall was a group of pictures of JP in elementary school. More JP pictures jockeyed for position on the end table. Charlene packed each and every picture. *Tomorrow I'll see if I can find a new rug.* She could not afford anything lavish, but even a small rug would get her started. *Maybe purple, maybe yellow. No more brown. Then I'll decorate the walls again.*

A FEW DAYS later, Margaret Hawthorne called Morrisey and got right down to business. "Do you have plans Tuesday night?" Margaret asked.

"No."

"You do now."

"I do?"

"You have a date."

Morrisey's heart stopped. "What?"

"You and Janet aren't serious, right? You can see other people?"

"We're not seeing each other anymore."

Margaret tut-tutted. "You weren't going to tell me?"

Morrisey pressed the phone to her ear. "I just hadn't. Okay, what's this about a date?"

"I have met a most wonderful woman named Yolanda. She runs a gardening shop for her father."

Morrisey said nothing. There were no words for it. Her mother was setting her up on a date? With a woman? Hell had frozen over.

"My roses were dying off, so I went there to get help. And Yolanda surely did assist me. You'll love her. She certainly loved your picture."

"Oh, God." Morrisey rubbed her forehead. "Mother!"

"You two will look good together. She's Hispanic. Tall and dark, like you. Nice voice. Strong. She's twenty-five years old. She's slender. Gorgeous."

"I am not going on a blind date!"

"Why not?"

"Why not? Because I don't want to! Mother, okay. I know you mean well. I appreciate it."

"Just go," Margaret urged. "What will it hurt?"

Charlene flashed into Morrisey's mind. Lovely Charlene who made Morrisey feel so alive, who made her heart ache. Charlene, whom Morrisey had no plans to see again. Charlene whom Morrisey did not want to fall in love with. Charlene, Gareth's other grandmother.

"I told Yolanda you'd meet her at 7:30, downtown, at Metro," Margaret supplied helpfully. "Now, I'm not sure who's paying. I don't mind covering the tab, since it was my idea."

Morrisey's mortification increased. "You told her my life story, didn't you?"

Margaret harrumphed. "Of course not." Her voice softened. "Sweetie, Yolanda's such a nice girl. Try it. Please."

"God," Morrisey said through clenched teeth. She did not want to go on this blind date, but just maybe Yolanda would get her mind off Charlene. "Fine, I'll do it. Tuesday at 7:30. Fine."

MORRISEY SHOWED UP for her date right on time. Yolanda arrived five minutes later and turned every head in the restaurant. She was everything Margaret said she was—more, actually. She was sexy, exotic, fun and playful. Her hair was black, much blacker than Morrisey's, and shinier. Her eyes, too, were darker than Morrisey's. She wore a tight blue dress that showed off luscious curves and smooth tanned skin. Where Janet Raines was butch, Yolanda was thoroughly feminine. They both were dreams. Nice, sweet, intelligent women. Both seemed to be into Morrisey.

Morrisey was not into them, though. She had felt nothing for Janet, and she did not click with Yolanda, either. Despite that, Morrisey kept up appearances. She did a pretty good job of being a date. She and Yolanda talked easily, although when the conversation turned to gardening, Morrisey fought a few yawns. She had never been one for dating. She was too impatient. Superficial talk, social niceties, rules to follow. Blah. Waste of time. She used to just jump right into bed. Sleep with a woman for a week or two until it got old. Rebecca had been a little different, of course.

And maybe Charlene would be. *No.*

After dinner, Morrisey and Yolanda walked to the garage where their cars were parked. "Come back to my apartment," Yolanda suggested with a devilish grin. "I have whipped cream."

Morrisey smiled smoothly. A few years earlier, she would have gone along all too happily. Not now. She was not going to take her clothes off for just anybody and let just anybody touch her, caress her. "I can't, sorry. I have to get my son."

Yolanda froze. "What?"

"I have to get my son."

"You have a kid?"

"Yes. A four-year-old boy. He'll be five in September."

Yolanda fished her car remote out of her purse. "I don't do women with kids. It's too messy."

Morrisey blinked. "Sorry. I guess I figured my mother told you. Or something. I don't know. I'm really sorry I didn't tell you earlier."

"Whatever, no big deal. It happens. I'll see you around." Yolanda started to get into her car but stopped. "Look, one time, okay?" Her lips quirked into a half-smile. "I'll bend my rules for you. I wanna see what you have under here." She trailed her fingers across Morrisey's shirt.

Morrisey stepped backward. "That's very thoughtful, but no thanks."

"Your loss." Yolanda got into her car. "You really should've told me earlier about your kid. God." She drove off, a small scowl darkening her face.

MORRISEY DID NOT head toward her mother's house, where Gareth was waiting. Instead, her heart hammering, she drove to The Log Cabin. She had never been there. In fact, she had never heard of the place before Charlene mentioned it. Morrisey had no trouble finding it, though. The restaurant lived up to its name. It looked like a big log cabin, albeit one in a seedy part of town. It was between a sex shop and a run-down 'otel, according to a garish neon sign.

Morrisey doubted Charlene would be at work but hoped she was. Morrisey would go in and see her. *Just saying hello. I was driving by and thought I'd stop in.*

The time was 9:30 p.m., and only a few cars dotted the restaurant's parking lot. No Acclaim. No Honda Accord, which was what Charlene had driven for that Sunday lunch. Morrisey parked in the back of the lot and shut her car's engine and headlights off. She could see a couple of waitresses and a busboy inside. A handful of people ate at window tables, and thanks to streetlights and the neon sign, the restaurant took on a ghostly look.

A familiar, cold shiver ran through Morrisey. What was she doing, alone in her car after dark, in this area of town? She shrugged to herself. She would be fine. It was time for one of those episodes anyway, and this dimly lit, nearly deserted parking lot was as fitting a place as any.

She had been so numb in the days, weeks and months after the rape. When she did not have to be at work, she stayed in bed and stared at the ceiling. Sometimes, for a change, she pulled the bedcovers over her head. She thought about nothing. She was just numb. She was determined, too, that no one ever know she had been raped. She would be the same Morrisey as always.

Christmas, just a few days after the attack, had been torture. Around her family she pretended that she could walk, smile and laugh just fine. She had put on such an act that December 25th. A couple of months followed, with more deadness inside. Then she found out she was pregnant. There was the abortion that never happened. Constant anxiety replaced the numbness.

The numbness had been better in many ways. Through it all, Morrisey would sit on her couch or lie in bed, as still as a statue, and just think and worry. She fretted about herself and about her baby-to-be. After Gareth's birth, the episodes happened less and less. But here she was, thinking and worrying again. The heaviness was crawling back, and Morrisey hated it. She hated thinking about the rape. She hated being numb again. She wished Charlene was at work. Charlene would hug her, make her feel okay and whole again. "You're a fucking idiot," Morrisey whispered. "So what if she's his mother?" *Call her now. Go on, get the cell. She'd see you in a heartbeat. You know she would. Do it.*

Morrisey was about to cry, in her car, in the desolate parking lot, so she reached into her glove compartment for tissues. She knew what would happen after her tears stopped flowing. She would not call Charlene. She would go to her mother's house and get her son, JP's son. She would be the same Morrisey as always. No one would know she had been raped, except Charlene. And that was fine. It really was.

Chapter Ten

CHARLENE SPENT THE next two weeks staying busy. She bought a couple of medium-sized rugs for her living room, one orange and one blue. She visited used-car dealerships in search of what proved to be an ever-elusive bargain. She hiked the trails at the Peaks of Otter. She started the training classes necessary for her to take over as manager at The Log Cabin. She did not visit JP's grave. And she waited for Morrisey to call.

Morrisey did not phone. Charlene tried to remain upbeat. It was easier said than done, but she plugged on. Even if she never saw Morrisey and Gareth again, she would be forever grateful to them. They had shown her that a rich world awaited her. They had made her feel again. She was young—forty-one years old—and it was time to start living again, to start contributing again.

One night, Charlene was helping Jeremy, the busboy, wipe off tables because there was nothing else for her to do. It was 9 p.m. and one of Charlene's sporadic night shifts. The Log Cabin was empty.

"Water slide?" Jeremy suggested. "Charge $3 and a candy bar per trip."

Charlene laughed. They were joking about what she and Miriam could put in when they became co-managers. "That'd attract kids, and we don't need more here."

"True. How about—"

The door chimed. Charlene straightened and readied her Log Cabin smile.

Jeremy smirked. "What we need more of is her."

Charlene froze. Even though her back was to the door, she knew Morrisey was the person who had walked in. Jeremy's expression, his gaze said it all—one hot woman had just graced the lowly restaurant with her presence.

Charlene turned, hoping she was rid of the deer-in-headlights look. There was Morrisey, as beautiful as ever. Panic filled Charlene. *Why here, why now?* She was sweaty, weary and not smelling so great after eight tough hours on her feet.

"Excuse me," Charlene murmured to Jeremy. She went over to meet Morrisey. *God, I've missed you.*

"Hey." Morrisey stuck her hands into her jean pockets.

"Hey."

"I was just driving by and saw your car. Thought I'd say hello."

"I'm glad. It's good to see you," Charlene said.

"Really?"

"Yes. How have you been?"

Morrisey surveyed the restaurant and smiled at a decorative sign that read HONK FOR GEESE. "I've been all right. Gareth, too. I just wanted to say that lunch was fun the other week. Want to come over again sometime, maybe Sunday evening, and bake cookies with Gareth and me?"

Charlene wanted to pump her fists and jump around the room. She settled for a grin and calmly said, "That sounds great. Oh, hey. Can I get you anything? Soda, a slice of pie, some coffee? My treat."

"Thanks, but I need to get going." They chatted briefly about Sunday and decided to start at 7 p.m. After Morrisey left, Charlene skipped back to Jeremy.

"You're falling in love," he said.

MORRISEY TOOK GARETH out for lunch the next day. He had been clamoring for hot dogs, so they went downtown to the Roanoke Weiner Stand. They sat at the window and let the busy mix of passersby entertain them, until Gareth announced, "Grandpa told me a story."

Morrisey cocked an eyebrow. "Oh, yeah?" She had not taken Gareth back to the cemetery, but her mother had taken him along a few times, including the day before.

"Yeah! He told me when he was little, he used to climb up trees so he wouldn't have to come inside for dinner. His mommy called him bad names."

"Hmm." A purple-haired youth walked by, reminding Morrisey of the time she dyed her hair purple in college. "Was it really Grandma who told you that?"

"Grandpa!" Gareth hollered. "And he wants me to bring him cars to play with."

Morrisey bit into a fry. This "talking to Grandpa" business had been cute and endearing at first, but it was getting creepy. "Gareth, sweetie, your grandfather's dead. He can't tell you things or play with cars."

"Can too! Grandma said so."

Morrisey sighed. "Okay." *As long as your grandfather doesn't talk to JP.*

After lunch, Morrisey and Gareth petted a police horse then window shopped. "Look!" Gareth cried as they passed a florist. "King Arthur stuff! Which one's me?"

Morrisey peered at the display, which was filled with the sprawling, colorful cast from Camelot. She spotted Arthur, the same one Charlene had gotten her. Next to him was a knight sporting a mop of red hair. "That one," Morrisey whispered. "Let's go in for a second."

WHEN CHARLENE ARRIVED at Morrisey's house on Sunday, Gareth informed her in a no-nonsense tone to wash her hands. Charlene complied with a grin, and Gareth set about gathering an egg, a bowl and other baking odds and ends.

Charlene was amazed. She flashed back to the time she saw Morrisey and Gareth in the baking goods aisle. "Do you do this often?"

"Kind of. We started a few months ago." Morrisey reached into a cabinet that was too high for Gareth. "I let Gareth run the show. It's a good teaching tool. It helps him with his math, reading, baking and creativity."

"Charlie!" Gareth stopped in the middle of cracking his egg. He dropped it into the bowl. "I forgot all about your present!" He barreled down the hallway.

"What's that about?"

Morrisey avoided Charlene's gaze and finished up with the abandoned egg. Then she explained, "Gareth wanted to get you something."

Gareth ran back into the kitchen, hollering, "Here it is!" He shoved a small, wrapped box into Charlene's hands. She brought the present up and stifled a laugh. It was the worst wrap job she had seen in her life.

"I wrapped it!" Gareth proclaimed.

"I noticed."

"Charlie!"

"Yeah?"

"Can I open it? Please, please, please?"

"Gareth!" Morrisey intervened. "Let Charlene open her own present."

Charlene sat at the kitchen table and played the guessing game with Gareth. She held the present to her ear and shook it gently. Something clunked inside, and Gareth squirmed. "It's a horse," Charlene declared. "A real live horse."

"That's silly. Horses are big."

"Maybe it's a baby horse. A foal."

"No! Baby horses aren't that small."

"Good point." Charlene unwrapped her present, which proved tricky because of the tape and stickers Gareth had slapped everywhere. A few moments later, she opened the box to find a tiny Sir Gareth figurine, complete with a suit of armor and a messy thatch of red hair. "Wow," she whispered.

"That's Sir Gareth, like me," Gareth explained, puffing out his chest. "See, we even have the same hair!"

"So you do," Charlene murmured. Her next thought was automatic, and she hated herself for it. *The same hair JP had.*

Morrisey cleared her throat. "Come on, let's finish baking."

MORRISEY WENT TO the bathroom a few minutes later, leaving Charlene in charge of Gareth. "Can I have the bowl after?" he asked.

"Does your mom let you have the bowl?"

Gareth molded a blob of cookie dough into a recognizable circle. "She makes me share with her."

Charlene shaped several cookies as well. "So the present was your idea?"

"Mommy's. She said you were real nice to get us something, so we should get you something back. I helped her pick it out!"

Charlene finished up with her cookies. She tried not to think. She struggled not to feel. She went about her task as if she did not live in a world in which a beautiful, vulnerable woman got her presents.

"Oven's ready!" Gareth cried. He dug out the oven mitts for Charlene. She slipped the cookies in, then bent down to hug her grandson and laugh with him the best she could.

MORRISEY AND CHARLENE were almost finished with their last task, a chocolate cake, when darkness set in. Gareth had tired of baking a while before that and was crashing and vrooming with trucks and bulldozers in the living room. "You really didn't have to do all this," Charlene said as she inspected the cake. She would put frosting on it later. It was time to go home.

"Do what?"

"You know. Spend your whole night baking with me and then cleaning up the mess. I really don't mind washing the bowls and pans."

"Maybe you can wash them next Sunday."

Charlene stopped in the middle of putting her cake into a container. "What?"

"Would you like to do something again next Sunday? Not baking, though. Maybe we can have a picnic or go to the zoo."

Charlene was careful as she set the cake into the container, concealing her swirling, giddy thoughts. *Morrisey's going to let me be a part of her life, of Gareth's.*

Charlene could not have been happier, even as Morrisey tilted her head and said, "But…"

"I know," Charlene interrupted. "This is just a trial thing. As far as everyone's concerned, I'm an old friend of yours."

CHARLENE WENT TO Morrisey's the next few Sundays. She, Morrisey and Gareth usually stayed at the house, but one weekend they went to the zoo. Another time they attended a Salem Avalanche baseball game, where Gareth promptly became besotted with Mugsy, one of the team's furry mascots. Charlene loved her new Sundays, even if it seemed that all they would ever be was a few hours each week with her grandson and his mother. That was fine, more than Charlene knew she deserved. Still, she itched to touch Morrisey, to hug her once more. Morrisey seemed to be doing okay. She never mentioned the rape, JP or anything remotely personal. The Sundays were all about Gareth. Morrisey and Charlene were never alone together. There were no invitations to talk on the back-porch swing. There were no sly glances. There was no teasing or mild flirting.

Charlene began to wonder if she had imagined the attraction between her and Morrisey. She consoled herself, saying it was for the best if nothing happened. A romantic entanglement with Morrisey would be disaster. But every time she saw Morrisey and noticed something new about her, Charlene could not help falling even more in love.

ONE SUNDAY AFTERNOON after a trip to the science museum, Morrisey said she was going to put Gareth down for a nap. Charlene took that as her cue to leave, but Morrisey asked her to stay a few minutes. Charlene waited on the living room couch and twiddled her thumbs. Her mind turned over various possibilities. *Morrisey's had enough. She wants to stop the Sundays. Or do one Sunday a month. Or just holidays now. She's sick and tired of my face. Or maybe she wants to take me out somewhere, just the two of us. On a date. Or maybe she's met another woman. Oh, stop it!*

Morrisey joined Charlene on the couch. "Hey," Morrisey said.

Her voice, tone and expression were all business. "Thanks for staying a little longer."

"You're welcome. What's up?"

Morrisey shrugged. "I have to attend a teachers' seminar Thursday night. Would you like to look after Gareth while I'm gone?"

Charlene met Morrisey's eyes. "You mean baby-sit him?"

Morrisey maintained the eye contact. "If you want."

"Yes! I'd love to."

"Thank you."

"For what?"

Morrisey picked up a GI Joe. Charlene recognized it as the one from the night Morrisey had phoned and asked Charlene to come over. "For being here," Morrisey said. "If that makes sense." She tossed the GI Joe aside and leaned in for a long hug that silenced all of Charlene's doubts about whether Morrisey liked her.

Chapter Eleven

MIRIAM TOOK CHARLENE to the mall on Wednesday. "My treat," Miriam explained. "Get new clothes to knock Morrisey's socks off tomorrow." They went into JC Penney, and Miriam pointed out a few shirts she thought were cute.

"No." Charlene blanched. "They're too expensive."

Miriam held up a hand. "No arguments."

"I'll be in rags, and she'll be all dressed up for her seminar."

Miriam groaned. "You have it really bad for her, don't you?"

"Maybe."

Miriam led Charlene to a shelf of jeans. "Try some on."

"It'll be my first time alone with Gareth. Oh, we've been alone before, but only for a few minutes. What if I mess up? What if he gets hurt? Morrisey is trusting me with her son."

"It will be fine." Miriam selected two pairs of jeans and handed them to Charlene. "Try those on."

"It's been such a long time since I've taken care of a child. What if Gareth—"

"Charlene! Would you please try on those jeans?"

Charlene's gaze flickered to the jeans in her arms. "Oh. Okay. Thanks."

Miriam blew out a breath. "You're welcome. Here, try on those shirts, too." She reached over to a clothes rack, plucked a few tops and shooed Charlene into a fitting room.

Charlene bolted the door, hung the shirts and dropped the jeans onto a small bench. She studied herself in the mirror and held her stomach in. She had to admit, she was a good-looking woman. Her body was toned and trim and her skin was healthy. She tucked her hair behind her ears and grinned shyly. Yes, she had a great smile. Slightly off-kilter, just like Morrisey had said. Charlene brought her lips back to further expose her teeth, which were nice, straight and white. She stepped closer to the mirror and narrowed her eyes. "I'm hot." Her lips curled into a satisfied smile. "I'm hot."

She slid her sandals off. She undid the button on her worn,

light-blue jeans, which she had owned since before JP killed himself. She slithered out of them and tossed them onto the bench. Her gaze wandered back into the mirror and over her legs. She turned around and craned her neck so she could study her behind, which was snug in blue bikini underwear. "Not bad. Not bad at all." She pulled her shirt off and pitched it next to the jeans. She turned again to study her front. Now clad only in underwear and a bra, Charlene cocked an eyebrow. "Still not bad," she whispered. Her stomach was taut, and there was little fat on her arms and her legs. Her breasts were as nice and round as apples, with no sag.

A knock sounded at the door. "How's it going?"

Charlene flushed in embarrassment. "Almost done! Just a minute." She grabbed the top pair of jeans and pulled them on. Next, she tossed a silk blue shirt on. She surveyed the results in the mirror and grinned. "I'd do me." She opened the door for Miriam and threw her arms around her best friend. "Thank you so much," she whispered in Miriam's ear. "Thank you so, so much for doing this, for putting up with me."

Miriam drew back, a smile crinkling her face. "You're welcome. I'm happy you're happy. Now, let's see." She held Charlene at arm's length and she whistled appreciatively. "If this doesn't make Morrisey drool all over you, I don't know what will."

WHEN CHARLENE ARRIVED home, shopping bag in hand, the telephone was ringing. She ran to it and muttered a breathless hello.

"Well, hello," came the reply, and Charlene froze at Morrisey's soft voice.

"Hello?" Morrisey asked.

Charlene blinked, afraid that Morrisey had changed her mind about the baby-sitting. *She regrets hugging me, letting me hug her. She thinks we're moving too fast.*

"Charlene?"

Charlene moistened her lips. "Hey. I'm here."

"Good. Glad I caught you. I was wondering if you'd like to join Gareth and me for dinner tomorrow before the seminar. We could order pizza."

Charlene tightened her grip on the telephone receiver, unaware her knuckles were turning white. *Yes. Yes. She hasn't changed her mind.* "Sure. That sounds great."

"Hey, it's fine if you can't or don't want to."

"No, I want to," Charlene exclaimed.

"You sure? You okay?"

Charlene pressed the telephone receiver to her ear. "I'm fine. I just walked in the door, actually. I was shopping."

"Oh, okay. Sorry. I tend to call people at bad times."

"It's not a bad time." Charlene twisted the spiraling telephone cord around her finger. "When do you want me to come over?"

"How about 5:45? I'll have the pizza delivered by then. What do you like?"

Charlene's mind was a blank. "What do I like?"

"Yes."

"What do you mean?"

Morrisey's tone took on an amused quality. "On your pizza. What toppings do you want?"

Charlene wished there was some way she could track down her brain cells and start the conversation over. "Whatever you like is fine," she answered.

"Pepperoni and extra cheese?"

"Wonderful."

Morrisey chuckled, causing Charlene's stomach to flutter.

"So." For the first time in the conversation, Morrisey seemed hesitant. "How are you? Did you have a good day? What were you shopping for?"

Charlene's eyes glanced at the plastic bag that held her new clothes. *I was shopping to impress you.* "Um, I was shopping for bags."

"Bags? You mean purses?"

"Right. Yes. Purses. I needed a new one, and I went with a friend of mine from work. Miriam. Actually, she's my best friend. She needed one too. We had a good time."

"Great. That's great. So you had a good day?"

Charlene pulled up a chair from her kitchen table and sat. "I had a pretty good day. One of the customers at work left a huge tip." *And I thought about you a lot.* "How was your day?"

"Eh, it was all right. Want the long version or the short version?"

"Long. I love stories."

"Well, okay. First, Gareth and I went to get our hair cut at a new place. The hairdresser had a really big—I mean, gigantic—mole on her chin. This mole even had moons orbiting it. I knew it would be trouble, and sure enough, Gareth piped up immediately. 'What's that thing on your chin? It's ugly!' The poor woman was so embarrassed. She kicked us out. We went to the mall for the haircuts. And Gareth asked me if he could get a dress to wear tomorrow. I had no idea what to say. I mean, I want him to be open-minded and all, but I don't want social services coming after me." Morrisey laughed, and Charlene grinned, wishing she had been there.

"So," Morrisey continued, "I did what all good parents would do. I changed the subject. He forgot all about it. Then when we got home, he went to play with the neighbor's puppy. Poor Gareth. The puppy bit him. Sank her teeth really deeply in Gareth's arm. Left marks and everything. Poor kid. He was crying all afternoon."

Charlene winced. "Oh, no. Will he be all right?"

"Oh, he'll be fine. He just got a bit too rough. Gareth learned his lesson. I doubt it'll happen again."

Charlene smiled. "Good. So you just did stuff with Gareth today?"

"Yes. It's really nice having the summers off, but, yeah, I need to get out more. Ha. Anyway, about tomorrow night. The seminar shouldn't take more than two hours. I should be home by 9:30. You'll probably need to put Gareth to bed. We can go over all that tomorrow."

"Okay. That's fine. Take your time at the seminar. And, Morrisey, thank you again. I really appreciate this."

"No need to thank me. I'll see you at 5:45."

"Okay." Charlene pressed her eyes shut, willing the conversation not to end, for Morrisey not to say goodbye and hang up. But of course she would. What else was she going to do?

"Well, do you like your new purse?"

Charlene's eyes flew open. Morrisey was not saying goodbye. She was not hanging up. Far from it. "Actually, I couldn't find one I liked," Charlene said. "Maybe another time."

"Oh, that's too bad. I don't have a purse. Just a wallet. I like to keep things simple. I don't have the desire to haul a hundred tubes of lipstick around with me."

Charlene leaned back in her chair, trying to relax. She pictured Morrisey, laughing. She remembered Morrisey at the grocery store with Gareth. Morrisey, with her deep tan, long legs and that vibrant red shirt. "It's not like you need makeup or anything," Charlene pointed out. "You're so beautiful. You're perfect."

Morrisey did not answer for a moment, and Charlene nearly choked on her tongue, her words belatedly registering in her brain. Had she actually told Morrisey she was "so beautiful?" "Perfect?" *That's what you get for relaxing.*

Morrisey gave a half-laugh. "Thank you. That's kind of you to say."

"I didn't mean it," Charlene blurted out.

"What? You didn't mean that I'm beautiful?"

"No, I meant that." Charlene's tongue twisted and turned. "I just meant to say that...Oh, never mind. I'm not making sense."

Morrisey said tentatively, "I understand. Well, I better be going now. I'll see you tomorrow. Thanks for the chat."

"Uh huh." Charlene managed a smile for her own sake.

"Goodbye."

"Bye."

Morrisey hung up, and Charlene held the phone to her ear a while longer.

GARETH FLUNG OPEN the door seconds after Charlene rang the doorbell. "Hi, Charlie! Do you have a present for me?"

Charlene dropped to her knees. "How about this?" She hugged Gareth, stood and closed the door. "Where's your mother?"

"Here I am." Morrisey rounded the corner. She literally took Charlene's breath away. She was wearing a black pantsuit that showed off her long, trim body. Her dark hair was a few inches shorter, and it brought out even more intensity in her eyes.

Jeans and a blue silk shirt. Charlene suddenly felt horribly, severely inadequate.

Gareth giggled and proclaimed, "Charlie has white on her shirt!"

Charlene's heart contracted, and her gaze dropped to her shirt. There it was, just above her right breast, a dried glob of toothpaste. Somehow, in all her hurried preparations, the repeated check-overs, all the times she inspected herself in the mirror, she had overlooked the toothpaste. How? It came to her. She had brushed her teeth last, when time was running out. She had not looked herself over after that except to check her teeth in the rearview mirror. *Stupid, stupid, stupid.* Everybody knew you put the clothes on last. The door was right behind her. She could run out and never have to see Morrisey and Gareth again. *Problem solved.*

Gareth's laughter increased. "Charlie has white on her shirt!"

Morrisey, her heels clicking on the wood floor, crossed to her son. She put her hands on his head. "It's not that big. I hardly notice it. Hey, don't you think that's a nice shirt?"

"Charlie has big white on her shirt!"

"Gareth, stop," Morrisey warned. "Let's help her clean it off."

"Okay!" Gareth grabbed Charlene's hand and dragged her through the living room to the kitchen sink. Morrisey was not far behind, and she ran a rag under the faucet. Charlene took the cloth and rubbed it against her shirt, all too aware that the corners of Morrisey's lips were twitching.

The doorbell rang. "That's the pizza. Be right back." Morrisey's heels clicked across the floor again. Charlene scrubbed furiously, and in a few moments, the toothpaste was replaced by a dark-blue water spot. Morrisey, bearing a pizza box, strode back into the kitchen. "Let's eat."

"Yay!" Gareth made his pleasure clear. "I'm hungry!"

Morrisey reached into a cabinet and drew out three plates. She took three glasses out of another cabinet. "Be right back." She disappeared down the hallway leading to the bedrooms. Charlene helped Gareth get his pizza, and then Morrisey, wearing a plain blue T-shirt and the same pants as before, ambled back. "Hey." She flashed a big smile. "I figured I'd better change my shirt before we ate."

"So you won't get pizza on it!" Gareth cried.

Morrisey gave her son a pointed look. "That's right. Because I wouldn't like it if I got pizza on my shirt and you laughed at me."

Gareth's face fell. "I wouldn't laugh at you."

Morrisey cocked an eyebrow, and Charlene felt her cheeks flush a hot red. She raised her hand. "It's okay."

Gareth tugged on Charlene's jeans. "I'm sorry, Charlie."

"It's fine," Charlene mumbled. "It was funny."

"Are you mad at me?"

"No," Charlene said gently.

"Okay." Gareth took his pizza into the dining room.

Morrisey joined Charlene at the counter. "I'm sorry about that," Morrisey whispered.

"Truly, it's fine. It was funny."

Morrisey scooped three slices of pizza onto her plate. "That really is a nice shirt. It brings out your eyes."

Charlene tried to stifle a grin of pleasure, but it broke through. "You like it?"

"Oh, yeah."

"Your haircut's great too." *Did you do it for me, like I got new clothes for you?*

Morrisey jerked her head toward the dining room. "Come on. Gareth's been waiting all day to tell you about a fish he saw."

THIRTY MINUTES LATER, the pizza was gone. Morrisey went off to brush her teeth and change her shirt again. She returned with a piece of paper. "Here's my cell number." She handed Charlene the information. "I'll have the phone on vibrate. Just in case I don't feel it, right there is the number of the place I'll be." She clasped her hands together. "I won't make you give Gareth a bath. You two have fun, all right? His bedtime's 8:00, but this summer, I've been letting him stay up a little later, up until 9:00 if he's behaving. If he acts up, send him to a corner for five minutes. Don't let him sweet talk you out of that. And he's done, ab-so-lutely done, with his TV allowance for the day, so no more of that. Oh, and no more food. If he really wants something, let him have an apple. I figure you guys can just play a board game, color, draw, or go outside. It'll be light for a while yet."

Morrisey lowered her gaze for a split second, and Charlene felt the weight of the task upon her shoulders. If she messed up, just one little thing...Morrisey was making a huge leap of faith by leaving her child alone with a woman she had known only for a few weeks, a woman who could easily take Gareth and run.

"Hey." Morrisey reached for Charlene's hand. "Don't worry. It'll be fine. I trust you. I wouldn't have asked you otherwise."

"Are you sure?"

"Yes." Morrisey glanced at the clock. "Okay, I better get going. You know where to reach me. I'll see you later. And, remember, don't let Gareth sweet talk you into anything he shouldn't be doing. He has my charm." The minute Morrisey pulled out of the driveway, Gareth ran to Charlene. "Can we watch *Finding Nemo*?"

"I don't think you're allowed to watch any more TV."

"I can watch one movie a day. That's different from TV time." Gareth went to the entertainment center and corralled the *Finding Nemo* DVD. He slid it into the player. "Come sit with me!" he cried.

Charlene ran a hand through her hair. Gareth's grin was too broad, too smug. "Hey, Gareth. Want to play a game or go outside?"

"I wanna watch Nemo!"

"Your TV time's up. How about we do something else?"

"I can watch one movie a day!"

"Are you sure you didn't watch a movie earlier today?"

Gareth shook his head solemnly, his eyes unnaturally wide and round. "I'm sure."

Charlene got to her knees and met Gareth's so-called innocent gaze. "My movie time's up. I can't watch this with you. Will you play with me?"

Gareth's jaw fell. "You can only watch one movie a day?"

"That's right."

Gareth wrinkled his nose. "Okay. Let's play hide and seek. I'll hide!" He leaped to his feet.

"Wait!" Charlene grasped Gareth's shoulder, preventing him from darting off. "Where are you going to hide?"

"I'm not telling!"

"I didn't mean that. I meant that this is a big house. What if I can't find you?" Charlene imagined Gareth getting trapped in a trunk shoved in some obscure, dusty corner. She would not be able to find him until it was too late.

"I won't go far."

Charlene wiped her sweaty palms on her jeans. "Why don't we play a board game? Or you could read a book to me. Hey! Let's draw pictures."

"I wanna hide!" Gareth howled.

"Let's go for a walk outside."

"No! The dog's gonna bite me!" Gareth shoved up his shirt sleeve to expose a deep, red ring of teeth marks on his upper arm.

Charlene winced, but she held her ground. "So you don't like dogs anymore?"

"Just that one." Gareth crossed his arms. "I went to pet her, and she bit me!"

"We'll play in the back yard. What do you like to play?"

"Can I hide outside?"

"There aren't many places where you could hide out back."

"Mommy and I play hide and seek in the neighborhood."

"The whole neighborhood?"

Gareth nodded eagerly.

Charlene gave in. "You know what? Let's watch your movie."

"You already watched yours today."

"Don't tell anybody."

"Okay! Come sit." Gareth plopped down on the floor. Charlene joined him, her heart thrumming with guilt. Watching a movie with Gareth was just about the only way to ensure he would stay safe, but she was directly and knowingly disobeying Morrisey's instructions. If Gareth went outside, and he ran off, and got bitten, or lost, or kidnapped—or if they stayed inside and she could not find him...

The movie started, and Charlene studied Gareth out of the corner of her eye. He watched in rapt fascination, his head slightly tilted, at the colorful undersea world that filled the television. He was so adorable, so infinitely beautiful and innocent, full of so much life and promise. And to think she had once worried about not being able to love him.

Gareth's eyes widened. "Did you see that?" He turned excitedly to Charlene. "Look! Look!"

She edged closer to him. "Okay, okay, I'm watching." She slid an arm around her grandson, her heart swelling with pride and love.

GARETH'S EYELIDS DROOPED shut right as the movie ended. With a bit of effort, Charlene scooped him up and carried him to his bed. It was still light outside, and Gareth's bedroom curtains were pulled back. His eyes flew open just as Charlene tugged the bedcovers over his chest. "Charlie?" he murmured.

"Yeah?"

"I don't wanna go to bed. I'm not tired."

"You sure about that?"

Gareth shot up, narrowly missing Charlene's head. "Will you tell me a story? Tell me a story about JP."

Charlene stared stupidly at Gareth.

"Will you? Tell me about JP."

"Go to sleep, sweetie."

Gareth crawled into Charlene's lap and rested his head on her breast. "Do him and Grandpa have fun?"

Charlene brought her arms around Gareth's small body. "I don't know. I hope so."

"Will you tell me a story about your daddy?"

Charlene blinked at the shift in questioning. "My daddy?"

"Yeah." Gareth looked up, into Charlene's eyes.

"I never really knew him. He died when I was a baby."

"Really?" Gareth clambered out of Charlene's lap and stood. He seemed wide awake now. "I don't know my daddy."

Charlene managed a weak grin. "Right."

"I don't really have a daddy. I have a donor."

"Your mother went to a sperm bank."

Gareth nodded. "I miss my granddad."

Charlene cupped Gareth's cheek and kissed it. "I'm sure you do."

"He was fun to play with. He wasn't boring, like Grandma."

"She loves you, though. She just wants what's best for you."

Gareth scrunched his face. "Did you see your daddy?"

Charlene tried her best to ignore the knot in her stomach. "I told you he died when I was a baby."

"Yeah, but did you see him? When he was alive, like I saw Grandpa?"

Charlene averted Gareth's open, curious gaze. "Yes. I was just a baby, so I don't remember it."

"Do you got pictures of him?"

"I have one," Charlene whispered. "At home."

"Was your daddy tall?"

Charlene swallowed. "Yes. And thin, really skinny. He had blond hair, like me, but his eyes were brown." She chuckled at a sudden memory. "My mom told me he liked to eat a lot. He'd never get full. He could eat a horse and then two. Never gained weight."

"I don't want to eat horses."

Charlene hastened to explain. "Well, he didn't actually eat horses. It's a saying, an idiom."

"Where's he? With Grandpa and JP?"

"I don't know."

"How come?"

She shrugged. "My mom never told me."

"Grandpa had a heart attack. Mommy says it didn't hurt."

"That's right, sweetie. It didn't hurt."

"I don't got a picture of my daddy," Gareth said. "I think he's a fireman."

"Why?"

"'Cause. Or a policeman. Or Superman."

"Superman?"

Gareth nodded. "My friend Aaron's daddy came for him last week!"

Charlene injected cheer into her reply. "That's great."

"Mommy says my daddy won't come for me. Grandpa says Mommy's wrong."

Charlene had heard enough. "Come on." She pulled Gareth's bedcovers back. "If you lie down, I'll tell you a story about when I was little, and I got in trouble."

Gareth's eyes lit up. "Yeah?"

"Yep."

Gareth clambered back into the bed. "Was that a long time ago?"

Charlene snorted. "Yes. It was a very long time ago."

"When there were dinosaurs?"

"No. Way before then."

"Before dinosaurs!"

"That's right." Charlene proceeded to tell Gareth about the time she and a friend had gotten lost in the woods, which was really a rather boring story, and in just a few minutes, he was sound asleep. Charlene adjusted his pillow, and he let out a little sigh of contentment. She remained sitting on his bed, her legs crossed, her eyes fixed on her grandson. He wanted his father to come for him. Charlene wanted that too, more than anything, for JP, the good JP, to come back, but it was not going to happen.

Gareth would never have his father, and Charlene would never have her son again. She shook a tear from her eye and lay down on her side. She memorized every detail of Gareth's face: his long, fine eyelashes, the sprinkling of freckles on his nose and his cheeks. The way he breathed just slightly out of his mouth. The longer Charlene looked, the more differences she found between Gareth and JP. That did not bother her. She wanted to love Gareth for who he was and not merely because he was JP's son and not just because he looked so much like JP.

Charlene closed her eyes for a moment, letting her body relax. It felt so good. She had not slept well lately. She had been tense because of Morrisey. She was vaguely aware she was drifting off to sleep, but she was powerless to stop it. *Just a little nap for a few minutes.*

Chapter Twelve

MORRISEY FIDDLED WITH her keys before finding the one for the house and inserting it in the lock. She took a deep breath and stepped inside. She might as well have stayed home. She had not learned one damned thing at the seminar because Charlene had been on her mind the whole time. When the first speaker had discussed new learning technologies, Morrisey had tuned out and wondered whether she should offer Charlene a drink. A little glass of wine?

When the second speaker began to lecture about steps to ensure productive parent/teacher conferences, Morrisey stifled a yawn and shifted her thoughts to Charlene's eyes. They were fantastically, uniquely blue and they conveyed so much depth and emotion—grief, anguish, indescribable joy, shyness.

During the third and final speaker, Morrisey's attention wandered to Charlene's lips. They were so full and enticing. She wanted to kiss them, to feel them roaming over her body, maybe stopping at...

That had startled her wide awake, and she rethought her decision to offer Charlene a glass of wine. They had been taking it slow the past few weeks. What would it hurt to wait a few more weeks before offering the proverbial glass of wine?

After the seminar ended, Morrisey had dawdled, trying to collect the courage to go home. Now here she was. She set her keys on the kitchen counter. She went into the living room and frowned. The room was brightly lit, and the television was on. The logo for the DVD player was flickering across the screen. Morrisey's lips twisted into a wry smile. How had Gareth done it this time? "Charlene?" Morrisey called softly. "I'm home." There was no reply. Morrisey slid out of her high-heeled shoes, turned on the hall light and headed to Gareth's bedroom. The door was open, and the light spilling inside illuminated Charlene and Gareth, both fast asleep, facing each other, their noses almost touching.

Morrisey leaned against the doorway, hesitant to approach the sleeping figures. She did not want to awaken Charlene and let reality back in. She waited a few heartbeats before tiptoeing to Charlene's side of the bed. Charlene's breathing was slow and measured. Her hands were bunched near her chin. "It doesn't matter who she is," Morrisey reminded herself. *She's great with Gareth and makes you happy.* Morrisey rubbed Charlene's arm and whispered, "Hey. Wake up. I'm home."

Charlene did not stir, so Morrisey tried again. "Charlene, wake up." Charlene's eyelids fluttered, and Morrisey smiled in triumph. "Hey, sleepyhead."

"Mmm?" Charlene's eyelids closed again. A second later, she bolted upright. "What happened?"

Morrisey pressed a finger to Charlene's lips. "Shh, it's okay."

CHARLENE WAS MORTIFIED as Morrisey led her into the living room. She rubbed the sleep from her eyes. How was her hair? Was her breath sour? Were there lines on her face? Was her shirt horribly wrinkled? Before she could excuse herself to the bathroom to investigate, Morrisey shot her a sly, knowing grin. "So how did Gareth get to watch *Finding Nemo*?"

Charlene froze.

Morrisey only laughed. "What happened? I'm curious how he swung this one."

"Well, first, Gareth said he was allowed to watch one movie a day, that it was separate from his TV time."

Morrisey was amused. "Not bad. He was lying, of course. I let him watch an hour of TV a day. If he wants to watch a movie, then no TV that day."

"I figured as much."

"And?"

"I knew he wasn't being truthful," Charlene said. "So I suggested we do something else. He wanted to play hide and seek."

Morrisey furrowed her brows. "Okay. What was wrong with that?"

"Well, I couldn't let him hide!"

"Why not?"

"Because I don't know the house well. I kept imagining all kinds of awful stuff. What if he got trapped in a trunk, the dryer, or something, and I couldn't find him? He didn't want to go outside or read or color. He didn't want to play a board game or do anything safe. If anything happened to him..." Charlene willed her rushed words to slow down. "So the movie seemed like the safest bet."

"Oh, Charlene." Morrisey voice and her expression were

sympathetic. "It's fine. I understand."

Charlene did not feel better, but she masked it with a smile. "Will you let me baby-sit him again?"

Morrisey rolled her eyes. "Of course I will. And before next time, I'll tell you all the little tricks he pulls on my mother and his other baby sitters. I won't let him play you again, all right? I promise. Other than that, how did it go? Have any trouble putting him to sleep?"

"No trouble." Charlene decided not to tell Morrisey about the "daddies" conversation. It would ruin the moment. "Gareth put his head on my shoulder. It was nice."

"Good."

"How was your seminar?"

"It was boring. I wasn't into it." Morrisey fiddled with a button on her shirt for a few moments. Charlene wondered if that was a signal for her to go home but kept quiet. After Morrisey was satisfied with the button, she said, "Want a drink? You probably know what I have. You also probably saw that I have wine. Want some?"

"Wine?"

Morrisey resumed twiddling with the button. "I've wanted to finish that bottle. I'd hate to waste the wine."

Charlene's chest was suddenly tight and heavy. There was no mistaking the meaning behind Morrisey's words. "Wine sounds great," Charlene replied slowly. "The last time I had some was when I went out with Miriam for her birthday last year."

"Your best friend, right?"

"Yes. The one I went shopping with."

Morrisey beckoned for Charlene to follow her into the kitchen. "Did you tell her about about Gareth? And me?"

Morrisey fetched two wine glasses from a cabinet, and Charlene licked her lips. *Please don't be mad.* "After I met you and Gareth for the first time, in the cemetery, I went over to Miriam's. I just had to talk to someone."

"I understand. I can't imagine what a shock it was."

"Yes. And later, well, I didn't quite tell her about Gareth. Or you. I know that's your business. She figured it out anyway."

Morrisey darkened, and she set the wine glasses next to the stove. "What exactly did Miriam figure out?"

"It'd been about two weeks. I'd been avoiding her, acting differently. She knew it had to be something bad. And then I just blurted it out. I couldn't hold it inside any longer, what JP did. So, yeah, I told her JP raped you. But that's all I said. No details. I didn't tell her about the other boys. I just had to get it off my chest and try to make some sense of it. I'm sorry."

Morrisey crossed her arms. "I see. Well, I do understand. I'm glad you had someone to talk to about it."

"Miriam can be trusted," Charlene rushed on. "She did tell Liz, her lover, but Liz won't tell anyone."

"Miriam's gay?"

"Yes. Actually, she's kind of my ex. We went out on a few dates a long time ago, when JP was four."

Morrisey's expression turned even darker. "All right." She reached into the refrigerator and drew out a half-full bottle of white wine. "What about the car you drove tonight and all those Sundays? Is it Miriam's?"

Charlene tried not to flinch. "Yes."

Morrisey, with great, catlike deliberation, set the wine bottle next to the glasses. "So you told her about the Acclaim."

"No, I swear. I know it's your business. I simply told her JP raped you."

"So you asked to borrow her car, and she said yes just like that because...?"

Charlene floundered for an explanation, and she decided to go with much of the same story she had told Miriam, except she would leave out the part about being attracted to Morrisey. "I told Miriam I wanted to impress you and that the Acclaim wouldn't cut it. Yeah, I know Miriam's Honda isn't much better, but it's better. It's all one color."

"Great. She thinks I'm all about looks and money. Thanks a lot."

Charlene wished Morrisey had something stronger than wine to drink. "No. I said I wanted to impress you as much as I possibly could, because you are the mother of my grandchild."

Morrisey began to pour the wine, doing so almost angrily. "Right."

"I had to tell her something, and it worked."

"You can stop."

"Stop what?"

"Borrowing her car. I'll be just fine. I'm a big girl."

"I know."

Morrisey sighed and seemed to deflate. "Sorry," she muttered. "I just hate that people know about the rape." She handed Charlene a half-full glass.

Charlene tilted it back for a tiny sip. The wine was rich and fruity, but she was not in the mood to appreciate it. Still, her anxiety prompted her to take a second, quick sip and then a third.

"Want to go out back, on the porch swing?" Morrisey asked. "It's a beautiful night. Lots of stars out."

Charlene took a fourth sip, her anxiety increasing. *Out back. On the porch swing. Oh, God.* She had wished for weeks for something to perhaps happen between her and Morrisey, but now that the possibility was all too real, Charlene found herself mumbling that she ought to be going. "I have to be up early for work," she explained.

"Oh." Disappointment, contained in that one little word, was clear in Morrisey's voice.

"I'm sorry. It's getting late, and when the alarm goes off at 6:30, it's—"

"I understand." Morrisey gave Charlene a tight little smile. "Do you need me to finish your wine for you?"

Charlene looked back to her wine glass. Suppose she went back to her apartment right this minute. Sure, two colorful rugs brightened the ugly carpet. Sure, JP did not stare at her from everywhere now. Still, would she really rather be there than here? She followed her heart and said, "You know what? Let's sit on the couch. It won't take me long to finish this."

Morrisey brought her glass to her lips, perhaps to conceal a smile. "All right."

Charlene followed Morrisey to the living room couch. Morrisey sipped her wine again and sighed in pleasure, her eyelids fluttering. Charlene could not believe just how sexy this woman, her grandson's mother, was.

Morrisey set her glass on a coaster. "So, you get up at 6:30 for work?"

"Most days, but as you saw, I have some afternoon or night shifts. Hey, are you still dating that woman?"

Morrisey raised an eyebrow. "Who?"

"I think she was a construction worker. That first day I came here, when everyone thought I was your date."

"Oh." Morrisey took a long sip of wine. "Janet. No. It wasn't working out."

"Why not?"

Morrisey indicated Charlene's glass. "You're not drinking."

Charlene brought the wine to her lips but did not drink.

"I just didn't feel anything for Janet," Morrisey explained. "Never did. We'd gone on four dates, so I figured it wasn't going to happen if it hadn't by then."

Charlene nodded and finished her wine in one long swallow.

"Well," Morrisey said. "You okay to drive?"

"I suppose so." Charlene was glad she had stayed longer. She wanted more—more wine, more conversation, more Morrisey.

"I'm going to have another glass," Morrisey declared. "Are you sure you don't want another?"

"I'll have one more. Thank you."

AFTER CHARLENE AND Morrisey refilled their glasses, they headed outside to the back porch swing. They sat close together, but their legs did not touch. The moon and starlight provided enough illumination that there was no need for the porch light. After a couple of minutes of awkwardness, Morrisey started telling Charlene why she had decided to become a teacher—for the money, she joked. Charlene's anxiety gradually disappeared, and before long, she was laughing and chatting easily with Morrisey. They finished their wine and kept talking and talking. They did not once mention Gareth or JP. Charlene loved having Morrisey so close, loved the way the moonlight framed her face and her sparkling dark eyes.

Maybe it was the wine, or the rush that accompanies falling in love, or both, but Charlene took a bold step. "An old friend of mine taught me how to read palms," she informed Morrisey. "She was a fortune teller for a few years."

"Really? Wow. She had a crystal ball and everything?"

"Yes. May I read your palm?"

"Isn't it a bit too dark out for that?"

"No. This is perfect. Give me your hand."

Morrisey shifted in her seat and offered Charlene her right palm. Charlene took it and ran her fingers over Morrisey's smooth, soft skin. She traced shallow, crisscrossing lines. Morrisey had the best right palm in the world.

"So what's my fortune?" Morrisey asked. "When do I win the lottery and retire to Italy?"

Here we go. Charlene brought her lips to Morrisey's palm. The first kiss was languid and sweet. The next few were quick and fluttery. Morrisey trembled under the ministrations, bolstering Charlene's confidence. "Mmm, that's nice," Morrisey murmured. "You're good. What else did your friend teach you about reading palms?"

"Well, my friend didn't know her anatomy very well." Charlene moved her lips past Morrisey's palm and a few kisses up her arm. Now she could feel goose bumps bursting across Morrisey's skin.

"Hmmm. God. That's good. Don't stop."

Charlene moved back to Morrisey's hand and took a finger in her mouth. She sucked softly, moans from Morrisey filling her ears. It was perfect. Everything was perfect. Then an owl hooted. *Hoo-hoo-hoo-hoo.* Morrisey stiffened and jerked her finger from Charlene's mouth.

Charlene looked up, afraid she'd been too bold. "What's wrong?"

Morrisey avoided Charlene's eyes and used her shirt to dry her finger. "Nothing."

"Did I go too far?"

"No."

Charlene knew it was time to shut up, at least about what had just happened. She sat back in the swing. Neither she nor Morrisey spoke as they looked into the starry night. Charlene wondered if the owl somehow reminded Morrisey of the rape. *Do something. Make her smile, make her laugh.* "I tripped at work the other day," Charlene blurted out. "Fell right on my butt."

Morrisey half-smiled. "Yeah? Tell me more."

IT WAS A FEW ticks shy of midnight when Morrisey walked Charlene to Miriam's car. Their conversation had recovered admirably after the owl incident, but there had been no more touches, no more flirting. They had put on masks and acted as if Charlene had not kissed Morrisey's hand and her arm. They had pretended that Morrisey's finger had not been in Charlene's mouth and that Morrisey had not moaned in pleasure. And now they were saying goodbye again.

"Want to get together Sunday as usual?" Charlene ventured.

Morrisey shrugged. "Doing anything tomorrow night?"

Charlene's heart leaped. *Tomorrow. Wow.* "I don't have plans. Hey, Gareth mentioned wanting to see that new Disney movie. How about it?"

Morrisey toyed with the button on her shirt again. "Or would you like me to get a baby-sitter for him? So you and I can do something on our own."

Charlene's stomach fluttered. *A date. We're going to go on a date! Oh my God.* "Yes. I would love that."

Morrisey grinned, obviously relieved. "Great. How about I come over to your place? You're here all the time. I can come over about, say, 7:00, and we'll go from there? Maybe to dinner or a picnic or something."

My place? Where JP lived, where his things are? Why? Charlene replied with a weak, "Sounds perfect," even though the suggestion seemed anything but.

Morrisey tucked her hair behind her ear. "Great. See you then. Drive safely."

"Good night."

Morrisey turned to go into her house but abruptly reversed course. She reached for Charlene's arm, and the next thing Charlene knew, Morrisey's mouth was on her own. Morrisey was impossibly soft and warm, and her kiss was gentle. Perhaps too gentle. Chaste, even. Charlene pressed into Morrisey, wanting, needing more.

Morrisey only whispered "Good night," grazing Charlene's earlobe and tickling it.

Then Morrisey was gone, and Charlene sank against the car. "Oh, God," she breathed. She needed a cold shower, and she needed it now.

Chapter Thirteen

MORRISEY STUDIED HERSELF in the bathroom mirror and willed herself to calm down, though in truth, she loved the flutters in her chest and in her stomach. She would not trade them for the world. Later that night, in just a few hours in fact, was her date. Morrisey was as giddy as a schoolgirl in love, and then some. *Charlene Sudsbury. So what if she's his mother?* Charlene was a wonderful, gentle, kind, funny, beautiful woman. She made Morrisey so happy and left her feeling alive.

Morrisey tore herself from the mirror and wandered into her bedroom. She flopped back onto her bed. She still could not believe what her mother had said a mere thirty minutes ago when she stopped by to pick up Gareth. "I'm more than happy to keep him overnight." There was no mistaking the sly glint in Margaret's gaze. Morrisey had scoffed, but even now, her mind reeled. She had never had anything remotely resembling a sex talk with her mother, and now this!

Did Morrisey want sex with Charlene? Of course she did. Only a fool would not. A delicious shudder ran through her as she imagined holding Charlene's naked body in her arms, or riding her. Or having Charlene straddle her, crying out in ecstasy. It would not happen that night, though, and probably would not for months yet. Charlene was struggling with her own feelings and with what JP had done. So was Morrisey, and she did not want anyone to get hurt in the process. Yes, they needed to take it slow.

Morrisey forced herself off the bed and ambled to her closet. She surveyed her shirts. *Hmm. No. Too formal. Too dark. Too casual. Too sexy. Not sexy enough. Maybe this one.* She wished she had not suggested meeting at Charlene's, but she had. So she would look at some pictures of JP, of Gareth's "father," and try not to flinch. She would get through it. Or maybe she would not bother to look at pictures. *Look another time.* She wanted tonight to be just about her and Charlene. She liked the idea of taking Charlene to the parkway for a picnic. Then maybe she would kiss Charlene, slide a hand under her shirt, and...*Stop.* Morrisey shook her head and tried to banish such thought. They kept coming back, stronger and stronger each time. Finally, she let out a little cry. Maybe it would not be so bad after all if something physical did happen soon. It had been more than five years since she had had sex, and Morrisey had found someone she trusted. She was ready — more than ready.

IN HER SMALL apartment across town, Charlene stepped into the shower. She washed and conditioned her hair. She scrubbed every inch of her body and shaved her armpits, her legs, her pussy. She was going to be Morrisey's lover, though not that night and maybe not for a while. But they had chemistry on all levels. They were right together.

Charlene wanted, more than anything, to be with Morrisey. She could not wait. But she was afraid of hurting Morrisey. What if she pinched Morrisey's nipple too hard, or accidentally bit her tongue? What if Morrisey was triggered back in time to that snowy night and Charlene awakened nightmares in her again? JP flashed into Charlene's mind — JP and his friends, mousy Ralph and two faceless boy-men, thrusting inside Morrisey, holding her down. Laughing and cackling as they devoured her.

Charlene shook her head and returned to the present time. She stepped out of the shower and began to get ready. She blow-dried her hair. She changed into jeans and a simple white shirt. She went into the living room and picked up a drawing she and Gareth had done together. The feeble green lines were supposed to comprise a tyrannosaurus rex, but it was impossible to tell. Charlene chuckled at the picture and at the memory. She wished she had a photo of Gareth. She closed her eyes and conjured him in her mind — her beautiful, lovely little grandson, with the sparkling eyes and the sunny face. JP was not worthy of this child. Charlene hoped she was.

AFTER MORRISEY KNOCKED, Charlene answered quickly.

"Hi, Charlene," Morrisey said, and Charlene's skin prickled at just how Morrisey breathed her name. *CharleneCharleneCharlene.* Morrisey brought a hand from behind her back to reveal a yellow rose, fluffy and soft in full bloom.

The gesture swept Charlene's breath away. "For me?"

Morrisey laughed. "Who else? Yes. Do you like it?"

"I love it. Thank you. It's beautiful." Charlene took the rose and brought it to her nose. The flower was sweet, clean and fresh. The next thing she knew, her arms were around Morrisey. She smelled even better than the rose.

"What was that for?" Morrisey asked after Charlene drew back.

Charlene shrugged, embarrassed. "I don't know. Just thanks, I guess. Come on in. I'll put the rose in some water." She ushered Morrisey into the apartment and shut the door behind them. Morrisey surveyed the living room, and Charlene tried to see it through her eyes. The room was, more or less, bare. A blank. Charlene had not gotten around to replacing all of the JP pictures she had torn from the walls and the furniture. There was no way Morrisey could know for sure that JP's pictures had, until recently, covered every inch of the space. Still, Charlene knew that Morrisey knew. There was a giveaway look in her eyes, in the tilt of her chin. Charlene retreated into the kitchen, her cheeks burning. She filled a vase with water and placed the rose into it. She returned to Morrisey, who had found the dinosaur drawing and was tracing its lines with her fingers.

"Charlene," Morrisey began.

"No, I didn't do it for you. I did it for me. A few weeks ago."

"Really?"

"Yes."

Morrisey sighed and kissed Charlene's hands. "All right."

CHARLENE SLOWLY TURNED the doorknob to JP's bedroom, and Morrisey sucked in a breath. She stepped inside and let her gaze roam from left to right. JP's bedroom was tiny, a mere shoebox of a space. The walls were white and bare except for a wooden shelf that ran the full length of the far side. On the bed were a large box and a bulging plastic bag. On the floor, various pictures and trophies peeked out of an untidy heap of boxes.

Charlene whispered, "After I found out about the rape, I packed. Then I unpacked. But I haven't been in here in a few weeks."

Morrisey indicated the bag on the bed. "Are those the pictures from the living room?"

"Yes."

Morrisey went toward the bag. She studied it, wondering what exactly she was doing. *Just get this over with, so you and Charlene can truly move on.* She snuck a hand inside. Her fingers gripped a wooden frame and she drew it out of the bag. She took in a broad, robust snowman sandwiched between a gap-toothed boy, JP, who looked about six years old, and a smiling blond woman, Charlene. They were bundled in heavy winter clothes, and the cold had painted their cheeks red. Morrisey was fascinated by Charlene's younger self, by the shining blue eyes, by the spark that Morrisey had only glimpsed in them. Then she focused on the child who would grow up to rape her, the boy who looked so much like her own son, the boy who had loved his mother, the same woman with whom Morrisey was falling in love.

In this picture, JP was simply a happy, grinning child, not yet a rapist. Morrisey reached into the bag for another picture. It was JP in his graduation cap and gown. He hardly resembled the cheery, red-cheeked boy in the previous photo. His eyes were dull, unseeing. His lips were pressed together into a thin line. This picture had been taken after the football accident—that was painfully obvious. Morrisey was looking at a young man, who, even though he was still breathing, still functioning and posing for a picture, was essentially dead inside. She hastily replaced the photo. She had seen enough. No more pictures, at least not today. That look on JP's face expressed exactly the numb disbelief Morrisey had experienced after the rape, of life being ripped into tiny, horrific pieces, the feeling that this can't be happening, not to me. JP had gone through it, too.

Morrisey glanced at Charlene, who was sitting on the bed and gazing distantly at a wall. She had not seen Morrisey's reaction, thank goodness. "Thank you for letting me look," Morrisey said. "My son is going to be a very handsome young man."

Charlene bit her lip. "I wish I knew why JP killed himself. I'd love the closure, but I'm afraid I won't ever find out."

"Why do you think he did it?"

"I don't know."

"Sweetie," Morrisey said softly, "perhaps there's no big underlying reason. Maybe it all just got to be too much for him. It could have been the football injury, the drugs—just a combination of things. Maybe he was just tired."

"Sometimes I wonder if he did it out of guilt, for raping you."

"Oh."

Charlene swallowed. "If that's why he did it, maybe I'd be glad, because at least he felt guilty about it. I'd know he wasn't a complete monster."

"I wouldn't be glad, I don't think."

"No?"

"Maybe. I don't know."

Charlene shuddered, and Morrisey went over to her.

"I found him on this bed," Charlene said. "This very bed. I saw the holes in his head, and his eyes…" Another shiver.

"I'm sorry," Morrisey replied helplessly. "I don't know what to say. JP would want you to be happy, wouldn't he?"

"I hope so."

"Well, you want yourself to be happy, right?"

Charlene gave a tiny nod. The desire, the sharp longing Morrisey saw in Charlene's eyes made her remember why she was at the apartment in the first place. "I want tonight to be just about us," Morrisey urged. "No JP or Gareth. I hadn't planned suggesting that I come here. The words just popped out of my mouth."

"Just you and me," Charlene whispered. Their gazes met and locked. Morrisey mentally replayed her finger in Charlene's warm, attentive mouth the night before. She remembered the soft kisses on her palm and her arm. And then last, but not least, there was the memory of how Charlene's body, clamoring for more, had responded to the goodbye kiss. Morrisey had not been ready then; now she was.

Pink, faint and wispy, but pink nonetheless, tinged Charlene's throat, her cheeks. Arousal. Morrisey knew Charlene was reading her mind, and an understanding passed between them. They both wanted the same thing. Tonight. Now. Sex, making love. Exploring each other, tasting each other.

Charlene stood and smoothed her shirt. "How about the grand tour? You haven't seen the kitchen or bathroom. I have a few closets, too."

"Do you happen to have a bedroom?"

CHARLENE, UNABLE TO believe what she and Morrisey were about to do, sat on her bed. Part of her wanted to put a stop to it, because logic told her it was too impetuous, too rash. Another, more insistent part of Charlene told her not to utter one damned word and to enjoy herself.

Morrisey was going to be in charge. That had been part of their silent understanding. She was standing just a couple of feet from the bed. Now she grinned slyly. "You're holding your breath, aren't you?"

Charlene blinked and realized she was, and had been for a few seconds. "Yes." She exhaled then inhaled, taking a deep a breath, one that would last a good while.

Morrisey laughed and fingered her shirt. "I'm not perfect, sorry to say. I have a little scar on my stomach, from the C-section. Gareth was in the breech position. And I'm afraid I have a sort of farmer's tan."

Charlene responded eagerly, betraying the extent of her desire. "You're perfect whichever way you are."

Morrisey winked. "I didn't think you would mind. Okay. What should I take off first?"

Charlene's gaze dropped to Morrisey's feet, and Morrisey

slipped out of her sandals. "All good?"

"Yes. Now your shirt."

Morrisey pulled her top off and let it drop to the floor. Her nipples were hard and straining against a black, lacy bra. Exactly as Charlene had envisioned. She stared, dry-mouthed, at the barely concealed breasts. Her fingers ached to reach over and touch Morrisey, to explore those breasts. Her tongue clamored to lick the nipples, taste them, suck them. "What next?" Morrisey asked.

"Your bra."

Morrisey said nothing. She simply reached behind her back and undid her bra. It landed on the floor, atop her shirt. Now Morrisey's breasts were on display for full appreciation. They were beautiful and round, with erect pink nipples. They were better than anything Charlene could have imagined.

"You like?" Morrisey asked.

"I like," Charlene managed to reply, not caring that she was staring and that her voice was hoarse. "I like very much."

"What now?"

"Pants."

Morrisey unbuttoned her jeans and gracefully slipped out of them. Her legs were long, smooth and tan. Endless. "You tan easily," Charlene observed, saying the first non-salacious thing that came to her mind. "I burn like a lobster."

Morrisey did not let Charlene get away with the sanitized thought. "Are you burning now?"

"Oh, God, yes."

Morrisey showed her approval by removing her underwear without Charlene asking. Morrisey was completely, totally naked. Her tiny C-section scar and barely noticeable tan lines just added to her womanly beauty. The hair on her pussy was black and neatly trimmed. Charlene couldn't wait to explore there, but she wanted to sample the breasts first. Morrisey twirled around, giving Charlene a long view of her butt. "Well?"

"Wow," was all Charlene could say. She was barely in control of her thoughts, much less her body.

"Your turn. Undress."

"Right." Charlene got to her feet and crossed to Morrisey. "Do you mind if I..."

"You want to touch me first?"

"Could I?"

"Of course." Morrisey took both of Charlene's hands and guided them to her breasts.

"Touching wasn't really what I meant, at least not with my hands."

"Your mouth? Tongue? Okay."

Charlene exhaled a breath. *OhGodOhGod*. She loved this. She bent slightly and brought her lips to one of Morrisey's nipples. She kissed it gently, and then her tongue took over, paying special attention to the tip of the nipple. Morrisey moaned and pressed her hands into Charlene's back. "Suck," Morrisey groaned. "Suck on it. Hard. Harder."

Charlene obeyed, her desire ratcheting along with Morrisey's cries. She ran her hand down between Morrisey's thighs and found nothing but slick, overwhelming wetness there. It was a wetness like none other Charlene had experienced. She abruptly stopped tending to the breast. She straightened and met Morrisey's eyes. "You're fucking dripping wet!"

"Mmm. Thanks to you." Morrisey took the moist fingers and guided them to Charlene's mouth. Charlene took a tentative lick then a more bold one. Morrisey's juice was sweet and natural, and Charlene flicked her tongue out for more.

"How is it?" Morrisey wondered.

"Better than the wine."

Morrisey laughed. "Come on. Let's get your clothes off."

Charlene stepped back, feeling self-conscious. She reminded herself she would be self-conscious for, what, thirty seconds? Then after that, bliss. She could live with such a deal.

"Do you remember last night when you kissed me?" Charlene asked. "As I was leaving."

"Most definitely. You liked it? I wanted to do more, but I was too shy."

"I loved it. Yes. God, yes. It made me so..."

"What? Horny?"

"Mmm-hmm. And when I got home, I..."

"You what?"

Charlene's mouth went dry. She was afraid Morrisey's face would flush with anger. *Using me without my permission, after your own son raped me?* Charlene swallowed. *Stop it.* "I masturbated. To you. I came three times in ten minutes, or less. It'd been a long time."

Anger did not color Morrisey's features. Quite the opposite, agitated desire, did. "Oh, Charlene," Morrisey murmured. "Are you trying to kill me?"

"No."

Morrisey's lips parted in a sly, shy smile. "Just when I think I couldn't possibly get any hornier."

"You're welcome."

"So, what happened when you masturbated? Did you fantasize or just get right down to it?"

"You undressed. Much like just now. Then I took my shirt off.

Like this." Charlene tugged her top off and dropped it with Morrisey's clothes. Her bra was white and standard-issue, nothing sexy about it. Morrisey seemed not to notice.

"Nice," she whispered roughly.

Charlene took a step back and then another, until she was inches from a wall. "Then, you pressed me against a wall. You slipped one of my breasts out of its bra cup then you took it in your mouth. "

Morrisey cocked an eyebrow. "Hmm. Hmmm." Her mouth was slightly parted. She was making little moans but seemed unaware of it. That turned Charlene on even more.

Charlene continued, "After you were done with my breast, you pulled down my pants and underwear. You didn't even bother to let me step out of them."

"Not very polite of me."

"Oh, it was simply boorish. But what you lacked in politeness, you more than made up for because you..." Charlene swallowed. "You had a magic tongue. And after that, after I came, after I exploded, you pushed me onto the bed and fucked me again. With your fingers. One, two, three, four, then five. In and out. It was so good. Then I got on one of your legs and straddled it, rode you, and came again." Charlene pressed her back against the wall. She was about to die. She needed Morrisey to do something, now now now.

But Morrisey was apparently enjoying the narrative. "Did we even kiss?"

"Yes! Yes, of course we did."

"When?"

Charlene struggled to remember exact moments and failed. It was all such a blur. "There was a lot of kissing, trust me. We kissed through it all. Before, during, after."

"Did I get anything in return?" Morrisey asked, teasingly. "You seem to have gotten a lot of good stuff. What did I get?"

Charlene's thoughts floundered guiltily. "Nothing. It was all me. You got to kiss me. I kissed you. Does that count?"

"Well, gosh. Talk about boorish!" Morrisey crooked a demanding finger at Charlene. "Come here, you."

Charlene bounced to Morrisey. "Yes?" Morrisey took Charlene's hand and guided it to her slick pussy, to her swollen clit. Charlene still could not believe how wet Morrisey was.

"There," Morrisey said. "Right there." Charlene started rubbing the clit, gently, and then with increasing urgency. "Yes, yes!" Morrisey moaned, her eyelids fluttering, her hips thrusting. "Right there. Yes. Jesus. Fuck!" Morrisey arched her back and exposed a creamy expanse of neck that Charlene yearned to smother in kisses.

It was such a wonderful, delicious neck. Charlene went for it and kept her hand working between Morrisey's thighs. Morrisey moaned and groaned and then nearly screamed into Charlene's ear. "Can't stand," she rasped. She dragged Charlene to the bed.

Charlene fought with her bra, pants and underwear, finally getting them off. Then she straddled Morrisey.

"God, Charlene." Lust glimmered in Morrisey's eyes. "You're so hot. Come here." Morrisey pulled Charlene down and devoured one of Charlene's breasts with her mouth and tongue. She drifted a hand up to caress the other breast. Charlene writhed and moaned under the expert touches. Her masturbation fantasies were long gone. This was better, so much better.

She was going to come. In just a few seconds. *nownownow.* It was starting, a crescendo bubbling up and up and up and up and up. Impossibly up. Up some more. It was getting to be agony now. *Oh, God, please now now now now please.* Up some more.

"Morris, Morris!" Charlene gasped, unable to bear it any longer. Morrisey did something, Charlene was not sure what, some kind of nibbling. It did the trick, sending Charlene soaring past the glorious point of no return. She arched her back and exploded. She clamped her mouth shut, trying not to let out a bellow that would bring everyone in the building rushing to the apartment.

Morrisey brought her mouth to Charlene's, pulling away only to say, "You're fucking loud." Then Morrisey's tongue found and fought Charlene's. It was their first real kiss, and it couldn't have been better.

Chapter Fourteen

ONE HOUR LATER Charlene tucked into the curl of Morrisey's arm and laid her head on Morrisey's chest. They remained for several minutes in blissful, contented silence, their sweat-drenched arms and legs entwined. Morrisey loved the feel of Charlene with her, of Charlene's racing heart, then of her gradually relaxing breaths. They fit together perfectly.

"So, how was it?" Morrisey drawled, expecting nothing but rave reviews.

"Good, quite good."

Morrisey slid Charlene up just a bit and nuzzled her ear. "I'm afraid I'll run up quite a tab," Charlene murmured. "I want a lot more."

"We'll work out a payment plan."

"Mmm." Charlene brought her lips to Morrisey's for a long kiss, and they tightened their holds on each other.

So, this was it. Morrisey was filled with an amazing sense of completeness. She had discovered true happiness and contentment. She had not thought once about JP or the rape during the romp in bed. All she had thought about was tasting Charlene, feeling Charlene, having Charlene devour her. Now their lovemaking was over, at least for the time being. It was time to return to Earth.

Charlene traced Morrisey's face with a finger. "You're so beautiful," Charlene murmured. "So sexy. I could do this all night, fuck like crazy."

"Mmm."

"You all right?"

Morrisey grinned. "Sure. I'm fine."

A touch of embarrassment flitted across Charlene's features. "I can't believe we did this."

"There's nothing wrong with it."

"You sure?" Charlene leaned over for another tantalizing kiss that lasted several moments.

"Two," Morrisey decided. "You owe me two. Make me come

now. Fuck me like crazy."

Charlene winked. "I'll give you three."

AFTER MORE LOVEMAKING, Charlene and Morrisey cuddled for a few minutes. Charlene did not want the moment to end, but Morrisey stirred and murmured, "I better get going. I have to pick up Gareth."

"I wish you didn't have to go."

"I don't want to." Morrisey lazily stroked Charlene's back. "Stay with me tonight. Please?"

"Yeah?" Charlene propped her head up and met Morrisey's eyes. Another delicious shudder heated her body, and she felt her nipples hardening. "What about Gareth?"

"What about him?"

"Won't he, I don't know, get confused? Wonder what I'm doing there? What if he wakes up while we're doing stuff?"

"He'll be fine," Morrisey replied simply. She grinned and kissed Charlene. "I'll help you be quieter."

"Am I really that loud?"

"Hell, yes. But I love it." Morrisey tumbled out of bed, and Charlene drank in her new lover's long, statuesque naked body.

"You're torturing me," Charlene complained.

"Good." Morrisey began to dress, and Charlene was content to just watch. Morrisey moved so very smoothly. She slid on her underwear with catlike grace and hooked her bra so easily, casually brushing hair out of her eyes. Charlene swallowed. *Morrisey. Morrisey. Oh, God.* They had done it. And it'd been wonderful. No, it was more than wonderful. She could not wait for more.

"What are you thinking?" Morrisey asked.

"That you suck."

"Didn't you like it?"

"Yes. You suck in a really good way."

Morrisey chuckled and pulled the rest of her clothes on. "I'll see you soon, right? Forty-five minutes? An hour?"

"Definitely." Charlene felt as if her chest would burst with happiness. She wanted so much to tell Morrisey everything she was thinking, all those jumbled, excited, giddy thoughts: that Morrisey was so good, that *they* were so good together, that she was head over heels in love and happier than she'd been in a long, long time. Maybe ever. Fear of saying too much, too soon, however, kept her quiet.

Morrisey seemed to understand. She winked at Charlene and told her to get her ass out of bed.

AFTER CHARLENE ARRIVED at Morrisey's house, they wasted no time jumping into Morrisey's bed and getting naked. Morrisey had two bowls at her side, one filled with strawberries, and a smaller one with chocolate syrup. Charlene's eyes gleamed as Morrisey picked up the strawberries. "You're spoiling me."

"Good." Morrisey dipped a strawberry into the chocolate. "You deserve to be spoiled." Morrisey let Charlene nibble at the strawberry but was easily distracted by the thought of Charlene nibbling between her legs instead.

"Morris?"

Morrisey got a strawberry for herself. "Yes?"

"You didn't think about—you know—at all? At my apartment?"

Morrisey gritted her teeth, wondering why Charlene had to bring it up, at this moment, and to cloak it in a 'you know.' "No, Charlene, I didn't think about the rape at all. Did you?"

"No. But I'm not the one who was..."

"Say it."

"I'm not the one who was raped. Gang raped."

Morrisey dipped a fresh strawberry into the chocolate and took a bite. "I'm fine. I've had time to deal with it. More than five years. I do understand it's kind of new to you and that you're still dealing with it. Please don't worry about me. I'm all good. I'm glad that you didn't hold back out of concern or worry for me. You didn't, right?"

Stains of scarlet appeared on Charlene's cheeks. "No. It was like another part of me took over."

Morrisey fed Charlene the rest of the strawberry. "I wonder which part."

"I never came with Mr. Burroughs," Charlene whispered. "He'd just, you know. We'd lie down, he'd mount me, get down to business and groan like a stuck pig. Every time. He took a minute. Maybe two. Sometimes only a few seconds. It wasn't all bad, though. There was something he did that I really liked. Something no else has done with me."

"What?"

"Doggy-style, in the ass. It hurt. It really hurt at first. Later, it felt so good."

"Huh." Morrisey opened her mouth to allow Charlene to feed her a strawberry.

Charlene blushed again. "Yes."

Morrisey ate the strawberry then placed fluttery kiss after fluttery kiss on Charlene's face and on her neck. "I can do that," she whispered. "We can buy a dildo."

"Mmm."

"Want me to use my fingers for now?"

"Eat me, and I'll use my own fingers. I've heard that feels really good together."

Morrisey stared at Charlene for a moment in amazement and wonder at how open Charlene was being. At how kinky they would be together. This was just the surface. They'd have a delicious future together. "I've never been fucked in the ass," Morrisey admitted. "So later maybe you could..."

"Of course," Charlene replied languidly, lazily. "I'd love to."

"I'm going in now. Just remember to keep it down. Gareth's sleeping." Morrisey dove between Charlene's legs and zoomed in on her clit, flicking her tongue every which way.

Hoo-hoo-hoo-hoo.

An owl made its presence known right outside the bedroom window, and Morrisey stopped instantly. In a flash, she saw blood, her own blood, mixing with the snow, and she felt it all again: the deathly cold, the unbearable, agonizing pain, the *hoo-hoo-hoo-hoo,* going back to her car, shivering uncontrollably and knowing she was going to freeze to death and welcoming it, trying the car, just to see, and having it start, as if nothing had happened.

Charlene's moans of pleasure continued, but they ceased a few seconds later as Morrisey did not resume her eager explorations. "Morris?" Charlene sat up.

Morrisey swallowed and lowered her eyes. The owl hooted again. "It's nothing," she said shakily. "Come on, where were we?"

Hoo-hoo-hoo-hoo.

"What's the matter?"

"Nothing. Really."

"Come on. It happened last night, too."

"No." Morrisey struggled to keep her voice steely. She would not let herself lose face in front of Charlene, especially not after all the protestations that she was fine, just fine. "Leave it alone."

"Is it about the rape?"

Morrisey gave up and crawled back to Charlene's side. "Yes, yes, okay."

"How so?"

"One of the guys kept saying *hoo-hoo-hoo-hoo* again and again and again. It was like a ringing in my ears. And now, whenever I hear an owl, I think of him."

"Which one?"

"Doesn't matter."

Charlene asked, in a tone devoid of emotion, "JP?"

"Yes."

"My son."

"Yes."

Silence followed. There was no touching, and the longer it went on, the more Morrisey was afraid she would cry. She was afraid to look at Charlene because she did not want to see whichever emotion was lurking on Charlene's face, be it repulsion, horror, sadness, or worst of all, realization. Her expression might say, "We can't be together. It's just too weird."

Finally, though, Morrisey had to look at Charlene, because not knowing was worse. Charlene was staring at a far wall, and her expression was neutral, unreadable.

Slowly, she spoke. "Aren't you afraid that you'll see them one day?"

"No. I wouldn't recognize them."

Charlene turned to study Morrisey. "So they could be any guy next to you at the store and you'd never know? That doesn't bother you?"

"Doesn't bother me at all. Now, where were we?"

"Maybe you wouldn't recognize them, but what if they recognized you? And what if they—"

"Jesus Christ, Charlene."

Charlene responded in a low, firm voice. "I bet I could track Ralph down. We wouldn't need to get the police involved."

"No."

"Yes."

"And do what?" Morrisey asked incredulously. "You'd beat him up? Yeah, good luck with that. Or bring him in to face me, make him get on his knees and cry and apologize? Wow! Great idea."

Hoo-hoo-hoo-hoo.

Morrisey slid out of bed and threw on her pajamas. "Just leave it alone, please."

"I can't. Those guys hurt you."

"Maybe this Ralph person you're thinking of isn't even the same guy who raped me!" Morrisey exclaimed. "A voice alone isn't enough to identify someone."

"Well, we can find out."

"I said no. I want nothing to do with him or the other two. Understand? Just leave it alone, please. Don't try to find them. The last thing in the world I need is to meet them. I've moved on. Period. I don't need them popping up."

Chapter Fifteen

THE NEXT MORNING, over a breakfast of pancakes, Morrisey admitted to Charlene that she missed her already. "Maybe Gareth and I could come in for lunch," Morrisey suggested. "What do you think?"

Charlene brightened, but then she frowned. "No."

"Why not?"

Charlene carefully stacked three pancakes on her plate. She squeezed syrup onto them. "Because." That was all.

"Because?" Morrisey prompted.

Charlene sighed. "A couple of the people at work knew JP. He came in sometimes. Some kids, when they grow up, look so different. JP's always looked the same. If they see Gareth, they'll ask questions. You don't want people to know, right? At least not yet."

Morrisey balled her hands into fists. "I see."

Charlene started cutting her pancakes. "I'll come by after work."

"I want to see you at lunch."

Charlene fed Morrisey a bite of pancake. "I want to see you, too."

"Then I'll come."

"What about Gareth?"

Morrisey reached for a fork and took a bite of Charlene's pancakes for herself. "We'll say that he's a distant cousin. Something like that."

Charlene speared another piece of pancake. "Hmm."

Morrisey snorted. "No. You know what? That's stupid. Tell them the truth. Tell them Gareth's your grandson and that I'm his mother."

Charlene nearly choked on her food. "What?"

"You don't have to tell them about the rape. That's not their business. Just tell them we're close and that he's your grandson."

"What if he overhears something?"

"I'll tell him this morning. I'll explain to him."

Charlene's eyes went wide. "What? That I'm his grandmother, that JP's his father?"

"Yes."

Charlene shoved half of a pancake into her mouth and took her time chewing it. She did not seem very happy. "I want our relationship to start off on the right foot," Morrisey explained. "We can't do that if we're lying to the whole world."

"Sweetie, why don't you think about this for a few days. Don't make any big decisions yet."

Morrisey crossed her arms. "Fine. I guess I'll see you after work."

AS THE HOURS went by at The Log Cabin, Charlene's elation turned into fear. She was in love with Morrisey. She truly, genuinely was one hundred percent in love. She could not wait to see Morrisey again. Their time together the previous night had been nothing short of magical. The sensations she had felt with Morrisey, those nerves in her body coming alive, were exquisite. But then the owl had brought to reality, in a stark, glittering moment, just what JP and his three conspirators had done. Had they truly had fun? Had they enjoyed Morrisey's cries, her struggles, her moans? Had Morrisey turned them on as much as she turned Charlene on? JP had been in the same places Charlene had, the same vagina and maybe the same lips. They had been with the same woman, under much different circumstances and with much different results. Charlene wanted to help Morrisey heal her scars and move on, but she wondered just how she could do it.

That look on Morrisey's face the night before seared Charlene's mind. Charlene had felt as though she had been there on that cold December night with Morrisey, watching her, watching JP rape her. Hearing JP gleefully cry "Hoo-hoo-hoo-hoo!" The pain, the cold, the blood—all were so vivid.

What if Charlene couldn't get that out of her mind when they made love again? And what if Morrisey was having doubts? They had jumped into bed so quickly and had not quite stopped to breathe since. Now Charlene was thinking, breathing. So was Morrisey. What if Morrisey was beginning to reconsider? What if Morrisey wanted to put the brakes on their relationship? Charlene's brain told her that was absurd. Morrisey had awakened early to fix pancakes for Charlene and to put her work clothes in the washer and dryer, but time and space to think did funny things.

What if Morrisey felt regret about what they had done? What if she did not want Charlene to come over after work anymore? At least Miriam's shift that day did not start until noon. Once Miriam came in, she would want to know everything. What would Charlene say? Would the guilty shifting of her eyes give her away, that she had fucked the woman her son raped, had fucked her hard? And that she had enjoyed every moment? Because she had, more than anything in her life.

A FEW MINUTES before noon, Miriam came in with her business face on. Her clothes were neatly pressed. Even her nametag gleamed. Charlene had never been a match for Miriam's business face. "Well?" Miriam sidled up next to Charlene. "How did the date go? Spill it."

Charlene managed a weak grin. "I'll tell you when I have my break. I need to drop an order off."

Miriam steadied Charlene before she could run off. "Good? Bad? So-so?"

Charlene's thoughts floundered. "Pretty good."

"Hm." Miriam puckered her lips. "Come on now. It's okay. Throw your arms around me. Dance with me, sing with me. You're in love, you're head over heels in love, and she loves you back. Celebrate!"

"Yes," Charlene said. "I am. It was so wonderful, but—"

Miriam held up a finger and scowled. "No buts. Charlene Sudsbury, let yourself enjoy this moment!"

Charlene shrank back. "What if she regrets what we did? What if she's changed her mind? Miriam, we had sex."

"How was it? Better than with you and me, I hope."

Charlene giggled. "Yes. It was mind-blowing."

"Still, no buts. No buts! Put a smile on your face and enjoy Morrisey and Gareth. Be happy! Be happy! You deserve it. Now, when do Liz and I get to meet them? We can't wait."

Charlene tried to relax. *Miriam's right. Enjoy the moment.* "I'll ask Morrisey. Sometime this week or next for dinner? She'd love to meet you guys, too."

WHEN THE CLOCK struck 5:00 p.m., Charlene decided to go home. She jumped into the shower, hell-bent on washing her hair, shaving, doing whatever she needed to do in the least time possible. Of course, when she was in the middle of shampooing her hair, the telephone rang. *Morrisey?* Charlene's eyes flew open, and the shampoo wasted no time making her life a living hell. Charlene whimpered in agony as she flailed about, trying to cleanse the burning suds from her eyes under the showerhead. By the time she was finished, the telephone had fallen silent, and her generic "I'm not home; please leave your name and number" message had kicked in. Charlene got out of the shower and dried off. She went to the answering machine, which was in the kitchen. There was one message. Charlene pressed the PLAY button.

A crackling teenage male voice grated on her ears. "Hey, Donnie. Change of plan. Meet at Pete's. Later." Charlene's heart stilled, and she listened again. She had subjected her poor eyes to such torture and had rushed out of the shower for a wrong number? She did not know if she should laugh or cry, although she felt more like crying.

"Fuck," she muttered. She found Morrisey's phone number and was on the line with her in two seconds flat. Yes, Morrisey wanted her to come over now. No, like yesterday. She had been thinking about it all day. Morrisey had even found a baby sitter for Gareth and would not need to pick him up until 9:00.

Charlene's knees went weak with relief. Morrisey did not regret what they'd done. Far from it. When Charlene returned to the shower, she sang and sang.

AN HOUR LATER, Charlene was on Morrisey's couch and pleasantly entwined in the other woman's arms. They had just finished eating Chinese takeout. "God, I'm so stuffed," Morrisey moaned, but she had the same grin on her face she'd had when Charlene arrived. "I missed you. You could've showered here. With me."

"I was worried."

"About what?"

"That you were having second thoughts and maybe regretted what we'd done. That it all had happened too soon."

Morrisey traced the contours of Charlene's face. "We did what we had to do." She continued gazing at Charlene and stroking her face, but eventually, her hands dropped to Charlene's breasts. "Are they sore from yesterday?"

"No." Charlene let out a low moan. She was trying to smother those nagging thoughts. Yet this was just what she had feared earlier at work. It was clear to her that Morrisey wanted to make love, to continue what they were doing when the owl had hooted, and so did Charlene. Desperately. But Charlene still had the memory of the emotional scars emanating from Morrisey's face and that image of JP in the snow thrusting inside Morrisey, of taking pleasure in it. Of Ralph with the girly, squeaky voice.

Ignore it. Charlene pushed her ghosts aside. Her lips, then her tongue, met Morrisey's in a hard, searching kiss. Charlene unbuttoned Morrisey's jeans, and her fingers found their way into Morrisey's underwear. In what seemed like a minute, although Charlene barely remembered it happening, they were both naked and panting. Morrisey was under Charlene, begging for release.

"Please," Morrisey rasped, "do something now."

Charlene's throat went dry. Had Morrisey wriggled like this on that snowy night many Decembers ago? "Please," Morrisey pleaded. That "please" could just as easily have been one to stop. Had Morrisey begged "please" then too? And had JP laughed and laughed and pounded harder?

"Please, Charlene. Oh, God damn it!" Morrisey pushed Charlene off her and sat up. Her breaths came in angry heaves.

"I'm sorry, I'm sorry. I can do it."

"This is what we're going to do," Morrisey replied. "I've been waiting all day for this. It's been agony. I need to do something." Morrisey held up one of her hands and wriggled her fingers. Charlene stiffened. Morrisey was going to finish herself off, because Charlene could not do it freely, with pleasure.

"Watch me," Morrisey urged. "Please. See how much I enjoy it. Imagine you doing it to me and imagine me enjoying it oh so much more. And then maybe you'll see that... Oh, I don't know. I don't know what you'll see. But I hope you do. I crave you, Charlene. I crave you. I want you to crave me too and not be afraid to be with me."

Charlene watched with a mixture of horror and oh God, oh God, is she really doing that? Morrisey lowered her hand to the dark curls between her thighs and closed her eyes. She moaned, her fingers apparently working their magic. Charlene's pulse pounded, and she felt like a jackass. She wanted to say, "No, no, I'll do it. Let me do it, please." She really wanted to. She just wanted to fling Morrisey's hand away and take care of her lover herself. The images of JP and of Ralph faded away like a mist. Words trembled from Charlene's lips, tiny, choked words. Morrisey apparently did not hear them. She kept going, her fingers working busily. "I want to do it. Let me do it," Charlene said, more strongly.

Morrisey went on.

Charlene swallowed at Morrisey's quivering breasts, at her heaving chest, at her dusty pink nipples growing erect. She wanted those in her mouth, she wanted her hand where Morrisey's hand was, but Charlene was so stunned, so rooted in place, by her own reaction, her own escalating desire, as she watched Morrisey take care of matters just fine on her own. A second later, Morrisey's eyes flew open, and Charlene's heart stopped. It was too late. But maybe not. Morrisey's lips curved upward in amusement.

"You can join me if you like," she offered.

She turned her hips just so and reached for Charlene. Charlene put her hand where Morrisey's had been seconds ago, and they came together not long after, in a shattering wave of ecstasy.

Chapter Sixteen

"SO, HOW'S IT going with Charlene?" Margaret Hawthorne asked. "What are you two up to tonight?"

Morrisey narrowed her eyes. She was at her mother's house to drop Gareth off. She and Charlene had been together for about two weeks. Things were wonderful, but Morrisey was still uncomfortable discussing Charlene with her mother. "I didn't say I was doing something with Charlene."

"You are, though."

Morrisey sighed. She just didn't have the heart to be her usual defensive self. "Yes. We're going to a movie."

Margaret um-hmm'ed knowingly. "Come on, just admit it. You're in love. I see it in your eyes, in your bounce, even in the way you breathe."

Morrisey could not keep a smile from spreading. "Yes, I am. Lay off me about it."

Margaret's eyes widened in pretend confusion. "I'm not doing anything. I'm happy for you. Why don't you and Gareth bring Charlene for dinner Saturday? I'll invite Bobby, Betsey, Carl and the twins. It'll be fun."

Morrisey smiled uneasily. Her mother's suggestion was not exactly appealing. "I'll see if Charlene's free."

"Are you happy?"

"I told you, I'm in love." And God, how she was. She and Charlene went to bed in each other's arms every night and woke up in each other's arms every morning. The owls were leaving them alone. Morrisey had never been happier, but her mother seemed skeptical.

"I'm glad for you, really I am," Margaret said. "I'm just thinking maybe you should take it a bit slower. Don't let her break your heart again."

"What's that supposed to mean?"

"I know she broke your heart before. I could tell the first time I met her, at your house."

"No, Mom. I told you. She's not an ex."

"So what happened?"

Morrisey forced herself to reply evenly. Her mother was just looking out for her. "I appreciate this, Mom, but I told you to lay off me."

Margaret drew back in hurt. "I want us to be close. I do. I love you, Morrisey. I never really said that when you were a child or when you were growing up. Or now, even. But I do want you to know that."

"I know you love me. I want us to be close, too."

"So tell me what happened before with you and Charlene."

Morrisey pressed her lips together and looked into her mother's eyes. She found simple, genuine concern there, and her mouth went dry as she realized she was going to tell her mother. Not right now, but she would. In a few days, on Saturday. With Charlene at her side, she could do it. It was time. She was as ready as she would ever be.

Morrisey inclined her head. "I'll tell you Saturday. You, Betsey, Carl and Bobby, okay?"

"You could tell me now."

"No. Saturday."

"All right," Margaret relented. "Thank you." She glanced at her watch. "When's the movie start?"

MORRISEY AND CHARLENE ended up not going to the movie. They stayed home, in bed, and made love. They broke in several newly purchased sex toys. They nearly broke Morrisey's bed, too. Afterward, Charlene asked Morrisey when she needed to get Gareth. Morrisey glanced at the nightstand clock. "In about an hour." She paused and cleared her throat. "Speaking of that..."

Charlene drew back, tensing at the subtle shift in Morrisey's voice. "Yes?"

"Mom invited us for dinner Saturday night. Think you'll be up for it after work?"

"I suppose, but she makes me nervous."

Morrisey took Charlene's hand and guided it to her own breasts. "I told her I'd tell her Saturday."

Charlene enjoyed the feel of her lover's smooth skin and lodged no objection to Morrisey directing her hand. "Tell her what?"

"The truth," Morrisey said matter-of-factly. "It's time. My brother, my sister, her husband and their kids will be there too."

"What truth do you mean?"

"About you. JP. Gareth. The rape."

Charlene was not sure how to respond. She was not ready for other people to know, but that did not matter. This was about Morrisey, and rightly so. "Whatever you want. It'll be a relief for you."

"I think so, yes. You're worried though."

Charlene bit her lip. "Your family's going to hate me. They're going to judge me for what JP did. I don't blame them. I do it, too."

"I imagine they won't be thrilled at first. Give them time, and they'll come around."

"I'm not sure it's a good idea for me to be there."

"I want you with me. Please?"

"Why?"

Morrisey's eyes darkened. "Why? Because I want you with me. I don't think I could do it alone. Will you go with me?"

"Of course," Charlene replied, ignoring her unease. "Whatever you need, I'll do."

"Thank you. My family will love you just as much as I love you. I promise. They'll just need time to absorb things."

"Are you sure you're ready?"

Morrisey lowered her gaze, and Charlene was afraid she'd angered her lover. But Morrisey looked back up a second later. "I'm not ready. I never completely will be. Who ever is? One thing I do know is that I'm tired of the lies." Morrisey's earnestness was a prick in Charlene's heart. God, how she loved the woman and hated seeing what JP had done to her. Charlene also thought about Margaret Hawthorne and the rose she had so kindly insisted JP have.

Chapter Seventeen

THE NEXT EVENING, Miriam and Liz came over for dinner and instantly fell in love with Gareth. Morrisey captivated them, too, and Miriam nudged Charlene several times, commenting that it was too bad Morrisey was not single, because Miriam would go after her otherwise. Charlene just laughed, glad that everybody was getting along so well.

Morrisey, though she remained guarded, seemed to like Miriam and Liz, too. After they left, Morrisey confessed to Charlene that she was jealous because Miriam and Liz were wonderful and really easy to bond with. "I wish I had friends like that."

"You have them now, too. Really. And me," Charlene pointed out.

"That I do," Morrisey said with a grin.

The rest of Charlene's week melted into a string of sweaty days on her feet and of fantastic evenings with Morrisey and Gareth. Then Saturday arrived, much to Charlene's chagrin. After a morning kiss goodbye from Morrisey, Charlene headed off to work. For the first time in recent memory, she dreaded the end of her shift, because she would have to go to Margaret Hawthorne's house. Charlene could picture it now. Morrisey's family would attack her and kick her out, as if she had raped Morrisey herself.

Charlene sighed as she parked Silver in front of The Log Cabin. Morrisey had good, pure intentions, but she would back out of telling her family about the rape. Charlene was sure of it. She could see it in Morrisey's eyes, in the way her breathing tensed whenever the subject came up. Morrisey was nowhere near comfortable enough with her family to tell them something so momentous. Charlene pulled her keys out of the ignition and pressed her lips together. She saw the task falling to her by default. Morrisey would back herself into a corner and be unable to blurt the words out. Charlene would have to tell Morrisey's family that her son raped their daughter, their sister. And she would do it, even if it took every fiber of her being, because Morrisey was right. Her family needed to know before she could truly move on.

A WELCOMING SMILE crinkled Margaret Hawthorne's face as she ushered in Morrisey, Charlene and Gareth. "Finally, you're here. I was getting worried."

Morrisey hugged her mother perfunctorily. "We're only five minutes late."

"Still." Margaret flashed her daughter a dark look and then turned to Charlene. "How lovely to see you again!" She took Charlene's hand. "Let me introduce you to everybody."

Margaret led Charlene through a living room that seemed bigger than her apartment. Charlene took in finely crafted furniture and thick, lush drapes. A blood-red rug covered most of the hardwood floor. "The furniture's handmade," Margaret remarked, pride seeping into her voice.

"It's lovely," Charlene murmured, feeling both intimidated and envious.

"Come on." Margaret guided Charlene into the dining room. A sideboard near the main dining table was resplendent with heaping dishes of food, and the delicious aroma of bread and chicken caused Charlene's mouth to water. The Log Cabin never smelled this good.

A second, smaller table had been set up for the children, and Gareth darted past Charlene to play with his cousins. A dark-haired woman, obviously Morrisey's sister, sat at the little table, coloring in books with two identical girls. Behind them, drinking from tall, thin glasses, were a brawny, mustachioed man with graying hair and a black-haired young man with sharp, handsome features and deep blue eyes.

Margaret beamed at the group. "This is my daughter, Betsey. Her husband, Dr. Carl Lewis." Margaret indicated the man with the graying hair, and he nodded in greeting. "Robert, my son." The handsome, curly-haired younger man gave Charlene a genuine smile and told her to call him Bobby. Margaret continued the introductions. "Betsey and Carl's twins, of course. Sophie and Warner." Margaret gave an indulgent sigh as her gaze settled upon the twin girls, whom Charlene pegged to be about eight years old. They wore identical pink dresses and shared their mother's slightly doughy face and pale skin. Amid the sea of dark-haired people, Gareth looked like a foreigner.

Margaret continued smiling. "This is Charlene, Morrisey's, ah, friend."

Ah, friend. Charlene prickled in embarrassment. Carl and

Betsey studied her with grave, perhaps even morbid, interest, their eyes boring into hers. Carl tugged at his moustache and narrowed his gaze. Nobody smiled, except Bobby. A knot rose in Charlene's throat. *Ah, friend.*

Morrisey, who had been behind her mother, crossed to Charlene and squeezed her hand. "This is Charlene, my lover,"

Betsey's eyelids fluttered, and she threw her daughters a panicked look. They kept coloring and chatting, oblivious to what was going on around them. Betsey recovered quickly and managed a smile. "How nice to meet you, Charlene."

"What do you do?" Carl asked. His voice was full of expectation.

Charlene's hands unconsciously crept to her shirt bottom. She twisted a wad of fabric and shifted her gaze from Carl's probing eyes to Gareth's friendly features. "I work at a restaurant," she muttered.

Carl craned his neck and cupped a hand to his ear. "Didn't hear you."

"I work at a restaurant."

"Oh?" Carl cocked an eyebrow. "You own it?"

"No." Charlene's voice seemed to come from a long way off. "I'm a waitress."

Disapproval lined Carl's face, as Charlene had known it would. He inclined his head and simply said, "Ah. A waitress."

"You're a waitress?" Margaret took a step back. "I thought you were a teacher too, like Rebecca and Morrisey. I thought you told me...hmm."

"No. But I'll be a manager soon."

"I see." Margaret clasped her hands together. "How lovely. Well, let's eat!"

As her family lined up to fill their plates, Morrisey put her arms around Charlene's waist, her breasts pressing into Charlene's back. She whispered into Charlene's ear, "You okay?"

"Gee, I'm on top of the world."

Morrisey chuckled. "They'll warm up. Just let them relax a bit."

"Excuse me."

Charlene looked up to see Betsey bringing a hand to her neck and wrinkling her nose. "Do you mind, well, refraining from public displays in front of the children?"

Charlene was sure her face turned a vivid scarlet. "Sorry," she stammered. She tried to break free of Morrisey, but Morrisey kept Charlene firmly in her arms.

"Actually, we do mind," Morrisey drawled.

Betsey narrowed her eyes and stepped closer. "Look, the girls are older now. They're impressionable."

"Then maybe they shouldn't be around you," Morrisey retorted. "Come on, Betsey. Don't be such a prude."

A snort sounded from Charlene's right, and out of the corner of her eye, she saw Bobby grinning. He set his plate on the table. "Don't listen to Betsey," he urged. "She doesn't know how to have fun."

Betsey immediately responded. "Is it so much to ask that they don't—"

Bobby held up a hand. "The twins won't be any more scarred than I was when I saw you making out with Tyler Moore. I survived that all right, don't you think?"

Betsey's jaw dropped open, and all she could manage was a sputter.

"Tyler Moore?" Morrisey asked incredulously. "Ew."

A heated blush overtook Betsey's features, and she looked toward the sideboard. "I'm going to eat now." She flipped her long dark hair back and stomped off.

Bobby gave Charlene a knowing wink. "Betsey's easy enough to handle. Don't let her get to you, all right? She's been an ass ever since she and Carl got into Catholicism."

Morrisey let go of Charlene. "Thanks, Bobby. Who else did Betsey make out with?"

"Oh, that's for me to know. And remember, I know everybody you made out with, too." He smirked and sauntered away.

Morrisey rolled her eyes. "He thinks he's cute."

For the first time since she arrived at the Hawthorne house, Charlene smiled genuinely. "I bet I could get him to spill some dirt on you."

"Don't you dare."

"Mommy!" Gareth ran up. "Grandma says I have to eat the broccoli. I don't wanna!"

"Just eat a little bit," Morrisey suggested.

"Sophie and Warner don't wanna eat it either!"

"You guys will figure something out."

Gareth crossed his arms and marched back to the kids' table, where Betsey's children were staring pensively at plates filled with salad and vegetables.

Morrisey took Charlene's hand. "Okay, let's eat. I won't make you suffer with the broccoli."

Charlene chuckled. Maybe the evening wouldn't be so bad after all.

CARL DOMINATED THE conversation during dinner. While Betsey and Margaret beamed adoringly at him, he recounted tale after tale of heroic, life-saving surgeries he had performed.

"We've heard those stories a hundred times," Bobby whispered to Charlene after Betsey left to bring the dessert out. "And with each telling, the exaggerations get worse."

Charlene gave him a shy grin. "So you're in college?"

Bobby inclined his head. "I'll be a senior in the fall. Majoring in physics."

"Impressive."

Bobby shrugged modestly, but he clearly enjoyed Charlene's reaction. "The ladies like it. And speaking of ladies, how did you meet my sister?"

"Oh. Uh." Charlene's heart skipped a beat, and she became aware that Morrisey's mother was listening to the conversation. "Morris?" Charlene turned to Morrisey, but Morrisey's attention was elsewhere.

"Sorry." Morrisey faced Charlene after a long pause. "I was making sure Gareth didn't feed the cat anything bad. What's going on?"

"Charlene was about to tell us how you met her," Margaret supplied.

Betsey returned to the table then, bearing a large chocolate cake. "Dessert! Made by yours truly." Charlene heaved a sigh of relief, and she squeezed Morrisey's leg under the table. How were they going to do this? Margaret was suspicious of Charlene and did not seem to like her much, and the same seemed true for Betsey and Carl. Bobby was nice and flirtatious. However, his tune would surely change once he found out who Charlene really was and what her son had done.

Morrisey gazed at the cake, but a faraway look clouded her eyes. Gareth and the twins ran to the table. "Cake, cake, cake!"

"Keep it down," Betsey warned.

"Can we have ice cream too?" one of the girls asked.

Charlene continued studying Morrisey, but she was in another world. Charlene squeezed Morrisey's leg again. "Morrisey?"

"Yeah?"

"You all right?"

"I'm fine," Morrisey murmured. "Can't wait to get this over with. I'll tell them right after dessert."

Charlene accepted a slice of cake from Betsey. She had not eaten much dinner, but an uneasy stirring began in her stomach.

Morrisey pushed her chair back. "Excuse me for just a minute."

MORRISEY WAS SPLASHING water on her face when a soft knock sounded on the bathroom door. "Morrisey?" Charlene asked hesitantly.

Morrisey studied herself in the mirror. "Door's open."

Charlene stepped in and closed the door behind her. "What's going on?"

Morrisey hated to cry, and she only did so alone. She had cried once in front of Charlene, when Charlene figured out she was raped and began to feel sorry for her. Even then, there had not been many tears. But now, as Charlene reached for Morrisey, she breathed in a shallow, quick gasp, aware that she was on the verge of losing control. She stepped back abruptly, pressing against the wall. "Don't touch me. Don't, please."

Charlene kept her hands to herself. "It'll be all right. They're not going to treat you like a leper. They want to help you."

"They'll be mad at me, won't they? That I didn't tell them before."

"Give them a chance. You're doing the right thing. Really."

Charlene's concern was so evident, so earnest, that a few tears escaped Morrisey. She wiped the back of her hand across her eyes, acutely embarrassed. She did not like feeling weak and out of control, especially in front of Charlene.

"I'm not going to do it," Morrisey decided. "Not today."

Charlene took a moment to weigh the statement. "What's going to be different later that makes it a better time? Won't it just be harder if you keep putting it off? You wanted to tell them the truth when you found out you were pregnant, didn't you? You couldn't do it, though. So you lied, and it's been five years. I really think you ought to give them a chance. Tonight."

Morrisey looked away, not liking how Charlene was in charge now, because it was she, Morrisey, who was supposed to be the calm and composed one, the one who did not look back or dwell in the past. But she couldn't bear to see the frowns on her family's faces nor their hard, judgmental eyes. The rape and how Gareth had been created were none of their concern and never would be.

"I'll do it if you want me to," Charlene continued. "I'll tell them."

"Why do they need to know, anyway?" Morrisey retorted. "It's not their business what happened. Not their life. God! What was I thinking? Why did I ever think they needed to know? I can't even tell my mother I love her. How am I going to tell her about the rape?"

"They deserve to know," Charlene said gently, "because they love you. You're their daughter, their sister. This will be good, really. It'll help you all get closer. So, come on, let's go back out, and I'll tell them."

Morrisey snickered. "No, you won't tell them. You can't tell them your *son* raped me. Because then, let's see — what are you afraid of? They'd think you were a bad mother, right? A bad person, et cetera."

If Charlene was angry, she did not show it. "Maybe they'll think that. At least they'll know what happened. And I'll tell them, I really will. For you, so this will stop eating you up. Look, Morris. I love you. I am here to support you, but I will not enable you."

"Fine," Morrisey replied grudgingly. "Fine. I'll tell them. I'll do it."

"Can I hug you now?"

Morrisey's anger evaporated at the little question, and she took Charlene in her arms. She breathed in Charlene's smell, her hair scented with strawberry shampoo, and, finally, Morrisey let her tears fall.

WHEN MORRISEY AND Charlene returned to the dining room, most of the cake was gone. "Everything all right?" Margaret asked.

"Just a little scare," Morrisey said. "Something I had for lunch."

"Glad you're okay." Betsey grinned widely. "Come on. Let's go in the living room. Carl and I have something wonderful to tell you all."

Morrisey forced to smile and nod. What now? How many more setbacks would there be? She guided Charlene into the living room with the others. Gareth and the twins were already there, playing with matchbox cars while Margaret's fluffy cat watched disdainfully from a window sill. "Sit down, sit down." Betsey shooed everyone toward the oversized couch and loveseat.

Charlene flashed Morrisey a curious look. "What's going on?"

"I'm not sure." With growing unease, Morrisey studied her sister. Betsey's eyes were shining, and her hands kept creeping to her belly. She had obviously put on a few pounds. "Huh. I bet she's pregnant. She and Carl have been trying to have another baby ever since the twins were born."

Charlene lowered her gaze. "Oh."

Morrisey shook her head. There was no way she could tell her family about the rape after Betsey made her big, joyous announcement. *Count on Betsey to ruin things.* Morrisey clenched her jaw. No. She would try to be happy for her sister. She would be happy for her sister. It was not Betsey's fault that Morrisey had something to say, too, and had waited five years to do it.

Morrisey's hand found Charlene's, and Betsey turned to Carl. They could barely contain their joy. "We're nearly four months pregnant!" Betsey exclaimed.

Margaret jumped to her feet. "Wonderful! Oh, this is magnficent news!" She threw her arms around Betsey and Carl. "Congratulations! Oh, this is wonderful!" She drew back and clasped her hands together. "Sophie, Warner! You're going to have a baby brother or sister!"

The girls and Gareth looked up from their play. "Mom told us yesterday," Sophie said.

"Aren't you excited?" Margaret asked.

"Mmm-hmm," the girl replied, but she did not look overly thrilled.

"Morrisey." Margaret whirled around, and Morrisey pasted on a big smile. "Isn't this wonderful?"

"Yes, it is." Morrisey crossed to her sister and gave Betsey a small hug. "I know you really wanted this." She squeezed Carl as well. Bobby was behind Morrisey and performed his round of hugs too. When Morrisey turned around, she saw Charlene sitting alone, the huge leather couch practically swallowing her up. Morrisey met Charlene's pained blue eyes. Charlene understood. She would not insist upon going through with it. Now was not the time. They could do it tomorrow, in a few days. Some other time, but not now.

Morrisey and Bobby returned to the couch, and Morrisey ended up sandwiched between her brother and Charlene. Margaret continued beaming at Betsey and Carl. "Do you want a boy or a girl?" she asked.

"It doesn't matter as long as the baby's healthy," Carl said.

Betsey added, "Regardless whether it's a boy or a girl, we were hoping to name the baby after Daddy. Would that be okay?"

Margaret stilled, and tears sprang to her eyes. "Oh, sweetie. That would be wonderful. Oh, come here." She wrapped her arms around Betsey once again.

Bobby nudged Morrisey in the ribs. "What a Kodak moment. Anyway, are you sure you're okay? You ran off pretty fast. What'd you have for lunch?"

"I'm fine." Morrisey paused. "I don't remember what I had."

"Did Charlene cook lunch? Is she that bad?"

"Hey!" Charlene exclaimed, indignation flushing her cheeks. "Like you know how to use anything other than the microwave."

Bobby shrugged. "Okay, okay. Guilty as charged, although I can grill, too. Really! So, hey, you never told me how you met my sister."

Morrisey squeezed her eyes shut for a nanosecond. *Great.* It wasn't like Bobby to be so single-minded. Their mother was putting him up to it.

"Morrisey should tell you," Charlene replied timidly.

"No." Morrisey avoided Charlene's eyes. *Please, not now.* "This is Betsey's day. It's her day, all right?"

Bobby's brows furrowed. "Huh?"

The tension inside Morrisey became almost unbearable, especially as Charlene began to speak. "Uh." Charlene was clearly struggling with how to respond. "We met through — well, kind of through — "

"Come on," Bobby prodded. "Mom told me that crap about you meeting in school or whatever. Yeah, right. You can tell me what really happened. What, did you guys meet in a bar and hop into bed? Come on, you can tell me."

Charlene shook her head. "Well, really, we met at the cemetery because of Gareth. Because he looked like my — "

Morrisey reached for her brother's shoulder. "Bobby, it's a long story for another time."

"Why not now? It's no big deal."

"It's Bestey's day. Let's just be happy for her."

"I was just asking how you two met. What's that have to do with Betsey?"

Morrisey became aware that the excited chatter around her had died and that her mother, sister and brother-in-law were eavesdropping.

"Morrisey had something to tell us, too," Margaret prompted.

Morrisey's throat constricted, and she waved her mother's comment away. "It's nothing."

Margaret crossed her arms. "Really?"

"She does have something to say," Charlene volunteered.

"No!" Morrisey exclaimed. "It's Betsey's day. Come on." She directed a panicked laugh at her sister. "Come on, tell us some more. I want to hear everything. When did you find out you were pregnant? Tell me all about it!"

Both Margaret and Betsey narrowed their dark eyes. They were not buying Morrisey's spiel one bit.

Charlene squeezed Morrisey's hand. "You can do it."

Morrisey tried to ignore the knot of betrayal and anger in her stomach. *She does have something to say. Something to say...something to say. Thanks a lot.*

"I have nothing to say," Morrisey muttered. "Never did."

Carl cleared his throat. "Come on, kids," he called. "Let's go outside."

The children jumped to their feet and practically dragged Carl out of the room. Morrisey was tempted to call after them. "Come back! We'll play in here." Or she could go after them for some hide and seek or to play catch. Anything to avoid her mother's hawk-like expression and searching gaze.

Margaret spoke apprehensively. "What is it?"

Morrisey forced her eyes up to her mother. Rarely did Margaret Hawthorne talk in such quiet, uncertain tones. What Morrisey saw, her mother's smothered worry and a pained frown, did nothing to ease her roiling stomach. *Concern now, anger later.*

Margaret spoke again, more firmly this time. "What happened, Morrisey?"

"Nothing. Not a damned thing happened."

"You wanted to know how we met," Charlene said in a low but steady voice.

"No! No."

"I'll tell them. Please?"

"It's Betsey's day."

"That's okay," Betsey countered. "What do you need to tell us? I think I heard Charlene say you met at the cemetery."

Morrisey dropped her gaze to the floor, to the red rug, so luxuriously thick, lush and vibrant. This was it. She was cornered with nowhere to go but ahead — if she lived that long. Her heart was about to jump out of her chest. "Fine," she began, her tongue thick and clumsy. "Remember when you moved? And I drove down to help you and Carl put some things together?"

"You mean last year? You didn't come."

Morrisey shook her head. "No. When you first moved to the lake."

Betsey thought for a moment. "Oh, right. That was a while ago."

"Yes," Morrisey murmured. "I suppose it was. But I still remember it as if it were yesterday."

"That's when you met Charlene? What about the cemetery?"

"We met at the cemetery. That's true. Five years ago is when I met her son."

"Didn't he kill himself?" Margaret asked.

Charlene answered for Morrisey. "Yes. My son, JP, killed himself."

"I didn't know you had a son," Bobby said. "I'm sorry. What happened?"

A twitch along Charlene's jaw gave away her pretend composure. "He blew his brains out. Suicide."

Bobby gulped. "Oh. I'm sorry."

"Me too," Charlene whispered.

"So you two met through her son?" Betsey asked.

Morrisey gave her sister a wry smile. "That's one way of putting it."

Margaret was becoming impatient. "Where is this going?"

"Why don't you two sit down?"

"I'll stand." Margaret's voice was cool. "Just tell me."

"Yeah," Betsey echoed, her hand straying protectively to her stomach. "Tell us."

Morrisey tried to reply, but her breath felt solid in her throat. She clasped and unclasped her hands. She picked at her nails and cuticles.

"Morrisey?" Betsey prompted.

Morrisey met her mother's gaze, and her heart sank. Margaret Hawthorne knew. Maybe she had just now figured it out, or maybe she had always known, somewhere deep inside. Or perhaps the knowledge had been somewhere much closer to the surface and she had not wanted to get into the messy details of it. The point was that she did know. She knew her daughter had been raped. She knew that Charlene was Gareth's other grandmother. Morrisey, reeling with the realization, continued to stare at her mother, willing Margaret to say, to do something.

Margaret's face was a mask of stone. The older woman turned on her heels and left the room.

Morrisey's chest tightened. "Oh, God."

"What's going on?" Betsey asked.

Margaret returned just then. Her jaw was set, and anger burned in her eyes. She crossed to Charlene and dropped Charlene's purse in her lap. "Please go."

Charlene shrank back.

"Did you not hear me?" Margaret's voice was hard and cold. "Go."

"Why?" Bobby asked.

Margaret made a harsh sound, almost a hiss. "Why don't you tell them, Charlene? Tell them what your son did to my daughter. I can't believe you. You accepted that rose. You laid it on his grave, right in front of me. Why don't you tell them why you and Gareth are both fair and light-skinned? I can't believe I didn't see it before." Margaret's voice was increasingly shrill. "After you tell them, get the hell out of my home and don't ever come back. Stay away from my daughter and my grandson. My grandson! Mine! You understand? Mine! Mine! What's wrong with you? Don't you see this is sick? You and Morrisey both. Don't you two see it? Are you using her, huh? Are you fucking my daughter to be with Gareth?"

Charlene got to her feet and stood ramrod straight. Her gaze was unwavering, and so were her words. "I love your grandson with all my heart," she said. "I would never do anything to hurt him and Morrisey. For what it's worth, after you left, I put the rose where it belonged, on your son's grave. I know JP didn't deserve it." Charlene softened a bit. "And I think you ought to...Look,

Morrisey needs..."

"Wait, wait. What's going on?" Betsey cut in. "I don't understand. What's this about roses?"

Morrisey forced herself to stand. She met her mother's eyes. "You're not kicking Charlene out. Deal with it."

An unreadable expression took over Margaret's features. "I don't understand you, Morrisey Hawthorne. I don't understand you at all. What is wrong with you? How can you even let that woman be around your son? She's using you."

Morrisey had had enough. She was tired of all of her mother's biting criticisms, all the aloofness, all the disapproval over the years. She said, clearly enunciating each word, "The question is why I let you be around my son for so long."

Margaret flinched, but Morrisey did not back down. "I can't believe I've been so afraid to tell you about Gareth because maybe you'd judge me or get that look in your eyes like it was my fault. Well, guess what? I don't give a shit anymore what you think. You're going to reject me? Go right ahead, because I don't want you, anyway." Morrisey turned to her brother and sister. "Bobby, Betsey, here's the thing. I was raped by Charlene's son. That's right! Raped. It's a lovely word, isn't it? But our mother just cares about kicking Charlene out. No hug for me. No asking me how I feel, how I'm doing. Nothing. We're not surprised, are we, Bobby and Betsey? Are we now?"

Bobby swallowed hard, and Betsey looked away. A chorus of excited voices and light footfalls followed by a heavier footfall sounded in the hallway, and seconds later, Gareth and the twins burst in. A grass stain colored Gareth's left knee, and his face brimmed with excitement. "Mommy!" he cried. "I almost caught a frog! But Warner tripped me!"

Warner stomped indignantly. "I did not!"

"Did too!"

Bobby and Betsey took simultaneous steps back, their eyes widening as if they were seeing Gareth for the first time, which, Morrisey supposed, they were. They were seeing him not as their nephew, but as Charlene's grandson, as a rapist's child. Morrisey hated it.

Bobby was the first to speak. "Morrisey, why didn't you tell us before? You shouldn't have had to go through that alone."

Morrisey's heart nearly broke at her brother's pain and concern. She had never loved him more than at that moment. "I just couldn't," Morrisey replied, some of her anger ebbing. "I'm sorry."

"No, don't be sorry." Bobby wrapped his arms around Morrisey and held her close. "Thank you for telling us."

"What's wrong?" Gareth asked.

"Nothing," Margaret answered. "Ms. Sudsbury was just leaving. You and your mother are staying a bit longer."

"Charlie came with us!" Gareth protested.

"I'll take you two home later," Margaret countered.

Morrisey broke free of Bobby's embrace. "Mother, Charlene and I came together. We leave together."

"Her son—"

"Goodbye. I am not going to call you, so if you want to talk, you come to me. Be prepared to beg your bleeding heart out. You don't have a heart, though, do you?" Without a backward glance, Morrisey took her son's hand and Charlene's hand. They left the house, and Morrisey walked with an extra spring in her step. She had told her family and had broken free of her mother's hold. She was with Charlene and Gareth, where she belonged.

Chapter Eighteen

ABOUT TWO WEEKS later, Morrisey and Gareth were on their back porch. Dusk was about to fall, and Gareth was peering through a jar teetering on the porch railing. Fireflies lit up the jar, much to Gareth's delight. "I got ten!" he crowed.

Morrisey frowned. "You beat me. I have nine."

"Yay!" The porch light broke through the dusk to illuminate Gareth's small face, so filled with the innocence of childhood. Morrisey took in her son with new, awed eyes. How had she gotten so lucky? She had been blessed with a remarkable child, and now she had an amazing woman in her life as well. Charlene was working a later shift at the restaurant and would be finishing up in a few minutes. It was her last Saturday shift, too. No more six-day work weeks. She was cutting back to five.

Gareth unscrewed his jar's lid and let the insects fly back out into the night. He held his hands out for Morrisey's jar. She obliged him, a small smile twitching at her lips because she had actually caught thirteen fireflies. After the fireflies were freed, Morrisey beckoned Gareth to sit with her on the porch swing. He crawled into her lap and rested his head against her chest. Morrisey held him for a few precious moments, savoring his steady breathing, his regular heartbeat. He smelled like grass.

"I don't wanna bath," Gareth said, as if he were reading her mind.

"I don't want one either," Morrisey murmured. "But I have to take one."

"Why?"

Morrisey ran her fingers through Gareth's fine hair, letting each strand fall one by one. "So I don't smell up the house. And I feel all nice and fresh after a bath. Don't you?"

"I guess," Gareth mumbled. "Can I play with the ships?"

Morrisey kissed the top of his head. "Sure."

"And the ducks?"

"Yep."

Gareth giggled and looked up. "The frogs too?"

"The toy frogs. Not the real ones."

Gareth's face fell.

"Mmm-hmm." Morrisey smiled, and then a realization hit her. It was now or never. It was time to tell her son who Charlene really was, who his father really was. Morrisey took a deep, calming breath. "Before we go in, I want to talk to you about something."

Gareth wriggled around in Morrisey's lap so that they were face-to-face. "Okay."

"It's about Charlene."

"Yeah?"

"About JP, too. Remember who he is? He's Charlene's son."

"I remember! Grandpa said JP's funny. JP tells Grandpa jokes."

"No."

"Does too!"

Morrisey swallowed, trying not to think about her father and JP cozying up like a couple of old buddies, telling jokes and swapping war stories.

"Grandpa misses me. Why can't I go with Grandma anymore?"

"Because."

"Is Charlie gonna be my daddy?"

Morrisey half-smiled. "You like her a lot, don't you?"

"I want my daddy."

"You know that—"

"Will Charlie throw football with me?"

"I throw football with you."

Gareth puckered his lips. "I guess."

Morrisey smoothed her son's hair. "Okay, sweetie. Charlene's a woman, not a man. She's not going to be your daddy. How would you like her to be your mother, like I'm your mother?"

"Is my daddy a doctor? Aaron's daddy who came back is a doctor, and he has a big car."

"I told you. You have a donor, because you're special."

Gareth shook his head. "My tummy hurts. I bet my daddy could make it feel better 'cause he's a doctor. He helps people."

Morrisey resisted the urge to retort something she would regret later. "Let's check your stomach out, sweetie." She stood and carried Gareth into the house, her calm demeanor masking the electric currents racing through her. She knew instinctively that she had blown the perfect chance to tell Gareth about his father—and she would pay for it, sooner or later.

CHARLENE WOKE MORRISEY up one morning in late August. "What is it?" Morrisey murmured, still half asleep.

"Do you ever get the feeling this is too good to be true?"

"No." Morrisey pulled Charlene to her. "Shh. Go back to sleep."

Charlene remained snug in Morrisey's arms, but she was wide awake. A dark foreboding was beginning to stir inside her, that her life would change very soon, and not for the better.

Throughout the day, as Charlene waited on customers at The Log Cabin, the feeling grew even worse. She was alternately clammy, cold and sweaty. Several times, she went into the bathroom to splash water on her face. Miriam came up behind Charlene one time. "What's wrong?"

Charlene dried her face. "I don't know. I just have a feeling something's going to go wrong soon."

"Such as?"

"I don't know," Charlene admitted. "Maybe Morrisey will get sick of me. She'll dump me and I'll never see her or Gareth again."

Miriam snorted. "That's just as likely as a pig sprouting wings and flying away. Baby, I saw how she was with you last night. Hell, I should be retching over the toilet."

Charlene smiled and studied her wan reflection in the mirror. "Well, maybe not that."

"She wants you to be Gareth's mother, you know."

Charlene's heart skipped a beat despite her glum mood. "You really think that? She hasn't said so yet."

"She will. Soon."

"I want that."

"She does too. Please don't worry."

"Maybe something's going to happen to Gareth."

"Hey, now." Miriam turned disapproving again. "Don't be thinking like that. Stop it. Just be happy, okay? There's nothing to worry about."

"We're going to tell Gareth that JP's his father," Charlene whispered. "Maybe that he was the sperm donor. Or maybe we'll tell Gareth that JP hurt Morrisey and leave it at that for a while."

Miriam's eyes widened. "When are you going to tell him?"

"Soon. We keep meaning to every day, but we never do."

"Why?"

Charlene shrugged. "Morrisey just says she'll know the right time when it comes. And it hasn't."

"It's got to be hard. Are you afraid Gareth's going to hate JP? Not now, but a few years down the road, when he's older?"

"Maybe," Charlene admitted. "I don't want him to experience what I'm feeling, all this confusion about JP. Love and hate at the same time is no fun."

AFTER WORK, CHARLENE headed to JP's grave. She hoped to find reassurance and peace there. It had been so long, more than three weeks, since her most recent visit. She sat carefully just to the left of JP's marker and wondered what to say. Should she apologize for not having visited lately? Should she update JP on her life and on how the boy who inherited his DNA was doing? *No.*

Charlene found herself uttering words she never dreamed she would say to her child. "I don't think I'm going to be back for a long time, JP. Maybe not even in a few weeks on your... Well, I guess we'll call it an anniversary after all." She bit back tears. "Three years, JP. Three years. Uh, anyway. This is going to be the last time for a while. If Gareth wants to come see you, I'll bring him. But I don't know if he will want to." Charlene cleared her throat.

"I'm going to explain to Morrisey that Gareth needs to know you hurt her. No details of course. He's only four years old. I'm not going to let him grow up with rose-colored glasses, thinking you're someone you're not. It'll hurt a lot less now than it will later. But, JP. John Patrick. I'm going to tell your son that for 17 years, his father was a good person. I hope that's right."

A breeze started up, as one always seemed to when Charlene was talking at the grave. *Heh heh heh.* Charlene froze. The wind was laughing, cackling, really. *Heh heh heh.* Then—*Hoo-hoo-hoo-hoo.* Charlene got to her feet, and her knees wobbled. She felt JP slamming her against a wall again, felt his dead, heavy body in her arms again. What exquisite pain.

"You asshole," Charlene fumed.

Hoo-hoo-hoo-hoo, said the JP breeze, louder and louder.

CHARLENE SAT IN her Acclaim in the cemetery parking lot for the longest time, trying to collect her composure. She ached to run back to JP's grave, fall to her knees and say she was sorry, that she didn't really mean what she said, that she'd visit more, really she would.

Charlene stayed in her car. After her guilt was exhausted, she put Silver into gear and drove away. She was going to the grocery store where she had seen Morrisey and Gareth laughing together. She would buy ingredients for cupcakes and muffins. She, Gareth and Morrisey would bake tonight. Charlene would tell Gareth about his father. It was time—it was past overdue—and then she could bury JP for good.

Charlene strode into the grocery store with purpose and confidence, her head held high. She grabbed a little shopping basket and headed for the baking goods section. As she had done on her first visit to the store, she stopped in her tracks right after rounding the corner of the aisle. Her chest stilled, and her entire body stiffened as she saw a young man staring at a can of frosting in his hand. He was wearing a red baseball cap, and he was at the very end of the aisle.

How could it be? His profile was unmistakable. She had held his body for hours, until he was cold to the touch. She had seen those dull, empty mannequin blue eyes and the holes in his head. He was dead, wasn't he? He was dead and buried right near Morrisey's father. He was in the very cemetery where Charlene had, only such a short time ago, called him an asshole. The police had come! Paramedics had declared him no longer living.

Charlene's heart dropped to the pit of her stomach, and she did not dare to breathe, because if she moved, even just a little bit, he would shatter and vanish like a dream upon waking, and Charlene would be left with a bloody mannequin of a son again.

There in front of her, way down aisle number five, was JP, her only child. It was JP, not a grave marker with a name and dates on it. No. This was her son, alive, breathing and trying to decide what kind of frosting he wanted. The person she saw was her JP, not at four like Gareth, not at ten and not at fifteen, not even at twenty-one when he died, but at twenty-four years old as he would be had he lived, He was thinner now, more pale.

The JP she saw now wore clean jeans and a yellow polo shirt. His hair was close-cropped, darker, rust-colored. There was no more bright carrot red, no crazy mishmash of colors. He no longer had an aura of anger, resentment or manic around him. He was at peace now, her son. He had become a man.

The shopping basket slipped from Charlene's hand and landed with a clatter on the shiny floor. JP did not look up. He replaced the red can of frosting and picked up a blue one. Charlene stared, her eyes wide, and still she did not breathe. She knew she should tell him that the frosting he had in his hand was not very good, that the red can was the one to get. Gareth liked the red can better.

A tidal wave of joy surged through Charlene. She had never experienced such an incredible, sheer joy. Never, ever, not even with Morrisey. JP was alive. Somehow, her beautiful little boy was alive. He was not the bad JP, either — he was the good JP: sensitive and caring, like before the accident. He had come back for her and for Gareth, hadn't he?

Morrisey would like him. She had to. She just had to. He was the good JP. JP would accept his punishment and pay his penance for the rape. There was a good explanation for the lifeless body, for the holes in his head. There had to be. He would not have made her suffer three years for nothing. Yes, there was a reason. All that could come later. Maybe he had been in the federal witness protection program. He had gotten tangled up in some huge drug scheme, and the feds had needed him to fake his suicide. *Something, something!* The important thing was that JP was alive.

Charlene stared some more. Her son bit his lip and shook his head. He put the blue can back and chose a green can. *No, no, no,* Charlene wanted to say. *That brand tastes like wax.* Still, she could not move, could not breathe, could not do anything except stare. She wondered if she'd finally snapped, if she was hallucinating. Or was this a ghost? Was JP content no longer to haunt her in her mind? Had she infuriated him so much at the cemetery that he felt the need to rise from the dead and appear before her himself?

Whatever the case, he dropped the green can in his shopping basket and looked up, right at Charlene. Recognition flooded his features. His eyes widened, and he went deathly pale. He stood rooted in place, just as still as Charlene was. They stared at each other for a minute that stretched into infinity. At long last, Charlene breathed. She trembled, every nerve in her body thawing from the stunned disbelief. She wanted so much to rush into his arms, to hold him, to have him hold her, but her shock was too overwhelming.

She was incapable of moving, so her son did — finally. He stepped toward her. He took another step, drawing ever closer. She half-expected him to vanish into thin air, proving he was just a figment of her imagination. He did not. He lifted his head just so, tilted it ever so slightly. Charlene saw that the blue eyes were gone, that this young man before her had eyes more green than blue, and not very many freckles. JP was dead, still dead. He would always be dead. He was still a name on a grave marker — still a bloody mannequin of a son.

The young man spoke. "Hello, Ms. Sudsbury," he said. "How are you? I'm glad you're here. I've been wanting to talk to you."

And then Charlene knew who he was. Ralph. Ralph, who raped Morrisey. Ralph looking like JP.

Chapter Nineteen

RALPH WAS ALL cleaned up. He hardly resembled the greasy, long-haired, beady-eyed youth lodged in Charlene's memory. When he spoke, there was no denying who he was. His squeaky, feminine voice had deepened and become richer, but hints of it still resonated. Charlene, her throat constricting, could only stare at Ralph, who had raped and hurt Morrisey, who was partially responsible for that haunted look in her eyes. How the hell could he look like JP, making Charlene think, for one perfect, glorious moment, that the world was right again and that her son was alive?

Charlene bristled with anger but said, "Get the red frosting."

Ralph's gaze dropped to his shopping basket. "Okay," he whispered. "I will."

"The other kinds taste like wax. They're not very good at all."

"Thank you, Ms. Sudsbury." Ralph slid his baseball cap off and held it at his side. His blue-green eyes, so beautiful, intense and flecked with gold, studied her. Charlene knew that look, had known it since she was sixteen years old. It was Mr. Burroughs' look — JP's and Gareth's, too.

"I'd like to talk to you," Ralph said.

"About what?"

"About JP. I've wanted to for a while. I never could get the courage to do it. But here you are. It's time you knew what happened. There's a Starbucks nearby. Will you let me buy you something?"

Gooseflesh covered every inch of Charlene's arms and legs. "No."

"Don't you want to know about JP?"

Charlene shook her head. She just wanted to flee this young man, this young man who had no right to look like her own son and like Gareth.

Ralph furrowed his brows. "You don't want to know about JP?"

"I need to go home. People are waiting for me."

"Remember at the funeral, I ran from you? I wasn't brave enough to face you then. I am now. I want to help you."

Charlene gritted her teeth and met Ralph's concerned eyes. God, he looked so much like JP that her whole body hurt.

"JP never introduced us," Ralph said tentatively. "Well, let me introduce myself properly. I'm Ralph Burroughs Jr. You knew my father, JP's father."

Charlene could no longer deny the things, the obvious and the inconsequential, that she had been trying so hard to ignore, to chalk up to coincidence: the perfectly symmetrical smile, the long eyelashes, the way he looked at her. *My wife's pregnant too. I love her. We're going to move to be closer to her parents. Take this money and get an abortion. Forget about me, okay?*

"Did JP know?" Charlene asked.

"Yes," Ralph said. "After my parents separated, I moved back here with my mother. We'd been living in Chicago, but she hated it there. She always said she did her best writing here. Anyway, a couple of years later, right after I dropped out of community college, I went to the mall. I saw this guy and I knew. I knew. He was my brother; he had to be. Even with his long, tangled hair, he was nearly the mirror image of my father. Our father."

"You went up to him?"

"Yes. I introduced myself, said my name, and his face changed. He knew. We both knew. That's how I met my brother."

Charlene looked numbly into the young man's eyes. "Why didn't JP tell me?"

"I guess he didn't want to hurt you."

"Hurt me? How would he have?"

"He wanted to meet our father. He told me he'd always wanted to, but he didn't want to hurt you or be disloyal to you." Ralph tugged his baseball cap back on. "One day, after I told JP that Dad had just moved to Northern Virginia, from Chicago, and that he and my mom were getting back together, JP says, 'Let's go see the bastard. I mean it, I mean it this time.' So, we went. We got to the house, and well, we'd had a lot of beers, JP especially. He stormed in, all angry, and he greeted our dad with a fist to the face. He started hollering about how our father had taken advantage of you and abandoned you." Ralph grinned wryly. "JP beat Dad up bad."

"JP did it for me?"

"Yes, pretty much. My brother loved you. There was no question about it. You were the most important thing in his life — even more important than football, I reckon. That's why it killed him, that knee thing. 'Cause he felt like he was breaking his promises to you. Big house, money, nice car, all that."

Charlene's tongue felt like sandpaper in her dry mouth as Ralph continued, his voice low and pained. "Dad said some bad things, like how JP wasn't his son, how JP should have been carved out and tossed in the trash a long time ago, how you'd been just a fun, ah, fuck to him. Stuff like that. On the drive home, JP was quiet, subdued. He didn't say a word, hardly. When I dropped him off, he just stalked into the building. He didn't even say goodbye.

"Look, Dad's not exactly a stand-up man. You know that. What he did to JP, he wasn't much better with me, you know? JP thought I'd had a wonderful, ideal life. He didn't understand that I hadn't been happy either. Uh, you know, I told JP all that." Ralph's voice became even more strained. "I told him what a bastard the old man was. It didn't matter. JP still wanted so badly to have his father, even if it was just to punish him for leaving. And when JP couldn't... The next day, JP was dead." Ralph's eyes filmed over with tears, and his voice trembled. "That was the worst day of my life. 'Cause JP was my brother. I loved him."

Charlene's shock gave way to fury. "Three years! Why didn't you tell me this before? It's been three years!"

"I couldn't!" Ralph pleaded. "How could I? You know I was messed up. On drugs. I've been straight for almost a year now. Almost a year." He tried to take Charlene's hand, and she jerked back. He flinched but went on. "Last year, I nearly killed myself with an overdose. I finally persuaded myself to check into a clinic."

"Three years," Charlene retorted, her voice scalding. "Three years!"

Gareth. Morrisey. The little boy and the dark-haired woman slammed back into Charlene's mind, larger than life. Morrisey was so beautiful and vulnerable. She made Charlene feel so alive. And Gareth, the child who had made Charlene's heart jump for joy at the cemetery, her grandson, the boy she loved so dearly.

Charlene looked at Ralph again, and stiffened with a dreadful realization. He was fidgeting with his ball cap, his gaze concerned. How had she missed it, even all those years before, with his long, greasy hair dyed purple and blue and green, even with his thin, lanky body and his acne-covered face? Now he had bulked up. He was no longer a stick of a boy; he had become a man. Still, how had she missed it? He was easily recognizable as JP's brother. He practically could have been JP's twin! Was he Gareth's father? Charlene told herself it was not possible. Gareth looked just like JP, save for the freckles and a few tiny things here and there, but damn it, in his own way, Gareth looked as much like Ralph as he looked like JP.

"Oh, God." Charlene saw that she was going to lose JP all over again. And how was she going to tell Morrisey that her little boy's daddy might not be safely buried after all?

CHARLENE STUMBLED ONTO Morrisey's front porch ten minutes later and jabbed a finger at the doorbell. Morrisey answered in seconds, but the smile developing on her face froze. "What's wrong, hon? And you know you don't need to ring the doorbell!"

Charlene looked into Morrisey's dark eyes. God, how she loved this woman.

"Charlie!" Gareth careened into Charlene and wrapped his arms around her legs.

"Hey." Morrisey took Charlene's hands. "What happened? You look as if you've seen a ghost."

Charlene was tempted to laugh in despair. It was like that day with Miriam all over again, when Charlene had seen Gareth at the cemetery. But unlike what she had told Miriam, Charlene was going to lie to Morrisey — for now, anyway, until she figured all this out.

"Sweetie?" Morrisey prompted.

Gareth ran back into the house, hollering, "Come play trucks with me!"

"Charlene's not feeling well," Morrisey called after her son. She led Charlene into the living room and sat with her on the couch. She snaked an arm around Charlene's shoulders. "What's wrong?"

"Nothing," Charlene whispered, and she broke from Morrisey. She clambered onto the floor to play with Gareth. *Please, please be JP's son.* Charlene was no longer ashamed that her son raped Morrisey. She needed for this boy to be her grandchild, for both her sake and Morrisey's.

Charlene picked up a truck, and Gareth dropped the bulldozer he had been holding. "Why are you sad?" he asked. Charlene drew back and looked into Gareth's eyes, into the blue eyes that could have been JP's. Gareth had to be JP's son. He just had to be, but Gareth's hair was already getting darker, there was no denying it.

"Charlie?" Gareth spoke again. "Are you okay?"

"I'm fine. Come on, let's play."

Morrisey joined them on the floor. "What's wrong?"

Charlene stood abruptly. "I have to go to the bathroom." She headed into the half-bathroom off the hallway. Morrisey was right behind her.

"What is it?" Morrisey asked.

Charlene grabbed her toothbrush. She wet it and squeezed

Crest onto it. She brushed, avoiding Morrisey's scrutiny. She took her time but finally had to spit the toothpaste out. She rinsed her mouth for as long as she could. She was afraid that if she met Morrisey's eyes, she would become unglued and confess everything. Morrisey was trying so hard to move on with her life, and to bring up the possibility that Gareth's father was alive and nearby would set her back. Hadn't she pleaded with Charlene on their first night as a couple to leave her rapists alone, to not try to find them?

"You went to the cemetery, didn't you?" Morrisey asked. "What happened? Oh, God. Not my mother?"

Charlene returned the toothbrush to its holder. "Not your mother. I'm just thinking."

"Thinking about what?"

"I'll tell you later—maybe tomorrow. I have to do something first."

Morrisey was silent for a few moments. "All right," she said at last. "Fine."

Chapter
Twenty

CHARLENE TURNED ONTO the quiet, tree-lined street and consulted her directions. Less than twenty-four hours ago, before seeing Ralph, she had wondered what her life would be like today. She had wondered if the knot in her stomach would be gone. The knot not only was far from gone, it was ten times worse. Charlene had never imagined she would be seeing JP's father. Mr. Burroughs' house would be just a few more down, on the right. And then there it was.

Charlene squirmed as she came upon the house, a cute yellow Cape Cod. It was like Morrisey's, except hers was blue. Mr. Burroughs's yard was bigger, and a sleek black BMW gleamed in the driveway. Charlene pulled Silver to the curb and took a deep breath. It was time to visit the man she thought she would never see again. "Good luck," she told herself, her voice faltering. She clutched her purse to her side, got out of the car and took slow, anxious steps to the front door.

She had called in sick at The Log Cabin to make the trip. Of course, as far as Morrisey knew, Charlene was at work. She had spent fifteen minutes that morning at the library, tracking down Mr. Burroughs' address via the Internet. Now here she was, in picturesque Loudon County, Virginia. She pressed the doorbell and wondered if, thanks to Ralph, Mr. Burroughs was expecting her.

A statuesque platinum blonde with unnatural cleavage answered the door. She looked about ten years older than Charlene and wore a suspicious smile on her sagging features. *A caricature of youth,* Charlene thought, almost shamefully. *That's what she is.*

"May I help you?" the blonde asked. She was probably Mr. Burroughs' wife, Ralph's mother, the well-known author of children's books who wrote under the pen name Bunny Winkerbeans.

"Hello. I'm looking for Mr. Burroughs. Is he home?"

"My husband is at work. May I tell him who stopped by?"

"You're Mrs. Burroughs? Clara?"

The blonde narrowed her eyes. "What do you want with my husband?"

"I just wanted to say hello. I was one of his students a long time ago."

"Oh?" Clara's features darkened. "What kind of student?" she asked.

"Eleventh-grade English."

"No. You know what I mean. A student student or a student he fucked?"

Charlene recoiled.

"Yeah." Clara Burroughs crossed her arms. "My husband and I have started over. We're in love with each other again. I'd appreciate it if you left him alone, if you left us alone."

"No! Please. I need to see him. Please. It's about my son, his son. Did he tell you? My son's name was JP, and he killed himself."

"Goodbye." Clara slammed the door, and Charlene gaped at the shiny door knocker. If Clara Burroughs thought all it took was a slammed door to get rid of her, she was woefully wrong. Charlene would wait all day and all night, even all week, for Mr. Burroughs to get home. She was not going to let him get away with what he had done to JP.

Charlene headed back to her car. She circled the street and found a suitable surveillance spot. She glanced at her watch. It was 3:00 p.m., and the car was unbearably hot. Charlene climbed out of the Acclaim. She would stretch her legs, walk to the Dairy Queen she noticed down the street, and have a late lunch.

During the walk to the restaurant, Morrisey flashed into Charlene's mind. Morrisey and Gareth. Charlene would tell Morrisey that night. She dreaded it but set her haunting thoughts aside as she reached the Dairy Queen. The heavenly coolness of air conditioning welcomed her, and she sighed happily. She ordered a hamburger, fries and iced tea. She sat by the window and slowly ate her lunch, studying cars and passersby. What would she say to Mr. Burroughs? *Hello, long time no see. Hey, you look good. What the hell's wrong with you? You killed my son!*

Charlene could not say that, though, because Mr. Burroughs had not killed JP. Maybe Charlene herself had. Her heart hurt even more for her son and with the knowledge that she had screwed up. Morrisey was right. Charlene should have held Mr. Burroughs accountable, at least financially, for his child. She should have done everything in her power, even if it meant taking Mr. Burroughs to court and suing for financial support. She had not done so, though, and JP was dead.

Charlene poked at her uneaten hamburger. Her stomach felt full of lead. She had just wasted four dollars and some change. She glanced at her watch. It was 3:45. If Mr. Burroughs was teaching summer school, he most likely would be home soon. Charlene got up and threw the remainder of her food and trash away. She trudged to the door. Just before she reached it, she stopped in her tracks, her heart stilling. She turned and surveyed the cash register area.

He was there.

Mr. Burroughs was the sole customer at the cash registers. He was there, right there, a few feet from her and getting an ice cream cone. If she took a few steps, she could touch him. Her legs took over and propelled her to her former teacher. "Mr. Burroughs?" she asked, more haltingly than she would have liked.

He turned. Recognition flooded his face, and he took a shocked step back.

"Mr. Burroughs." Charlene felt disconnected from reality.

"Here you go, handsome." The bosomy young blonde cashier handed Mr. Burroughs his change and fluttered her eyelashes. "Enjoy the cone. See you tonight."

Mr. Burroughs pulled Charlene aside. "Well, ah, hello." He took a lick from his vanilla ice cream. He had hardly changed in twenty-five years. There were strands of white in his red hair now and some wrinkles on his face, but his eyes were the same strong, steady blue, and his smile was as brilliant as ever.

"Hello." Charlene struggled to keep her voice cold, even as the man acted like there was nothing out of the ordinary. "I see you remember me."

"Ah, Charity? Yes, that's it. Charity. Or is it Charlotte?"

"Cut the crap."

Mr. Burroughs glanced toward the door. "Ah, it's nice running into you, but I need to be going."

"No," Charlene countered icily. "Sit." She pointed toward the closest table, and after a long moment, Mr. Burroughs nodded his assent. He sat. He licked his ice cream as if he had not a care in the world, but a twitch along his jaw gave him away. Charlene sat too and just stared at her son's father. He nibbled at his cone. Charlene stared some more. When it became evident he was not going to say a word, she spoke. "My son, *your son*, killed himself the day after he visited you."

Mr. Burroughs' jaw stopped twitching. "I believe Ralph mentioned that."

"You believe?"

"It was a few years ago."

"You're a piece of work," Charlene seethed, not sure whether she ought to laugh or cry. "How could you do that to your own son, say the things you did to him?"

Mr. Burroughs wolfed down the rest of his cone. He fixed Charlene with an unwavering gaze. "Look, that kid wasn't my son. I paid you money to get rid of him. As far as I'm concerned, that's where it ended. It is not my fault you didn't go through with it."

"Is that what you told him?"

Mr. Burroughs shrugged easily. "He had no right coming into my home and punching me, that drunk, loser bastard."

"Oh, my God." Charlene wondered how she had ever been vulnerable enough to fall under the spell of this psychopath. Was it all a game to him?

"Hey." Mr. Burroughs reached for Charlene's hand. "I'm sorry about the kid, okay? Really. Understand this, though. He was a big boy. It's not my fault what he did. It's not your fault, either. All right?"

"Maybe it was my fault."

"No," Mr. Burroughs said, and he tightened his grip on Charlene. "He was a big boy."

"Big boys hurt, too, though. Do you even know what JP stands for? What your son's full name was?"

Mr. Burroughs glanced toward the door again, and there it was, a slight softening of his features. A humanization. "John Patrick," he whispered, still avoiding her eyes.

"That's right. You had the same middle names."

"The John must have been from your father."

Charlene blinked, surprised Mr. Burroughs remembered that. He sighed and let go of her hand. "I'm sorry," he said kindly. "Look, I have to go, okay? My wife, you know. I promised my wife I'd be home by four o'clock every day."

"You're fucking the cashier, aren't you. How old is she? Sixteen, like I was?"

Mr. Burroughs stood. "I'm not fucking her. Do us both a favor, all right? Don't come back here." He made his way out of the restaurant. Charlene buried her face in her hands and willed herself not to cry. Then she went over to the cashier. It would probably do no good, but she had to try.

DUSK WAS FALLING when Charlene arrived back in town. She did not go to Morrisey's house. Instead, she went to her own apartment. She headed right for JP's nightstand, for the gun. It was time to hold it. JP had bought it from a friend of his, unbeknownst to Charlene. After the death investigation, the police asked her if she wanted it. She thought a moment and then said, "Sure." She hated the gun, but she kept it around. It was the weapon that killed her son. It was also the last thing he held, the last thing he touched in life.

After three years of being unable to open the nightstand drawer, Charlene yanked it free easily enough. It was just like the police and Miriam had said: porn magazines, odds and ends, some pictures—though none of her or JP—and the gun. Charlene picked it up and fumbled the chamber open. It was empty, so she handled the gun less carefully. *Hmm.* She had never held a gun before. For some reason, she had expected it to be heavy, and maybe most handguns were. This one was light as a feather. She traced the gun's lines, feeling its sleekness and power.

Charlene tried to put herself in JP's place, to feel his pain, his intense, burning ache at the words his father had spoken to him. She imagined she was her son, that she wanted to die just as much as JP had wanted to die, that she had nothing to live for. She imagined that as far as her father was concerned, she did not exist, that she had a bum knee and no future. She tried to feel as though she had resorted to hitting her own mother, that she had hit rock bottom and could not go up. Charlene took a deep breath. *Okay.* She brought the gun to her temple, just as JP had.

What had her son's last thoughts been, his last words? Maybe, *I love you, Mom. Forgive me.* Maybe, *Screw you, world. Fuck you, Dad. You too, Mom.* Maybe, maybe nothing. No matter how hard she tried, Charlene could not understand, could not feel, just why her son pulled the trigger. He had been kicked down some, true, but he could have picked himself up. He had her and, apparently, a brother who loved him very much. He had brains, a good heart. Plenty of young men suffered career-ending injuries and ended up just fine. Plenty of young men had childhoods and fathers much worse than Mr. Burroughs. JP had just chosen to wither into himself, into his alcohol and drugs. Was there anything she could have done?

Charlene racked her memory, as she had time and time again, analyzing JP's behavior for any signs that he was suicidal. She could not think of anything. In the last days of his life, JP had been the same as always—moody, angry, violent. She had labored almost three years to make sense of his death so she could forgive him. She had been trying three years to understand, to feel. She was no closer to figuring it out.

Had it been revenge, pure and simple? To get back at her, to get back at his father, to get back at the three football players who sacked him? To get back at everybody? He never should have lived, according to Mr. Burroughs. *Carved out.* Maybe JP had figured, "Hey, I'll make that bastard sorry for what he said. See how he feels after I'm dead." Maybe JP hoped that, with him dead, his father would finally want to find out about him and maybe even come to love him.

Revenge. And love? Charlene's heart ached at the thought. This was the son she wanted, a sensitive young man who cared about people, who wanted to be loved. He was completely gone now. He did not even live on in Gareth, did he? Charlene wished she had never gone into that grocery store. She wished she still lived in blissful ignorance. It did not matter that Ralph would have found her eventually. It would be so much easier to forgive JP for killing himself if Gareth was his child, because then JP would not be gone completely.

Charlene let out a little whimper. Her thoughts and emotions were all over the place. She was no closer to finding out any truth about her son's death. Revenge. Love. Hate. Despair. Loneliness. Depression. She did not know why JP killed himself. Maybe he had not known, either. Maybe he just felt it was something he had to do. Maybe he had seized death on the spur of the moment. Maybe it even had been an accident. Maybe he'd just been playing around, and the gun had gone off. Or maybe it had been Russian roulette. Maybe JP had been courting death for a week already. September 25th just happened to be his unlucky day.

Charlene kept the gun at her head. Eventually, she pulled the trigger.

Chapter Twenty-One

MORRISEY KNEW CHARLENE had something important and difficult to tell her. Charlene did not stop by until about 10 p.m., and she was withdrawn and contemplative. Morrisey did not press. Charlene would share soon enough, in her own time. First, they made love, and it was wonderful, slow and sad all at the same time. Afterward, when they were sweaty and comfortably entwined in each other's arms, Charlene talked about the gun and about her struggle. Then she said, "I went to see JP's father."

Morrisey's breath caught in her throat. "Why?"

A shudder ran through Charlene. "Mr. Burroughs was one of the last people to see JP alive."

"How do you know that?"

"Ralph told me."

Morrisey froze, even as the name seared her brain, whirring and rattling and shrilling. *Ralph, Ralph, Ralph, Ralph, OhMyGod.* "Ralph?"

"Yes. Ralph who raped you."

"You hunted him down after I asked you not to?"

"No," Charlene whispered. "I saw him. I ran into him at Kroger yesterday. I was going to get things so we could bake and tell Gareth who his father was. I was ready. But then I saw Ralph."

"Oh." Every nerve in Morrisey's body was on alert. Ralph, in her neighborhood. Ralph, shopping in her store, breathing the same air she did. "He lives near here?"

Charlene's eyes widened at the thought. "I don't know. Oh God, Morrisey, Morrisey. Would you still love me, still want to be with me if Gareth and I weren't related?"

"What kind of question is that?"

"Just answer it."

"I love you. You. I fell in love with you from the moment I saw you in the cemetery, before I knew who you were. I love you no matter what. Please know that."

"You'd still love me even if we didn't share a bond over Gareth anymore? He's who brought us together in the first place. It's why you talked to me about the rape. It's why you let me help you."

"What are you getting at?"

"I think Ralph might be Gareth's father. Gareth's father might be alive. I'm so sorry, Morris. I'm so sorry."

Morrisey laughed out loud, ignoring the agony in Charlene's expression. Better to laugh than to contemplate the unthinkable. "That's impossible. Gareth looks just like JP."

"Gareth also looks just like Ralph. He is JP's half-brother, but they could almost be twins."

Morrisey struggled to reconcile ping-pong thoughts. All she could manage in the end was, "You knew all this time Ralph was JP's brother?"

"No. Of course I didn't know. And Ralph looks so different now. I'm not sure how to describe it." Charlene went on to tell Morrisey everything that had happened at the store.

"I don't believe this," Morrisey said when Charlene finished. "You really think..."

"Yes." The misery on Charlene's face intensified. "I'm so sorry."

Morrisey drew Charlene in for a hug. "Gareth is JP's son. He has to be. I have no doubt about it. When I see you and Gareth together, your bond is so natural. You have the same nose, same eyes, same expression."

"People see what they want to see."

"Okay, look, why don't we test you and Gareth? I don't need a test, but maybe it'll put your mind at ease."

Charlene looked up, horrified. "No! What if it says Ralph's—"

"It won't!" Morrisey snapped. "Ralph is not Gareth's father." She refused to entertain the thought for even a second. "So his name is Ralph Burroughs?"

"Junior. Ralph Jr."

Morrisey got out of bed and did not bother to dress. She strode into the kitchen for the phone book and located Ralph's name and address. He lived only a few minutes' drive from her, in one of those sprawling apartment complexes. He had been there, such a short distance away, for goodness knew how long.

"What are you doing?" Charlene joined Morrisey and peered at Ralph's entry. "Isn't that—"

"We have to move," Morrisey declared.

"Move?"

"Move. We could. Charlene, we could move to California. Or Florida. The three of us. Please?"

"Running away won't solve the problem."

Morrisey let the phone book drop. "You know what? I do need

to have a test. I'm sorry."

"Yeah. I understand."

Morrisey wrapped her arms around Charlene and melted into her lover's bare skin. The moment was not perfect. It was not romantic at all. It would do, though, for a very simple reason. Morrisey already had blown her perfect chance to tell Gareth who his father was. Somehow, however irrational and illogical it was, she knew that if she had told Gareth amid the fireflies, amid the encroaching darkness, that JP was his father, that Charlene was his father's mother, there would have been no Ralph. She had to stop running from the world.

Morrisey whispered into Charlene's ear, "No matter what happens, I want us to spend our lives together. You are meant to be Gareth's mother, not his grandmother. What do you say?"

Chapter Twenty-Two

"ALL RIGHT." A gray-haired nurse held up the first of four cotton buccal swabs. "I'm just going to brush this inside your cheek."

Charlene smiled, trying to mask her anxiety so that she wouldn't stoke Gareth's fears. "Swab on."

Gareth, who was in Morrisey's lap, craned his head. "Is that gonna hurt?"

"No." The nurse threw him an indulgent grin. "It won't hurt at all."

"It's gonna hurt!"

Morrisey patted her son's head. "It won't hurt. It might tickle the inside of your cheek, but that's all."

Charlene opened her mouth for her swabbing. "That's right," the nurse said as she brushed the inside of Charlene's cheek. "It doesn't hurt at all."

"It hurts, doesn't it, Charlie?" Gareth asked as the nurse finished taking the samples.

"No pain." Charlene went over to Gareth and mussed his hair. "It tickled a little bit, so try not to laugh when you go."

Gareth nodded solemnly. "Okay, Charlie. But I don't wanna go."

Morrisey rose from her seat and stretched her legs. She seemed the picture of coolness, but Charlene knew better. "All right. I'll go next."

"Good!" The nurse grinned. "Do you want a lollipop after?"

Gareth let out a cry. "She gets a lollipop?"

"She surely does. And so does Charlene." The nurse reached into a cabinet and brought out an oversized purple lollipop. "Here you go." She handed it to Charlene.

"I want one too!" Gareth exclaimed.

"You'll get it in just a little bit, darling." The nurse motioned Morrisey into the chair Charlene had just vacated.

"No! Now!" Gareth howled.

The nurse sank to her knees. She took Gareth by the shoulders and looked into his excited blue eyes. "It is supposed to be your mommy's turn now. Do you want me to do you instead?"

Gareth bobbed his head eagerly. "Okay!"

"Okay. Can you open your mouth nice and wide?" Gareth stretched his mouth to its limits. "Very good!" the nurse exclaimed. She finished with Gareth in no time. While he sucked happily on a red lollipop, the nurse took Morrisey's samples. Just twenty minutes after they had arrived at the doctor's office, Charlene, Morrisey and Gareth were on their way out.

Gareth reached Morrisey's car first. "Can we go back?" he asked. "I want a lemon one! Can I have yours?"

Morrisey clutched her lollipop to her chest, her eyes narrowing playfully. "No. This is mine."

Gareth stomped his foot. "I'm almost done with mine!"

"Well, take your time with it," Morrisey advised. She tousled his hair then placed a fluttery kiss on Charlene's lips. "I wish you didn't have to get back to work."

"Me too," Charlene replied. She felt so safe and secure when she was with Morrisey, like nothing could go wrong. When she was apart from Morrisey, doubts crept into her mind that were black and desolate: Gareth was not her grandson, Ralph and the two other men were going to hurt Morrisey all over again.

Well, they would get DNA results in a few days.

Charlene walked the few parking spaces to Silver and got in. "Goodbye," she whispered, to no one in particular.

MORRISEY DID NOT know what she would do if Ralph was the father of her son. She tried not to dwell on the matter. It was no use worrying about something that might not even turn out. Nevertheless, the idea kept haunting her, and at the oddest moments. Ralph had not been on her mind while she and Gareth were washing her car after they got home from the doctor's office, but when she reached for the wax, he had popped into her head out of the blue.

Ralph might be Gareth's father. What are you going to do?

Morrisey had not been able to dislodge the thought in the hours since. She hated how she was allowing that one man to dominate her life, her movements, her shopping habits, where she took Gareth to play. And even if Ralph was not Gareth's father, Morrisey dreaded running into him. One glance at Gareth, and Ralph would know something odd was going on. Then he would look at her, and his eyes would glimmer with recognition—that woman in the snow years ago. He'd notice her red-headed, blue-eyed son. In the best case, Gareth was Ralph's nephew. That certainly was nothing to cheer about.

Morrisey's heart had nearly stopped the previous morning, when she had been fixing cereal for Charlene and Gareth. She had looked out the front window to check on the weather, and a red-haired youth walked past with a golden Labrador retriever. Morrisey went stiff, and she had only been able to stare.

Was that man her son's father?

Charlene had come up, taken note of the young man, and said, "No, sweetie. That's not Ralph."

Morrisey did not want to react like that again every time she saw a red-haired man. She had done it for a couple of years after Gareth's birth but had gradually stopped. Now it was starting again. She wondered if Ralph ever thought about her, the woman he raped, the woman he left to die.

CHARLENE TOOK A long look around her son's room, at the bare shelves and dressers, at the bed stripped of its coverings. She had figured she would wait until the very last minute to pack up JP's room before moving in with Morrisey. Instead, she had torn into his things with gusto, packing with a maniacal cheerfulness that concealed the desolation and dread within her. Now she was finished with it and more depressed than she had been in a long time. Packing JP's things so soon had been a mistake because now he was hidden away. She was happy to be moving in with Morrisey and Gareth and yet she felt as if she were leaving her son behind. This apartment was the only home JP had known. This was where they had shared their Christmases, his birthdays, his joys and sorrows.

A thousand memories overwhelmed Charlene. She recalled her first night at the apartment, in this very room, with her tiny son. She had been terrified. She was so inexperienced and afraid she might drop her baby. She had been happy, too, though, to have someone who needed her. She had found a measure of peace at last, some sense of belonging She was no longer aimless or lonely, thanks to her beautiful little son, who looked at her unblinking, with his big round button-blue eyes.

JP, at five, was afraid of monsters under his bed and in his closet. Charlene had to inspect his room countless times, often in the middle of the night, to try to reassure him there was nothing lurking in those dark places.

JP, at thirteen, had brought his first girlfriend over for a "study date." Charlene arrived home late at night from work to find his bedroom door closed. She had not known anyone else was there, and she knocked on the door. The knock was answered with scrambling and rustling, with excited voices and footfalls. JP opened the door a crack and peeked out. "Yeah?"

"Who do you have in there?"

"Nobody."

Charlene sniffed at the air. "This nobody has perfume?"

"Mom, be cool. Please."

Charlene bit her lip. "I'm cool. You know I'm cool."

Her son gave her a little smile and a wink. "I know."

God, how she loved him. And of course, in this room, on this very bed, JP ended his life. Charlene drew in a harsh breath and let her tears fall. Morrisey and Gareth were her new family, her future. She would not have it any other way, but damn it, she missed her son. "I hope you're happy, wherever you are," she said. "Goodbye, John Patrick."

DNA TEST RESULTS day dawned bright and early. Morrisey rose before the 6:30 alarm to fix breakfast for Charlene. They acted as if nothing was out of the ordinary. They ate their muffins and drank their orange juice and coffee. Morrisey promised to call when she knew something. They kissed goodbye, and Charlene went off to work.

Gareth woke up about 8:00, and at first, things were okay. He quickly became a chore, though, hammering away at Morrisey to watch television or a movie. He knew something was up and was trying to capitalize on it. At 11:40, he flashed Morrisey an impish smile. "Can I watch TV?" She frowned, annoyed. "Can I? Can I?" he asked again, bouncing in place on the living room floor, where he was scribbling in a coloring book.

Morrisey scowled from the kitchen table, where she was paying some bills. "I've already said no—fifty times."

"But I wanna!" Gareth howled.

"No!"

"Pleeeeeeeeeeeeeeeeeeeasssssssssssse."

Morrisey slammed down her checkbook and crossed to her son. She towered over him, feeling the scowl on her face deepen. "I said no! If you ask again, you're going to your room, with no toys!"

Gareth's chin quivered. "Why are you mad?"

Morrisey snorted. "You know why. Because you keep asking if you can watch TV. You know full well you may not!"

"Sorry."

Morrisey took a deep breath then plopped down on the floor. "Why don't you come with me and color at the table?"

Gareth's eyes lit up. "Can I watch TV?"

"Oh, God," Morrisey mewled. She slumped against the couch.

"Can I, can I?"

Morrisey was so tempted to cave in, to say, "Yes, fine, fine, you may watch TV," but she was not going to do that.

"Can I? Can I? I wanna watch *Finding Nemo*."

Morrisey pointed a finger toward the hallway. "Go to your room. Now."

"But—"

"No buts! Go!"

Gareth jumped to his feet. "You're mean!"

"Go. Now."

Gareth turned on his heels and stomped down the hallway. He slammed his bedroom door shut. Morrisey rubbed her temples. She hated yelling at her son and hated it when he got into that stubborn streak. Sometimes, though, he could be such a kid. The telephone rang, and Morrisey stiffened. What if that was the doctor's office? It probably was. In just a few seconds, she would find out who Gareth's father was—either JP, dead and buried, or Ralph, alive and nearby. Morrisey trembled as she got up and crossed to the phone. She grabbed it on the fifth ring.

"Morris?" Charlene's voice, worried and breathless, brought a small smile to Morrisey's lips. "Did you hear from the doctor's office yet?"

"No. I told you I'd call when I did."

"I know, I know. I had a minute, so I was just making sure."

"How's work going?"

"It's going all right." Charlene chuckled awkwardly. "Not one of my finer days. How's Gareth?"

"He's being an ass. I just sent him to his room."

"Oh, no. What did he do?"

Morrisey rolled her eyes and pressed the receiver to her ear. "He kept asking over and over and over again if he could watch TV. He would not take 'no' for an answer."

"He takes after you."

"Hey. What's that supposed to mean?"

"Oh, come on." Charlene's voice took on a mischievous tone. "You know how you are when there's something you want. Nothing can stop you."

"Yeah, I suppose," Morrisey grumbled.

"Yeah, yeah, you suppose."

Morrisey could imagine Charlene sticking her tongue out.

"Well, I need to get back to work. Give me a call when you hear from the doctor's office."

"Of course. I love you."

"Love you more." Charlene hung up before Morrisey could react.

CHARLENE HAD BEEN on edge all morning, and the nightmare customer who had complained endlessly about his eggs had pushed Charlene nearly to the brink of homicide. As noon approached and then passed, Charlene's anxiety approached monstrous proportions. The telephone call from Morrisey could not come soon enough.

At 2:57, Charlene ran a washcloth under a water faucet, grabbed some cleaning supplies and headed to a dirty table. She needed to keep busy, and it was a slow time. She wiped bread crumbs off the table, her thoughts centering on Gareth. She did love him. She had watched him drift off to sleep the night before, the expression on his face so much like his mother's. Charlene loved watching Morrisey fall asleep; it was one of her favorite ways to end a day, wrapped in Morrisey's arms, listening to her steady breathing and the little noises she made.

If JP was not Gareth's father, that meant JP was gone, forever. There would be no part of him left, except in Charlene's memories. That made her sadder than anything else, to think that her son might be gone so completely, that he had not left anything behind. She was fortunate that she had Morrisey at her side, and Morrisey wanted her to be Gareth's mother. Charlene's heart swelled as she remembered Morrisey's words that blood did not matter. Genes did not matter. Gareth was Charlene's, no matter what a test said.

After Charlene finished wiping off the table, she grabbed an apple and headed outside behind the restaurant. She sat on a wooden crate and studied her apple. It was big, and her stomach lurched. *Should've brought a smaller one.* She considered going back inside to clean more tables. Instead, she opened her mouth and took a tentative bite.

"Hey." Miriam sat down next to Charlene. "What's wrong? Your eyes have been glued to the clock all day."

"I'm waiting for a phone call."

"What about?"

Charlene shook her head. "I'll tell you later. It's pretty slow today, huh?"

"Yeah, it's slow." Miriam cleared her throat. "I'm not here to check on you, actually. There's a young man here to see you. He says he's a friend of JP's. His name is Ralph. Ralph Burroughs."

Charlene's heart stopped. *Not Ralph, not now.*

"He looks like he could almost be JP's twin. Ralph Burroughs. JP has a brother?"

"Oh," Charlene whispered, suddenly feeling as if the sky were crashing down on her.

"Charlene? Charlene? Did you know? Charlene?"

"Don't bring him back here. I don't want to see him."

Miriam did not reply right away. When she did, her words were slow and measured. "He seemed pretty eager. Maybe you ought to meet with him. He's JP's brother. Maybe he can help you."

"Make him leave."

"You've met him before, haven't you? You know about him."

Charlene swallowed. "Yes." She glanced at her watch, and her heart sank even more. Why hadn't Morrisey called yet? Ralph showing up could not be a good sign.

Heavy footfalls sounded, and Charlene and Miriam looked up. Ralph had taken it upon himself to find Charlene. He glanced uncertainly between Charlene and Miriam. "Hey. Uh, can we talk? I won't be long."

Miriam squeezed Charlene's shoulder. "See you soon, hon." She headed back into the restaurant.

Ralph tugged at his ear. "How are you?"

"Why are you here?"

Ralph's eyes were wide and earnest. "I apologize for bothering you at work, but you ran away so fast the other day. I wanted to make sure you were okay. I stopped by your apartment a few times. You were never home. Calling would be too impersonal. Look, I'm sorry I sprang all that info on you the other day. I wanted to talk with you to maybe clear up some things or answer any questions you might have."

Charlene crossed her arms and willed her trembling hands not to betray her. "I'm fine."

Miriam reappeared at the back door. "Morrisey's here."

"What?"

"Morrisey's here."

"No, no, no." Charlene's throat constricted. "Tell her to—tell her I'll just—Miriam, get rid of her, okay? Tell her I'm not here!"

"She's upset. I told her you'd be out in a minute."

"Yes, fine," Charlene said. *She's upset.* That could only mean one thing. Charlene took a deep breath. "Ralph, you have to go. Now. Please."

"Let me give you my number, okay?"

The atmosphere changed in an instant. The air became motionless yet electrically charged. *Morrisey.* Charlene looked up and met Morrisey's pained gaze. That expression told her all she needed to know about Gareth's father. Then there was a shrill, excited voice, Gareth's. He toddled toward Charlene, his face bright as usual. "Hi, Charlie! Mommy won't let me watch TV. Can I, can I?

Tell her to let me watch TV! Please?"

Charlene's stomach reeled, Ralph's eyes went wide, and Morrisey went pale as she finally saw the young man who was gaping at her son.

Gareth did not notice all the tension. He cracked a broad smile and held out his hand to Ralph. "Who are you? I'm Gareth." Ralph clamped his jaw shut and took Gareth's hand.

"Who are you?" Gareth repeated. "Do you think I'm JP, too?"

"I..." Ralph's hand still covered Gareth's, and Charlene was seized by an overwhelming need to separate their touch. She had to stop it, had to stop this, could not let one of the men who raped Morrisey touch her son, the boy who was his biological child. It was all so surreal, all so slow-motion, as though it was not happening. Charlene was powerless to move, to talk, to stop it.

"It's okay," Gareth said. "Charlie thought I was JP, too."

Ralph gulped, and his voice returned to him. "Is JP your father?"

Gareth furrowed his brows and turned to Morrisey. "Mommy!"

Morrisey kept staring at Ralph. He let go of Gareth's hand. "Wow. I didn't know. Wow! I'm an uncle." Ralph turned an excited grin onto Morrisey. "Are you his mother? How did you know my brother? Wow, I can't believe this. I'm an uncle!" Ralph's grin expanded. "What's your name? I didn't know JP was seeing anyone. Oh! I'm sorry. I didn't introduce myself. My name's Ralph." There was absolutely no glimmer of recognition in the young man's sparkling blue-green eyes.

Charlene managed a reply. "You should go, Ralph."

"Why?"

"You're my uncle?" Gareth asked. "I like Bryan's Uncle Chris. He took us fishing!"

"Ralph, please go. Go!" Charlene said.

"But he's my uncle!" Gareth cried.

Charlene threw the boy a despairing look, and the confusion on Ralph's face grew. Morrisey had not taken her gaze off Ralph for one second. She was fixated on him, and her expression was slowly turning into disbelief. Ralph held his hands out and surveyed the people in front of him. "What's going on?"

"Do you like to fish?" Gareth asked. "And play baseball? Do you have a dog? I want a puppy!"

Ralph chuckled. "I don't have a dog yet. I live in an apartment, and the mean old landlord doesn't allow dogs. But I have fish. Some of mine glow in the dark."

"Ooh!" Gareth's eyes grew as big as saucers. "Your fish glow in the dark? What color? Can I go see them?"

Charlene grabbed Gareth's hand. "Come on. I'll walk you and your mom to your car."

"I wanna talk to my uncle!"

"No!"

"Are you my grandma?"

Charlene froze in mid-step but recovered quickly. "Gareth, let's go."

Morrisey blinked and shifted her eyes from Ralph to Charlene.

"Are you my grandma?" Gareth repeated. "Is JP my daddy? Can we go see him at the cemetery? Grandpa told me he thought JP was my daddy."

Charlene faltered.

Morrisey returned her gaze to Ralph. She spoke, her voice low and pained. "You truly don't recognize me, do you?"

Ralph looked sheepish. "I'm sorry. I really didn't know JP was seeing anyone. And, uh, well, you know we were out of it most of the time anyway. I hardly remember a thing."

Morrisey's eyes iced over. "You think that's funny?"

Ralph turned contrite. "No, not at all. Look, I've changed. I've gone sober. I don't do drugs anymore. I'm getting myself through college, and I'm working too." He threw Gareth an admiring, proud look. "Man, I can't believe I have a nephew. Look, let me take you guys to lunch. We can eat here. Or go somewhere else. Wherever. And we can get acquainted. I'll be a cool uncle, you'll see."

Morrisey snorted. "Leave me and my son alone."

"Why? Come on! Let me buy you lunch."

"No."

Ralph shook his head in annoyance, but then he stopped. He froze. His eyes went wide, and he stared at Morrisey. There it was: understanding, realization, remembrance. "Oh, shit," he said. "Oh my God. I can't believe—oh my God." He and Morrisey held each other's gazes for what seemed like an eternity. Ralph was white and looked scared to death. Morrisey's expression was harder to read. "I am sorry," Ralph pleaded. "I am so sorry. You have no idea how. Not a day goes by that I don't think about you."

"You couldn't even be bothered to recognize me. It took you long enough."

"No! No."

"You raped me. You left me to die."

Ralph swallowed. "I've changed, though. I have. Really. I promise."

Morrisey dug her fingers into Gareth's shoulders, and the boy's mouth twisted in pain. She scooped her son into her arms, and they vanished around a dumpster.

Ralph turned to Charlene. "Oh, my God." He pointed a quivering finger toward the dumpster. "She—she—I—Gareth. Gareth. Wait. Is he—he's mine, isn't he? He's my son."

"You're not a father. You're a rapist." Charlene stalked off to find Jay. She needed the rest of the afternoon off.

Chapter Twenty-Three

MORRISEY WINCED EVERY time she remembered that long, awful gaze between her and Ralph. She would never forget his sickened, confused, yet numb expression. It was the same look she herself had had after the rape, the same look JP had after the football accident.

"Mommy?" Gareth ventured from the back seat as Morrisey turned the car into the driveway. "That man's my daddy? Or my uncle? Is Charlie my grandma?"

Morrisey looked straight ahead and turned the car off. "Time for your nap."

"No!" Gareth protested. "I already napped!"

Morrisey got out of the car and opened the back side door for her son. She unbuckled him from his child seat, but he dug his heels into the floor. She had to practically drag him into the house.

"I don't wanna!" he cried. "I wanna see my daddy!"

"No!"

"He has fish that glow in the dark!"

Morrisey dropped to her knees and fixed Gareth with stern eyes. "Go to your room."

"No!"

"Fine!" Morrisey strode to the television and turned it on. "Watch your fucking TV then!"

Gareth slunk to the couch, and Morrisey exhaled a heavy breath. She trudged into the kitchen and hung up her car keys on a hook. So Gareth knew now about his father. He had met and liked his father.

Moments later, Charlene burst through the kitchen door. She pulled Morrisey to her. "I'm so sorry. I tried to get rid of him before you could see him."

"It's all right."

"No, it's not. I'm sorry."

"What was he doing there?"

"He wanted to see if I had any questions for him. The other

day, when he told me about JP and I pieced together that he might be Gareth's father, I kind of just ran out of the store. I was in shock."

Morrisey crossed her arms. "Isn't it convenient? You've seen him twice in just a little more than a week. Are you really being truthful with me? You sure you didn't try to track him down? You sure you didn't tell him about the little test we did? Maybe you never lost touch with him over the years. Hmm?"

Charlene's mouth fell open, and Morrisey immediately regretted her accusations. "I'm sorry." She reached for Charlene's hands. "I don't know why I said that."

"Do you really think I'd do that? I respect your wishes, Morrisey."

"I know. It's just been a bad day."

"So, JP isn't Gareth's father, huh?"

"The tests showed you and Gareth most likely aren't related. I'm sorry."

Charlene's blue eyes darkened with unreadable emotion. "Me, too. How's Gareth?"

"Charlie!" Gareth barreled into the kitchen, right on cue. "Are you my grandma?"

Charlene did not answer, so Morrisey took it upon herself. "Remember last week when we went to the doctor and the nurse took swabs from our cheeks?"

"Yeah."

"That was a test to see if Charlene was your grandma. We found out she's not."

"What about Ralph? Is he my daddy? Is he going to live with us? He can sleep with me!"

Morrisey slumped into a chair. She could not bring herself to look at her son, at his eager, excited face. "Charlene, please, can you take him somewhere? Just please, get him out of here."

"Yes," Charlene replied, none too firmly.

"I can't do this right now. Please take him somewhere."

Charlene held out a hand to Gareth. "You hungry?"

"Are we gonna see my daddy?"

Gareth's question was the last straw for Morrisey. She pushed her chair back and fled down the hallway.

CHARLENE STUDIED GARETH over a jumble of French fries and chicken nuggets. They were at McDonald's, one of Gareth's favorite places, but they both had hardly touched their food. Gareth had been pounding Charlene with questions about his father. "How come Ralph's not your little boy? 'Cause Chris is Bruce's brother, and Chris is Bryan's uncle."

"Ralph and JP have the same daddy. The difference is that I'm JP's mother. Ralph has another mother."

Gareth furrowed his brows. "Oh."

"I guess it's a little complicated."

"Are we gonna see my daddy now?" Gareth asked for what seemed like the hundredth time.

"No, sweetie." Charlene repeated her answer.

"Why?"

"I don't know," Charlene replied.

"Do you like me?"

Charlene snapped her head up. "What do you mean?"

"Are you mad at me?"

Charlene lowered her gaze. "No. I love you. Now eat your food."

Gareth, his blue eyes solemn, studied Charlene. "I wish you were my grandma. You're better than Grandma Hawthorne."

"I want to be your mother. Is that okay?"

"Will you let me watch TV more?"

Charlene chuckled. "Oh, sweetie."

Gareth dipped a French fry into his ketchup. "Charlie?"

"Yes?"

"Can I go play on the slides?"

"Yes. Go on."

Gareth jumped to his feet. The second he raced through the doorway between the dining area and the outdoor playground, hot tears slid down Charlene's cheeks, scalding her skin. JP was gone. Really, truly gone, forever. Charlene sat at the table until enough tears had fallen. She wiped her eyes then forced herself to the playground. Gareth was standing next to the slides. He was regaling three blond girls and a blond woman with tales about his father, who apparently was a veterinarian. Charlene listened for a while from a distance, her heart dulling because she could not take the pain anymore, just could not take it anymore. She went up to Gareth, but he kept chattering.

"Last week Daddy saw a dog on the road, and the dog was bleeding and really yucky, but Daddy saved his life, and Daddy says we can keep the dog. It's a lab dog. Big and yellow."

The woman laughed and looked up at Charlene. "You must be so proud of your husband. I have to beg and whine to get my Jeffrey off the couch."

Charlene managed a weak grin. "Right. Yes. Well, uh, Gareth, let's go."

Gareth's eyes lit up. "We're gonna see my daddy at work now and pet the dogs and cats! My grandma has a big cat named

Regina."

Charlene led Gareth to her car. "Hey, I have a great idea. Let's go to the park. I'll push you on the swings."

Gareth stomped his foot and howled, absolutely howled. Several adults in the parking lot glanced curiously at him and Charlene. "I wanna go see my daddy at work and pet the cats and dogs and rabbits and snakes!"

"Gareth, he's not a vet. Okay?"

"I wanna pet the cats and dogs! And I wanna get the doggie that my daddy saved last week. Daddy said I could name him!"

"There are no cats and dogs, sweetie."

"Are too!"

"No."

"Are too! My daddy saves dogs and cats and rabbits."

Charlene took a deep breath and flexed her fists. She knelt so she was face to face with Gareth. It was not quite her place to tell Gareth what she was about to tell him. It was Morrisey's place. To Charlene, Morrisey had been putting it off too long and would delay for years if she had her way. "Gareth," Charlene said, "your father hurt your mother. That's why she doesn't like him."

Gareth furrowed his brows. His silence filled the air, but at last he replied with an "Oh." Then he asked, "Daddy hurt Mommy?"

"Yes."

"How?"

"He hit her," Charlene explained. "He made her cry. I think maybe he's getting better now. He's in college, and—well. Never mind. Do you want to go to the park and swing, sweetie? We can talk or just play and have fun. Whatever you like." Charlene reached for Gareth's hand. She pressed their palms together. Her hand was easily three times as big as his.

Gareth giggled. "You have big hands, but not as big as Mommy's."

MORRISEY FLOPPED ONTO her bed and covered her face. All this daddy talk was exhausting her. She forced herself up and wandered into Gareth's room. It was a small, bright, cheerful space. The walls were painted a sunny yellow, and Gareth's bed, shaped like a race car, stood in one corner. Miniature cars, trucks and bulldozers were spilled on the floor near the bed. On Gareth's wood dresser was a picture of Adrian, Morrisey's father, with an infant Gareth in his arms. Morrisey allowed herself a smile and fingered the picture. "I could use you right now, Daddy." She choked back a tear. After Gareth's birth, she and her father had really bonded, in a way they never had before, and in a way

Morrisey knew she never could bond with her mother and siblings. She, Gareth and Adrian had started doing things together, with Adrian seemingly aware of the fact he was the main man in his grandson's life. But then he had died, keeled over in the kitchen.

Morrisey wondered what her childhood would have been like without her father. She would have turned out all right. She knew that, yet she could not deny she was all the richer for having known her father. And now what was she supposed to tell her son about his father? What was she supposed to do about his father? She did not want Gareth to grow up confused, or consumed with hate and anger.

Morrisey returned the picture of her father and Gareth to its proper place. She trudged to Gareth's bed and lay down. She clutched one of his bulldozers to her chest. "I was raped," she whispered. "I was raped." *It's time to stop hiding. You're not alone.* She closed her eyes and took a deep breath. Then the doorbell rang.

BETSEY HAD NEVER stopped by Morrisey's for a casual visit. Why would she? They were not close, emotionally nor geographically, but here she was, on Morrisey's doorstep. "Betsey," Morrisey managed to say. She ushered her sister in, wondering what in the world was going on. She had heard nothing from Betsey since that Saturday dinner at their mother's house, not that she expected to. Bobby had called a few times, though, and he had taken Gareth out for pizza twice.

Betsey flashed a wide, fake smile at Morrisey. "How are you?"

Morrisey ignored the knot in her stomach. "I'm fine. Why are you here?"

"I wanted to see how you were doing. Where's Gareth?"

"He's out with Charlene. Care to sit?" Morrisey indicated the couch.

Betsey nodded, and they sat. "I'm sorry," Betsey began haltingly, "about the dinner at Mom's, about what happened. I'm sorry, too, that it's taken so long for me to call or come by. I guess I've been, well, in shock a little bit, also angry and hurt that you couldn't tell me what happened. I suppose that's partly my fault, too." Betsey inched closer and took Morrisey's hand. "I'm glad you told us. I want to help you in any way I can. I know I haven't been the greatest sister. I'm very happy you've met Charlene. I've never seen you smile the way you did that night around her. I'd like to get to know her better, if you will let me."

Morrisey swallowed. "Betsey."

"No, no. Look, I've been an ass about you being gay. And—"

"You're here because you feel sorry for me. This is exactly why

I didn't want to tell anyone, most of all you people, that I was raped."

Betsey's jaw fell open. "You people? You mean your family? We don't feel sorry for you. We just want to help you in any way we can."

"Oh, yeah? Helping me in any way you can means waiting weeks before coming to see me? And to Mom, it means never calling? Yeah, boy. What a jolly bunch. You people have been a lot of help to me. You people have hurt me almost as much as the rape did!"

Tears sprang to Betsey's eyes, and she blinked them back furiously. "You're right. I'm sorry." She tightened her grip on Morrisey's hand. "After, well, after yesterday, I realized I needed to get over myself and to see you and talk to you."

"What happened yesterday?"

"I lost the baby."

Morrisey sucked in a breath. "Oh, no."

"That was probably my last chance."

"Oh, Betsey," Morrisey was at a loss for words. "Is there anything I can do?"

"Yes. Yes, actually there is something you can do."

"What? Anything."

"Take me out. Let's have some fun. Remember when we were kids? We used to go to the arcades. You always kicked my ass."

Morrisey laughed, suddenly glad her sister had come to see her. "Sure. Of course."

Betsey shifted uncomfortably. "There's another reason I couldn't bring myself to come see you for a long time. Something else you should know too."

"Yes?"

"It's about Mom. I can tell she wants to help you. She does. She just doesn't know how to do it. You know how she is."

Morrisey sniffed. "It's her loss. It's sad for her, more than it is for me."

Betsey pressed a hand to her forehead. "There's something else, though. No one's supposed to know this. Not even me. The only reason I know is because I was at home one day when I wasn't supposed to be." Betsey cleared her throat and continued. "In my freshman year of high school, I overheard Mom and Daddy talking. Morrisey, our mother was raped too."

Morrisey stared at her sister. Betsey's expression was genuine. Pained. "What? No way!"

"Their bedroom door was open just a little bit, and she was crying her heart out to Daddy."

"It happened while they were married?"

"Before, but I gathered she was telling Daddy for the first time."

Morrisey felt as if the wind had been knocked out of her. "How'd it happen?"

"I didn't stay long enough to get all the details," Betsey admitted. "I felt like I was intruding, which I suppose I was. Basically, Mom was in high school. She went out on a date, and the guy, well, you know." Betsey sighed, and she looked just as miserable as Morrisey felt. "I didn't know what to do. I felt so bad for her."

"I can imagine," Morrisey said. "Oh, I can't believe it. Do you think Dad was the only person she told? Why'd she tell him? I mean, that was years and years after it happened."

Betsey shrugged. "I don't know. Maybe she just woke up one day and had to tell him."

More thoughts assailed Morrisey. "Hmm."

Betsey looked away for a second. "I needed to get it off my chest. I wanted to help her so much. I mean, Morrisey, she was crying her eyes out. I could hardly understand what she was saying. Ever since then, I..." Betsey grinned wryly. "I've tried to forget about it. I couldn't, and I haven't told anyone else. It's not their business. Even Carl doesn't know. Look, I hope that, well, I don't know. I've wanted to come see you, to help you, ever since that dinner at Mom's. But I couldn't face you, look you in the eyes, and keep Mom's secret."

Morrisey jerked her head. "Yeah. All right." She and her mother were long overdue for a talk. So were she and Betsey. Morrisey plunged ahead, even though she was sure she would cry and turn into a mess in front of her sister, but it had to be done. She had been raped; time to stop pretending otherwise. "I need to tell you something, too, Betsey," Morrisey said. "Four guys raped me, not one, and it turns out JP isn't Gareth's father after all."

Chapter Twenty-Four

MORRISEY AND BETSEY had a great time at the arcade. Betsey even gave Morrisey a run for her bragging rights a few times, but the fun could not go on forever. Soon enough, it was time to say goodbye. The sisters parted with a hug and made plans to roller blade with their kids the next week. Then Morrisey took a deep breath and went to visit her mother—not just for Margaret Hawthorne's sake, but for Morrisey's too. Perhaps for some insight, also, about dealing with Ralph.

Morrisey drummed her fingers on the steering wheel as she drove into her mother's quiet neighborhood of stately mansions. She was not sure how to approach the visit, so she would just wing it. She pulled into her mother's spacious driveway, and there was the elegant Margaret Hawthorne, clad in gardening clothes and kneeling over some flowers. She stood and watched in obvious trepidation as Morrisey emerged from her car. The knees of Margaret's pants were grass-stained. A bucket and small spade were at her feet.

Morrisey was careful to stand a few arms' lengths from her mother. "Hello," Morrisey said quietly. "How are you?"

Margaret took a step back. "I'm fine. And you?"

"I could be better. You haven't called. It's been a long time."

Margaret's nostrils flared. "I called once. She answered. It's not my fault you insist on having that woman around your child after what her son did to you!"

"Look," Morrisey said, grabbing her mother's wrist. "Charlene isn't the issue here. I was raped. That's right. I was raped," Morrisey repeated as her mother flinched. "Raped, raped, raped. I can say it. And I sure could have used a hug from you, or maybe just a kind word or two. You knew, didn't you? You knew all along, from the minute I told you I was pregnant. And you did nothing!"

"I did not know," Margaret said emphatically.

"You suspected, then!"

Margaret sniffed haughtily. "I suspected no such thing."

Morrisey slumped back, suddenly weary. "Why? Why can't you just..."

Margaret crossed her arms. The gaze she sent Morrisey was just as unloving as it had been on the night Morrisey had announced the pregnancy.

Morrisey knew Margaret Hawthorne was a proud woman. There was no way she would ever admit she had been raped. It must have been agony for her to tell her husband, and Morrisey understood her mother's need for secrecy. The secret was safe with her. But she just wanted a hug, just something.

"Would you like to come in for tea?" Margaret asked.

Morrisey met her mother's eyes. Tea was probably all she would get for now. Tea was all her mother could offer. "Okay," Morrisey said. "Fine. Tea. Just for a little bit."

FIVE MINUTES LATER, Morrisey and Margaret were seated in the living room and sipping iced teas. "Did I tell you that the children's AIDS foundation elected me president for another year?" Margaret asked. "I was so gratified, of course, and—"

Morrisey jerked a hand up. Suddenly, tea was not enough to appease her. "Mother, that's wonderful. But I'd rather talk about something else."

A shadow crossed Margaret's face. "What?"

"You know what."

"I'm afraid I don't."

"About what happened to me."

Margaret lifted her tea glass and daintily brought it to her lips. She could not conceal the flash of panic in her eyes. "Morrisey." She took a deep breath and set her glass down. "What do you want me to say? I'm sorry it happened." She gave Morrisey a bleak, despairing, completely hopeless look that lasted all of a half second. It was enough to send chills up Morrisey's spine.

Her mother had no idea what she was doing. Why would she? She had never been close to Morrisey and had been just as distant—although more approving—with Betsey and Bobby. Morrisey gulped from her tea, then she stood. "You said you wished we were closer."

"I do."

"So." Morrisey fingered a button on her shirt. "You really hurt me. Do you have any idea how hard it was, just how unbelievably hard it was for me to tell you what had happened? And what did I get from you? You're my mother!"

Margaret's expression crumpled into a tired sadness. "You're right. I'm sorry. What's wrong with me? I want to help you. I do."

Morrisey's stomach clenched at the desperation in her mother's voice. "How about a hug?"

Margaret inclined her head. "A hug. Okay." She stood, crossed the few steps to Morrisey, and gingerly pulled her into an embrace as if Morrisey would break,. An instant later, Margaret was holding on for dear life. "Sweetie," she said, tears choking her voice. "I love you. I love you. I'm so sorry."

"I love you too, Mom," Morrisey answered.

Margaret drew back and wiped at her eyes with the back of her hand. "Yes, I knew," she muttered. "I knew, deep down, when you told us that you were pregnant, that you had not been artificially inseminated. I ignored that knot in my stomach. What was I going to do? What should I have done?" She shook her head dismissively. "No, I know what I should have done. I suppose I just—sweetie." Margaret fixed a serious gaze on Morrisey. "I'm sorry. I'm sorry about how I acted toward Charlene. I really am. You are a wonderful person, a wonderful mother. I trust your judgment a hundred percent. I can't imagine how you were able to invite your rapist's mother into your son's life, into her grandson's life. That took courage."

Morrisey could not look at her mother. "I don't know about that. If it had been any other woman it might not have been the same."

Margaret sighed. "Still."

"Anyway, it turns out Charlene isn't Gareth's grandmother. They're not related at all."

Margaret's eyes flew open. "What did you say?"

"They're not related," Morrisey repeated in a hushed whisper. "Four men raped me. It wasn't just JP. And it turns out he had a half brother, Gareth's father."

Margaret's expression was disbelieving. "Four men?"

"Yes."

Margaret's jaw worked its way up and down, but she could not say anything.

"I have a question," Morrisey ventured.

"Yes?"

"What did you do about the man who raped you? Or was he a boy then?"

Margaret stiffened. "Excuse me?"

"Answer me."

Margaret did not give in. "I said, excuse me."

"I asked you a question."

"I haven't the foggiest clue what you're talking about."

"So what did you do about him?" Morrisey persisted.

"If you're going to keep up this ridiculous line of questioning, you should leave."

Morrisey held her hands out. "Mother, please. I just want to help you."

Margaret stayed ramrod straight, her eyes unwavering. After a moment, she ground her lips and looked away. "Nothing. I did nothing."

"Who was he?"

"The golden boy, class president, homecoming king to my homecoming queen, football stud. Everything. I knew no one would believe me, that no one would care. Back in that day, rape just didn't happen. It was unheard of. I felt as if it was my fault, anyway, that I'd done something wrong. I sucked it in and went back to school the next morning. Because our names fell just right alphabetically, he sat next to me when we graduated. I acted like nothing happened."

"That's how I've been acting too, but something did happen."

"Yes. Something did happen."

"You were raped. And you know it wasn't your fault, right? You did nothing wrong. He did."

Margaret flinched, and slowly, she covered Morrisey's hands with her own. "Yes, I was raped. I know now that it wasn't my fault. I'm so sorry you had to go through it alone. If I could do it over again and help you, I would. Four men. My God."

"I'm afraid, Mom," Morrisey blurted out.

"Oh, honey, why?"

"I saw Gareth's father today."

"What?"

Morrisey's words spilled out. "He saw Gareth. Everything. I'm afraid. I'm so afraid. I don't know what to do. I think have to go to the police. I have to do something. Part of me has been numb since the rape because I've been avoiding what happened. I've been trying to pretend everything's the same as always, that I was never raped. But I was. I was raped, and now I could be sending my son's father and two other men to jail."

Morrisey looked into her mother's eyes and beseeched her. "Please, Mom. Help me. Tell me that everything will be okay, that Gareth will understand. Reassure me that he won't hate me for putting his dad—his dear old dad who's sober, his dad with the glow-in-the-dark fish, his dad who raped me and who left me to die—in jail."

"It will be all right," Margaret said emphatically. "It will be just fine. I promise. You're raising a good boy who loves you."

WHEN MORRISEY GOT home, Charlene and Gareth were on

the couch. They were sound asleep. Gareth was on top of Charlene, and her arms were around him. Morrisey approached them quietly. Charlene stirred, but Morrisey made no move to wake her up. Not yet.

Who knew what the future would bring? More love, more heartache. Maybe more children. Maybe Charlene taking Gareth to visit his father in jail, maybe Ralph being released and going to see his son. Or maybe no one would go to jail. Maybe there'd be no trial due to a lack of evidence, the rapists' denials, or some other reason. Morrisey's gut told her that Ralph would step up and do the right thing, though. He would pay his penance. She had seen it in his eyes.

Morrisey smiled. *Don't worry so much. It will be just fine. Somehow.* She bent down to wake Charlene and Gareth. Life was waiting.

A FORTHCOMING TITLE
published by
Regal Crest

Rebuilding Sasha
by S. Renee Bess

Sasha Lewis, general manager for her gay best friend's construction company, flies back to Philadelphia after an unsuccessful business trip in Maine and deals with her disappointment by feigning sleep during the flight home. One more time she feels she's failed. One more time she's not sure how to believe in herself or her abilities. Because of her sense of failure, Sasha misses the opportunity to meet the attractive passenger seated next to her. Avery Sloan, a social worker, is returning from a conference. It's probably just as well that they didn't meet since Sasha has a live-in partner, Lee Simpson.

Though they didn't connect on the plane, Avery's path is destined to intersect with Sasha's because Whittingham Builders is hired to do the rehab for Avery's new project, conversion of an old house to a group home that will serve formerly incarcerated clients. Having recently ended a relationship calmly and without acrimony, Avery now finds herself alone and missing love.

Although Sasha is drawn to Avery Sloan, she is determined to maintain her relationship with Lee. Unfortunately, Sasha cannot trust Lee to be faithful, and when challenged, Lee targets Sasha with unfounded accusations, threats, and impromptu acts of meanness that begin to spiral out of control. When Lee goes on a destructive rampage that ends with a tragic loss, Sasha must deal with the repercussions. Will Sasha succumb to the violence, sabotage, and a shredded sense of self-worth? Or can she find a new foundation that rebuilds and restores her willingness to care about others and herself?

Coming in November 2008

OTHER REGAL CREST TITLES

Brenda Adcock	Reiko's Garden	978-1-932300-77-2
Victor J. Banis	Come This Way	978-1-932300-82-6
Renee Bess	Breaking Jaie	978-1-932300-84-0
L. E. Butler	Relief	978-1-932300-98-7
Q. Kelly	The Odd Couple	978-1-932300-99-4
Lori L. Lake	Different Dress	978-1-932300-08-6
Lori L. Lake	Shimmer & Other Stories	978-1-932300-95-6
Lori L. Lake	Snow Moon Rising	978-1-932300-50-5
Lori L. Lake	Stepping Out: Short Stories	978-1-932300-16-1
Lori L. Lake	The Milk of Human Kindness	978-1-932300-28-4
Greg Lilly	Fingering the Family Jewels	978-1-932300-22-2
Greg Lilly	Devil's Bridge	978-1-932300-78-9
Cate Swannell	Heart's Passage	978-1-932300-09-3
Jane Vollbrecht	Close Enough	978-1-932300-85-7
Jane Vollbrecht	Heart Trouble	978-1-932300-58-1
Jane Vollbrecht	In Broad Daylight	978-1-932300-76-5

Be sure to check out our other imprints,
Yellow Rose Books and Quest Books.

About the Author:

Q. Kelly lives in Virginia. She works at a newspaper as a copy editor and page designer. She started writing when she was a child and has won many awards for her short stories.

Check her out online at www.qkelly.net and www.myspace.com/q_kelly.

VISIT US ONLINE AT

www.regalcrest.biz

At the Regal Crest Website You'll Find

- The latest news about forthcoming titles and new releases
- Our complete backlist of romance, mystery, thriller and adventure titles
- Information about your favorite authors
- Current bestsellers
- Media tearsheets to print and take with you when you shop

Regal Crest titles are available from all progressive booksellers and online at StarCrossed Productions, (www.scp-inc.biz), or at www.amazon.com, www.bamm.com, www.barnesandnoble.com, and many others.

Printed in the United States
128128LV00003B/123/P